A TARNISHED PHOENIX

名折かし不死鳥

By the same author

The Wages of Zen
The Chrysanthemum Chain
A Sort of Samurai
The Ninth Netsuke
Sayonara, Sweet Amaryllis
Death of a Daimyo
The Death Ceremony
Go Gently, Gaijin
The Imperial Way
Kimono for a Corpse
The Reluctant Ronin
A Haiku for Hanae

A TARNISHED PHOENIX

James Melville

Barrie & Jenkins
London

First published in 1990 by
Barrie & Jenkins Ltd, 20 Vauxhall Bridge Road,
London SW1V 2SA

Copyright © James Melville, 1990

British Library Cataloguing in Publication Data
Melville, James 1931–
A tarnished phoenix
Rn: Peter Martin I. Title
823'.914 [F]

ISBN: 0–7126–3651–X

To my son, Adam Melville Martin

Author's Note

This is a work of fiction, and most of the principal characters are creatures of my imagination. Where real people figure or are referred to in the narrative they are given their correct names. The parts they play in my story, as well as their attitudes and attributes, are consistent with opinions and impressions recorded by contemporaries who knew them, as well as with photographic evidence and the published work of historians concerned with the Occupation and with Japanese politics and society in the early postwar years.

I found it impossible to avoid the frequent use of the acronym SCAP. The letters stand for Supreme Commander Allied Powers, and strictly therefore should refer to General Douglas MacArthur. In practice SCAP was almost invariably used – as I have employed it throughout – to refer to the administrative organization over which he presided from late 1945 until President Truman relieved him of his command on 11 April 1951. MacArthur was concurrently Commander-in-Chief of all US forces in the Far East and in this capacity had his general headquarters (GHQ) in Tokyo.

SCAP proper consisted of two branches, or "Sections", each under the direction of an American general officer, but staffed in the main by civilian experts. One was concerned with political affairs, the other with economic and scientific matters. There was, however, a *de facto* third branch, namely G2 or Intelligence Section under General Charles Willoughby. This formed part of MacArthur's Far East Command and consisted largely of military personnel. It should be borne in mind that while the Military Government had extensive legal privileges and powers, the Japanese government functioned throughout the Occupation, and in theory at least SCAP worked with and through the Japanese authorities.

The names and locations of the various buildings in which MacArthur's military and civilian staff worked and lived are authentic, and in all other respects I have done my best to present an accurate picture of the physical and political background against which the action takes place. In this endeavour I have been much indebted to the work of many historians, biographers and journalists whose books and articles have partially satisfied but continue to stimulate my curiosity about what really happened in Japan in the aftermath of World War II. What I suggest in this novel *might* possibly have happened is not, however, to be confused with history. Not yet, anyway.

Many Japanese, American and British friends generously recalled their own experiences of the period for me, or helped me to locate valuable material. Chief among these are Hisao Kanaseki whose friendship I have enjoyed for nearly thirty years and who lives in Tokyo, Jim Goodrich of New York State, and Hal Drake of the Tokyo bureau of *Pacific Stars & Stripes*. Special thanks are due to two generous American friends: John L. Apostolou of Los Angeles who read the book in draft and, skilled editor that he is, expertly helped me through the complexities (for an Englishman) of American usage; and Mark Schreiber of Tokyo. Mr Schreiber pointed me in the direction of much useful information, contributing many priceless nuggets from his own encyclopaedic knowledge of things Japanese. He also read the book in draft. I have profited greatly from his typically constructive comments, suggestions and criticisms.

James Melville

Principal Characters

Historical

Major-General Charles Willoughby   Commanding G2 (Intelligence
Section), GHQ, Far East

Yoshio Kodama ⎱
                     Detained as suspected war criminal
Nobusuke Kishi ⎰

Fictional

Military personnel serving in G2

Sgt Polly Horvath ⎱
Pfc. Angie Brewster ⎰   US Women's Army Corps
Major Mike Brooks   Staff officer
Lt-Cdr Arthur Reynolds   Royal Australian Navy
M/Sgt Joe Noonan   US Army Counter-Intelligence Corps

Civilian experts serving in Supreme Headquarters Allied Powers

Eleanor Curtis   Economic Section
John Prothero   Director, Labor Division
Jay Murakami   Prothero's deputy
Tom Berman   International Prosecution Section,
War Crimes Tribunal

Eijiro Nakajima   Locally engaged Japanese researcher, War Data
Department

Others

Fujiko Ueda   Murakami's housekeeper
Masao Suekawa   Bar owner and gangster

TOKYO, JANUARY 1947

1

The tall man emerged from Asakusa Station on the outskirts of downtown Tokyo and paused for a moment to sniff the air. A poorly dressed couple were putting up crudely printed Japanese-language posters on a wall nearby. One was already in place: it read SUPPORT THE GENERAL STRIKE! Next to it the man, who was no more than nineteen or twenty and looked as if he was a student, was smoothing a second one down. The slogan was different: SMASH THE PUPPET GOVERNMENT! His girl companion was holding a battered paint can with a brush-handle protruding from it in one hand, and had a modest bundle of posters tucked under her other arm. She looked even younger than the man, and flashed him a tender little smile when he finished and took the paste-pot from her to apply the brush to the wall again. When he was ready she handed him a third poster, bearing the Chinese characters for DOWN WITH THE EMPEROR SYSTEM!

The watcher shook his head slowly and thoughtfully. Not much more than a year before, death would almost certainly have been the penalty for the expression of such sentiments, even in private. Catching his eye, the girl cheekily raised a hand in the clenched-fist communist salute, and the couple moved off to take their message elsewhere. The tall man watched them out of sight before setting out in the opposite direction. It was a cold, miserable evening but the earlier rain had at least slackened to a drizzle, and he walked briskly eastwards along the street the Americans had decided to call Avenue Q.

A lot of things had been different not much more than a year before, he reminded himself. This entire district had been a wasteland. The incendiary bombs had left little but charred and blackened stumps of wood and the occasional crumbling plaster wall rearing up like decayed teeth from the rubble, from which the people could contrive only the most wretched of hovels. Many of those improvised shacks remained and were still occupied, and the light from kerosene lamps glimmered fitfully through chinks and crannies here and there. Mostly, though, houses of a kind and little open-fronted shops had been run up again on their original sites, and the lights that showed were from low-wattage electric lamps.

It was normality of a kind, but grim and austere all the same, and the faces of the few local people he passed looked pinched and drawn in the chill gloom. His own was effectively concealed, because the collar of his khaki raincoat was turned up and he wore a snap-brim hat well down over his forehead. Those who did glance at him assumed he was an American on account of both the smart raincoat and his height. So a few minutes later did the two white-helmeted military policemen, both corporals, who moved forward to bar his way when he turned a corner.

"Hold it right there, fella."

The lanky one had a soft southern accent and seemed amiable enough. His companion's tongue flickered over his upper lip as he drew his white night-stick from the webbing sling at his waist and then tapped the palm of his gloved left hand lightly with it.

"See that sign?"

He gestured towards the board fixed to the electricity supply pole against which he had been leaning. The black lettering – OFF LIMITS TO ALLIED PERSONNEL – stood out boldly against its white background. The man said nothing, but put up two fingers to the brim of his hat and pushed it an inch or two back from his forehead so that his face was illuminated by the street light further up the same pole. The tall southerner peered at him and then shrugged.

"Could have fooled me. OK, on your way, friend."

"Not so fast, bud." The other corporal spoke for the first time, the end of his baton now hard against the stranger's chest as he made to walk on. "Kind of husky for a Nip, aren't you? Let's see some ID."

The Japanese stood very still for a long moment, and then reached into the front of his raincoat, dislodging the night-stick so suddenly that the MP almost dropped it. His eyes narrowed as the silent man produced his identity card and pointedly turned aside to show it to the southerner, who glanced at it casually, paused, and then took it into his hand and scrutinized it for several seconds, his gaze flickering once or twice from the card to its bearer as he did so. Then the corporal straightened up a little, handed the card back and nodded to his partner.

"In order, Jim. Just dandy, in fact. So I believe we'll just wish this gentleman a pleasant evening and step aside."

Jim seemed not to catch the warning note in his colleague's voice and prodded the Japanese in the chest again with the stick.

"OK, wise guy," he said, irritably shaking off the hand the southerner at once reached out and placed on his arm. "So you have your ID. You also have a US army trench-coat, officer's use only. You maybe got a carton of Luckies in there too? Huh?" This time it was his partner who moved the menacing night-stick, pulling it to one side.

"I said let it go, Jim." The taller MP's voice was still quiet, though his manner was now urgent. It only served to make Jim the more aggressive.

"Hell, man, what's with you? Nobody around here right now but us chickens, the night is young and I don't like this guy. So I believe I'll just persuade Mister Wise-Ass here to open up a little."

He jerked his baton free from his partner's restraining hand. The Japanese glanced at it and then looked around unhurriedly. What the belligerent American said was true. The crossing was poorly lit, and there were no other pedestrians within sight.

The silent man turned to face his tormentor again and then moved very fast indeed. All at once Jim's night-stick was no longer in his hand but locked across his throat, while a powerful hand forced his head forward. The southerner at once reached with one hand for the whistle on its chain attached to the pocket of his greatcoat, while with the other he unbuttoned the holster on his belt.

The Japanese shook his head as he caught the southerner's eye. Then he spoke for the first time, and in English. His voice was deep and resonant, his breathing apparently unaffected by the effort of controlling Jim, who was flapping feebly in his grasp.

"No need for that, Corporal," he said. "I could break his neck, but I'm not planning to. He'll be OK." He released his victim and contemptuously shoved him to one side, then handed the baton over to the southerner. "A badly bruised windpipe that'll take a while to settle down perhaps, but you can explain it could have been a lot worse. Maybe he'll be a little more disposed to listen to you in future." Jim was retching and wheezing helplessly, murder in his streaming eyes but clearly incapable of action. "Mind telling me your name?"

"Uh . . . Roberts, Ted Roberts. Hell, you didn't have to treat him that rough."

"You seem like a sensible man, Corporal Roberts. Sensible enough to know that high-wire performers can do without goons fooling with the rope. Tell that to Jim while he's catching his breath."

With that he nodded and walked away, looking back only once just before he rounded the next corner, to see Roberts supporting his partner with his arm, the vapour clouds of their breath clearly visible in the pool of dim light from the street-lamp above them.

Former Commander Eijiro Nakajima of the Imperial Japanese Navy turned right. A few yards ahead of him was a noble wooden gateway: symbolic rather than functional, for though it had a gracefully curving tiled roof it lacked actual gates. A young willow tree grew to one side, and from above hung a great spherical lantern of oiled paper stretched over a framework of bamboo strips. Illuminated from within by an electric lamp, it was of a rich red colour, except for the bold black brush-strokes of the Chinese characters painted on it.

Nakajima passed through into what seemed like a different world from that represented by the austerity of the gloomy streets behind him. The light that spilled from almost every building was cheerful, warm and extravagant, as if defying the power to depress of winter, darkness and the continuing drizzle. As he penetrated further into the licensed quarter there were more people in the narrow streets, some of them westerners undiscouraged by the OFF LIMITS signs and the risk of being picked up by military police patrols.

Some of the Japanese were touts, men wearing short cotton happi-coats over shabby western-style clothes, often the remains of their old army uniforms. They carried Japanese umbrellas made of oiled paper and bamboo, and emblazoned like the great lantern at the willow gate with Chinese characters, representing the names of the establishments that employed them on commission. A few were fussily escorting actual clients, others beckoning and calling to potential customers wandering on foot, or trailing the rare taxi crawling at walking pace along the broader streets to enable its occupants to consider possibilities before deciding where to get out. None of the touts accosted the tall man, but a few paused to look over their shoulders at him after he had passed by.

Between a third and half of the buildings lining the streets and alleys looked like traditional Japanese inns. Two-storey structures of wood, they had an amplitude, solidity and dignity about their appearance contrasting strikingly with the scrimping shoddiness of the new houses in the respectable parts of Asakusa. The characters of their names – names like "Daffodil Teahouse", "Pine Tree Pavilion" and "Bridge Of Dreams" – were deeply incised and gilded or painted black on wooden panels placed above or to one side of their entrances.

In the first traumatic days and weeks of defeat in 1945 the highest priority had been given to rebuilding these old-style houses of assignation with the best materials available, and teams of professional prostitutes were directed to them. The municipal authorities so ordered things, convinced that with the arrival of tens of thousands of foreign soldiers only an efficient and attractive brothel service could protect Japanese women and girls in general from the horrors of indiscriminate rape. In the event the subtlely of the attractions of the old-fashioned houses turned out to be largely wasted on the young men with their Hershey bars and chewing gum, and few GIs ventured into them even before they were put off limits.

Most preferred to stand in line and wait their turn outside the mass-turnover establishments with their own US Army prophylactic stations: pick up a condom, pay three dollars and be briskly but politely serviced by girls indistinguishable, apart from their come-on clothes and bold make-up from shop assistants or assembly-line workers. Despite the work of the prophylactic stations, within a matter of months the incidence of VD began to worry the brass hats.

At the same time their pragmatic policies came under attack by Christian missionaries. During a much-publicized visit Cardinal Spellman of New York thunderously condemned sexual licence, and before long all military personnel were barred from Japanese brothels of every type, and transgressors were now and then picked up by patrolling service policemen. Enforcement was patchy, though, and there were always those prepared to take a chance. On that particular evening most of the doors in the Yoshiwara quarter were closed against the cold, but here and there a door stood open, a kimono-clad woman just inside the entrance inclining her head in decorous invitation to potential clients. Nakajima paused to exchange a few words with one such woman but soon pressed on.

His business was at a different sort of place altogether, one of the gaudy "western-style' establishments more to the taste of foreigners. These fast-buck places were quickly run up from concrete breeze-blocks, corrugated iron and cheap veneer. Coloured light-bulbs flashed on and off around their painted façades; they called themselves cabarets, bars, night-clubs, even "theaters". They had names to match, for the most part crudely lettered in English: "Sweetheart", "Boogie" and "Lover"; "Hi-Ball", "Starlite" and "Blue Moon" were among those he passed. The music which issued from their open doors was recorded, by Glenn Miller, Harry James and Tommy Dorsey, and by some of their emerging Japanese imitators.

Nakajima turned into the entrance of the Hotshot Cabaret, acknowledging with a curt nod the hasty but deep bow of the sharp-featured, dinner-jacketed man just inside, who then obsequiously took his hat and helped him off with his raincoat. A large mirror occupied most of one wall of the tiny lobby and the newcomer turned to face it, first smoothing his brilliantined hair with one hand and then combing it properly with a pocket comb produced from his grey tweed sports jacket.

Though he was a big man, without his hat and coat Nakajima looked like the ordinary Japanese he was, albeit fitter, more relaxed and certainly better fed than the majority in January 1947. He was thirty-seven years old, had strongly moulded, characterful features, the skin of his face swarthy but free from pock-marks or other blemishes, his black eyes glittering in the bright lights. His grey slacks matched the jacket perfectly and the maroon tie he wore would have made for a very stylish ensemble but for the fact that his crisp poplin shirt was pale khaki, obviously army issue like his raincoat. He addressed the doorman's reflection in the mirror while returning the comb to his breast pocket.

"I'm late. He here yet?" His accent in Japanese was that of the Kansai area; Osaka probably, or perhaps Kobe, but the doorman's when he replied was unmistakably local.

"Yes. He's been here about fifteen minutes."

Nakajima nodded again and turned, and the deferential doorman drew aside the curtain at the back of the lobby for him to enter a dimly lit room some thirty feet long and perhaps half as wide. Much of one side was occupied by a long bar which stopped short of a tiny stage barely big enough to accommodate a man at an upright piano, a string bass player and a woman in a long red evening dress crooning into a microphone.

Immediately in front of the stage two couples were swaying to and fro but not seriously attempting to dance, while most of the remaining floor area was occupied by people sitting at small round tables. Including the trio on the stage, half a dozen on high stools at the bar and the barman busily occupied behind it, there were in all only twenty or so people in the room. Of these, four of the men and all of the women were employed there.

Three noisy young Americans were sitting at two of the tables which had been pushed together. Each attended by a Japanese girl in western dress, they were drinking beer and obediently nibbling at the rice crackers and shreds of dried squid the girls were feeding them in the intervals of paying them extravagant and to them largely unintelligible compliments. None of the boys could have been much over twenty, and the new arrival barely glanced in their direction as he crossed to the bar.

Two other men were perched on stools there. The one alone with his drink at the end of the bar nearest the stage and with his eyes fixed on the singer was a heavily built Japanese in a dark suit. He looked out of place in such surroundings, and somewhat ill at ease. Nearer sixty than fifty, he had the air of a solid professional man: a doctor perhaps, or a lawyer. In fact he was a politician, but the little chrysanthemum badge that identified him as a member of the National Diet and which he normally wore with pride in his lapel was stowed away in his waistcoat pocket.

The other man at the bar was thin-faced, much younger and a foreigner. His suit didn't fit too well, and his lank, straw-coloured hair flopped over his high forehead. Two hostesses stood immediately to his right, and he had several packs of Camels on the bar in front of him. He was occupying himself, without much apparent pleasure, by dropping cigarettes one by one down the front of each woman's blouse alternately and inviting the other to retrieve it.

For the benefit of their customer the girls were doing their best to simulate sexual excitement as they ostentatiously fondled each other's breasts while at the same time taking great care not to crush the precious cigarettes: it was a childish game but easy money, since each had already assembled a pile of Camels worth a lot on the black market. The blond foreigner looked fairly drunk, but there was an air of authority, even a hint of menace about him, as though the situation could quickly turn ugly if one or other of his temporary companions were to betray any lack of enthusiasm; and Nakajima looked him over warily as he slid on to the stool beside the solitary drinker.

"I'm sorry I'm late," he said quietly in Japanese, using the polite form of the language.

"It doesn't matter." The politician kept his back turned as he spoke, but then swivelled round and looked Nakajima up and down. "I was slightly delayed myself." In spite of his age he looked healthy and vigorous, and the two false teeth revealed when he opened his mouth were, most unusually, of gold.

"I was held up by a couple of MPs on the way," Nakajima went on after the barman had placed a glass of beer in front of him and retreated hurriedly at an unobtrusive gesture of dismissal. "I showed my official G2 ID card to one of them and he behaved himself, but the other was looking for trouble. There was nobody else about, so I rather enjoyed dealing with him."

The Dietman nodded, but his eyes were cold. "If you mean what I think you do, that could have been inadvisable. That ID card of yours is worth a great deal to other people besides you, and you could lose it if you insist on indulging your taste for strong-arm stuff. Did he make a note of your name?"

"No. The one who saw it will probably remember, but he's a sensible fellow. I think you can trust my judgment in situations like that, *sensei*."

Something in Nakajima's tone produced a conciliatory gesture from the older man, who glanced past him at the foreigner further along the bar. "Very well, I expect you're right. I don't much care for the look of that *gaijin* over there. Any idea who he is?"

"No. Obviously not a Yank. Russian, perhaps. One of their prosecution or Allied Council staff. Or one of the German ex-diplomats waiting to be shipped home. They still get luxury rations from our Foreign Ministry; live very well. I'll ask the manager later, he can find out from the girls. Even if he understands Japanese he can't hear us from here, though. Besides, he's busy amusing himself."

"All right. Turn your back to him, though. Right. Now listen carefully. The gentleman wants to see you personally, and it'll be arranged shortly. He's well pleased with you, by the way. If only for that reason, quite frankly I'd have thought it wisest to keep your present distance. But there you are. I can only assume he may have one or two purely personal instructions for you that he's not prepared to pass through the usual channels. So stand by. We'll keep you informed."

He paused as a song came to an end and remained silent while the three young Americans applauded the vocalist, resuming only when the pianist and the bass player swung into another number.

"There's something else. Have you ever come across a G2 man called Brooks?"

"I know who he is. I've never met him, though. Why?"

"You'll know Brooks is an officer, then. A major, in fact. He's concerned with security at installations outside Tokyo, but a reliable American contact of mine in SHAPE thinks he might be interesting himself in matters that shouldn't concern him. There might be nothing in it, but to be on the safe side we'd like you to find out what you can in the way of personal information about this Brooks. Character, weaknesses and so forth, and if possible where he stands, politically. Can you do that?"

"I can try. I can't guarantee reliable information about his political opinions, though. People in sensitive jobs are beginning to think it advisable to button their lips about politics, or to say what they think's expected of them."

The older man made a sound half-way between a grunt and a chuckle. "Well, we both understand what it's like to be in that position, don't we? Do what you can, anyway. Now, one last thing. This is for your information only, no action called for on your part. There's a man called Noonan, small fry, an NCO I think, in counter-intelligence. He's one of the people my friends deal with for supplies. PX and quartermaster stuff. They've recently come to an arrangement with an up-and-coming man in Kobe and may want to increase their business with Noonan substantially. If he's up to it. As I say, there's no need for you to concern yourself with him directly, but we think you ought to know of the connection."

2

"Why call it a Mongolian dinner, for God's sake?" Angie demanded, fishing a slice of beef out of the broth and holding it poised in mid-air with her chopsticks. "Mongolians don't eat this crud."

Jay didn't take offence. Angie Brewster was a big woman with a big heart. Outspoken at the best of times, she could be counted on to be cheerfully argumentative after a few drinks. The nice thing was that most times she stayed that way. Angie might turn a little maudlin towards the end of a long evening and ask everybody within earshot why they thought she'd ended up an old maid, but she never quite lost her gutsy sense of humour or seriously upset people. It was one of the reasons they enjoyed having her around.

"How in the world do *you* know what Mongolians eat, Angie? Polly here's the real expert. Her ancestors slugged it out with them, isn't that right, Polly?"

Preoccupied though she was, Polly Horvath managed a smile. "Sure. All fired up with the local wine. Bull's blood, they called it. Still do, I guess. I wouldn't know about Mongolian eating habits in those days, but this is delicious."

There were six at Jay Murakami's table that same raw January evening, on the other side of Tokyo from the tawdry Hotshot Cabaret. The Washington Heights housing project was still in the early stages of development on the site of the old Imperial Army parade grounds, and only a handful of the more senior civilian officials on the staff of the Supreme Commander Allied Powers had as yet been allotted houses there. Jay had given a combined pre-Christmas drinks and house-warming party only a couple of weeks earlier, and now a few friends were helping to initiate his newly acquired "steamboat": a charcoal burner with a cylindrical chimney surrounded by a circular trough big enough to hold several pints of simmering beef, chicken or fish broth.

The meal was well under way, and they were on to the second huge platter of thinly sliced raw beef brought in from the kitchen by Jay's housekeeper Fujiko-san, who had also replaced a depleted flat vegetable basket with another, piled high with Chinese cabbage, leeks, bean-sprouts and cubes of palest ivory bean-curd. From these raw materials everyone was supposed to select whatever took his or her fancy, transfer it to the broth for a few minutes and then retrieve and eat it.

It seldom worked out that way, and it fell to Jay as an attentive host to make sure that the increasingly rich, aromatic broth was kept well stocked with slices of the meat and a selection of the vegetables, and from time to time personally to replenish somebody's individual bowl. It was not necessary to do this for Angie. She went on muttering disparagingly about Mongolians in general and their cuisine in particular, but was nevertheless tucking in heartily, and washing her food down with her fair share of beer.

Eleanor Curtis was sitting on Jay's right, as befitted her status, and Polly on his left. Though at twenty-six she was young enough to be Angie's daughter, as a senior economic analyst on the civilian staff Eleanor ranked about equal to an army captain. The other two women actually were in the army, but as an administrative clerk Angie was a humble WAC private first class, while Polly at twenty-eight was a sergeant. The American staff of SCAP and Far East Command took conscious pride in their democratic style and often joked among themselves about the absurd lengths to which their handful of British colleagues went to avoid bridging the great divide between officers and other ranks. All the same, it would not have occurred to Jay Murakami to invite a military officer to his dinner table at the same time as Polly or Angie, even when neither of them was in uniform.

Civilians like Eleanor, Tom Berman and his own boss the Professor were another matter. The Professor was probably equal in status to a colonel at least, perhaps a brigadier, and Tom Berman, leading a sizeable team in the International Prosecution Section, was just a step or so behind in the pecking order, like himself. The majority of the SCAP professionals disdained military protocol, and the others present were already acquainted with both Polly and Angie. Their gender in an overwhelmingly male expatriate community earned them invitations of a kind that never came the way of similarly low-ranking men. Jay was well aware that even Eleanor, the Professor or Tom might be put out if the niceties of social etiquette were not observed; and was too experienced in that area to put a foot wrong.

"How you doing, Professor?"

John Prothero started slightly as Angie laid a large, warm hand on his forearm, and then brushed a stray lock of silver hair back from his forehead. "What? Oh. I beg your pardon, Miss Brewster, I'm afraid I was miles away. I'm having a splendid time, thank you."

"I was wondering how you like the food. Mongolian dinner! Huh! Mongolians don't eat this crud, you know."

"So I have been gathering from you. It's a pleasant, sociable thing to cook at the table, though, wouldn't you agree." It was a statement, not a question, and without waiting for a reply Prothero unobtrusively detached his sleeve from Angie's grasp and smiled across the table at Polly. "Well, Miss Horvath," he said politely, "how nice it is to see you here this evening. Tell me, what news do you bring us of the great man's feelings about the forthcoming general strike?"

He spoke in his usual quiet, donnish manner, but Tom Berman at the other end of the table overheard him, and in order to pay attention to Polly's response at once abandoned the stilted conversation he had been having with Eleanor Curtis. The effects of present and future inflation on plans to reform the agricultural sector by enabling small tenant farmers to buy the land they worked with the aid of mortgage finance were no doubt significant, but of considerably less interest to him than they clearly were to her.

At five feet ten, fair-skinned blonde Eleanor was as tall as most men, and very much in command of herself in the office. On social occasions, however, she was prone to blush on being directly addressed by a man: a reaction which desperately embarrassed her and in large gatherings sometimes led casual observers out of earshot to suppose that the people talking to her were telling dirty stories or making improper suggestions. As soon as Tom Berman stopped looking at her, Eleanor's high colour faded and she too turned to Polly, who hesitated and sipped at her beer, acutely aware of the expectant silence which had fallen on the room.

"Which great man are you referring to, Professor? Not the Supreme Commander, I presume? My General Willoughby, or General Whitney? Hardly General Marquat, I guess. You surely know his feelings better than anybody else in this room."

Prothero smiled again. "No, Miss Horvath. Your general, not mine. It is common knowledge that Marquat shares Whitney's view, that having positively encouraged the formation of a vast number of trade unions during the past year or so, SCAP must respect the right of their members to go on strike – ”

“For *political* reasons, though? With the object of bringing down the Japanese government and installing a left-wing regime?” It was Tom Berman who interrupted, every inch the accomplished courtroom performer seizing on a weak point in an argument. Prothero inclined his head gently but raised a hand and continued imperturbably. He was famous for his impressively grammatical conversational style.

“ – as we have indeed already done on a number of occasions. Political slogans are indeed being displayed and shouted by demonstrators all over the city. All the same, I understand that General MacArthur is as yet by no means persuaded that the motives of those planning the national strike are, as you suggest, Tom, wholly or even primarily political. Nor, even granting for the sake of argument that they are, does it follow that the strike will in fact bring down the government. Our respected chief will no doubt as always take account of the advice of all three of his heads of sections.”

“Hey, Professor, is it true General Marquat takes his old cavalry whip with him into conferences?” Angie sat back, red-faced and beaming tipsily, but Prothero took her in his stride.

“That is so, Miss Brewster, but be assured that I have never seen him use it. It is also the case that between the wars he edited the automobile page of a West Coast newspaper, a fact some people profess to find amusing. Manifestly, neither consideration weighs against him in the Supreme Commander’s estimation. As I was saying, Miss Horvath, it would be of interest to know whether you and your G2 colleagues have reason to think that General Willoughby is taking a strong line on this issue.”

“Don’t ask me, Professor, I’m just a sergeant,” Polly protested. “He doesn’t take me into his confidence. But he doesn’t exactly conceal his views about the threat from the left, and I’d guess he’s trying to persuade the chief to prohibit the strike.” Clearly reluctant to say more, she picked up her bowl and busied herself by refilling it from the steamboat. Jay Murakami took up the conversation.

“Polly’s right, of course . . . in the sense that we all know the *Herr General* believes in *realpolitik*, hates communism and reckons all of us civilians are at best parlour pinks. Even you, Tom,” he added with a quick smile at Berman.

"Well! Listen who's giving us this 'Herr General' stuff!" Lowering her bowl, which she had been holding so close to her face that her glasses were partially steamed up, Angie drew on her ample reserves of outrage. "So what if he was born in Germany? He was an American citizen practically before you were born, Jay. And you're a *nisei*, right? How'd you like it if we called you Murakami the Jap?"

He shrugged. "Plenty of people do, Angie. It doesn't bother me. My parents are naturalized Japanese immigrants and I love them. As a native-born American myself, I certainly don't plan on changing my name to Smith. So I sometimes wonder why Charles Andre Willoughby wasn't content to stick with Adolf Weidenbach. Do you and Mike Brooks ever speculate about it, Polly?"

"For heaven's sake, Jay! Don't be ridiculous. Excuse me please, I'll be right back." Polly slipped out of the room and stood for a moment indecisively in the hallway, the back of her left hand to her suddenly hot cheek. There was a tiny lavatory for the use of guests on the other side and she took a step towards it, then changed her mind and headed for the stairs. Jay had urged the women as they arrived to make use of the dressing table in the spare bedroom if they wished, and Polly felt in need of peace and quiet for a few minutes. She guessed the others would assume not that she needed to visit the john but that she was embarrassed by Jay's reference to Major Brooks. In the circumstances it might be just as well if they did speculate about the possibility that she might have a crush on him. Better that than their suspecting anything else.

She was in no way bothered by Jay Murakami's hostile remarks about General MacArthur's long-time comrade and present chief of intelligence, Major-General Willoughby. Polly had heard enough scuttlebutt about him from other people in SCAP Headquarters to have been appalled when, three months earlier, she was first assigned to work for Mike Brooks, one of his aides, in the central administrative office of Intelligence Section or G2. Since then she had seen the general from time to time, and was impressed in spite of herself by his aristocratic good looks and his austere military bearing. He had never addressed a word to her directly, but in her hearing at least spoke courteously enough to Major Brooks, and Polly found it hard to understand why he had a reputation for being evil-tempered.

Still, Brooks himself was often given to remark that no man is a hero to his valet, and told Polly enough about the head of G2's style of command for her to decide to dislike him on principle and to pick up the habit of referring to him as the "Junker General", as most other people around the Dai-Ichi Building did. After a while she'd seen enough tart comments Willoughby had scribbled in the margins of memoranda and draft reports to form her own judgment, and gleefully passed on to one or two particular friends MacArthur's alleged description of his trusted adviser as "my lovable fascist".

The general strike was being planned by a joint committee set up by the unions of teachers, civil servants and other government workers, and was due to begin on 1 February. Along with the closing stages of the presentation of the case for the prosecution before the Tokyo International Tribunal, the strike was a prime topic of office conversation among military and civilian personnel alike, and therefore almost bound to crop up that evening. Everybody round the table worked for SCAP, so it would have been impossibly stuffy for Polly to plead confidentiality when faced with John Prothero's question. In any case what troubled her was not what Willoughby was thinking about the general strike or the line he was taking with the Supreme Commander. That was easy enough for anybody to guess.

Polly's problem was, so far as she knew, completely unrelated to the strike. It was to decide what on earth to do about the papers she had seen in the slim folder at the bottom of the safe in Major Brooks's office that afternoon, the safe to which he alone was supposed to have access, and in which he kept his bourbon.

It was a week or two after she began to work for the untidy, balding major with the pleasant lopsided smile that it dawned on Polly that he was an alcoholic. Like many of his kind, Mike Brooks employed great ingenuity in keeping himself topped up. At first, she thought the occasional hesitancies in his speech and slips of the tongue had a certain charm, as did his physical ineptitude and the rueful smile on his face when, as sometimes happened, he opened the matchbox upside down when lighting his pipe and she had to help him retrieve the contents from the floor. Polly once asked him why he didn't use a Zippo and was treated to a lecture on the dire effects of lighter-fuel vapour on the taste of tobacco smoke.

The major was, she thought then and still thought, a very nice man, and she enjoyed hearing him talk about his background. He had taught German in high school in civilian life, and told her it had been on account of his knowledge of the language that he had found his way into army intelligence. He had volunteered to stay on in the army for a spell at the end of the war on the reasonable assumption that he would be attached to the Allied Control Commission in Germany. He should, he admitted, have realized that the army would foul things up and ship his body to Tokyo while his heart was in Berlin. Now and then in a chatty mood he would propose elaborate and amusing hypotheses to account for his finding himself evaluating and collating with Polly's assistance the regular reports submitted to G2 by the security officers at Allied military installations all over Japan.

It was for the most part undemanding work. This was just as well since Polly soon found that she was expected to handle most of it herself, the major spending the greater part of his time away from the office. When he did show up he invariably approved her draft reports and recommendations to higher authority, and signed anything she put in front of him.

If a hero's shortcomings are inevitably apparent to his valet, a middle-ranking, gently cynical, indolent officer who was formerly a schoolteacher is unlikely to be able to hoodwink his personal assistant for very long. It was Polly's keen sense of smell that enabled her after a while to put two and two together; when she noticed that the lingering fug of Balkan Sobranie tobacco smoke in Mike Brooks's office was subtly different from the fumes which hung about Lieutenant Commander Arthur Reynolds, the Australian naval officer who worked just along the corridor. It was Reynolds who had introduced his American colleague to the exotic blend and who kept him supplied with it.

Once the seed of suspicion had planted itself in Polly's lively mind she soon began to notice other clues to the major's secret, and to put her own interpretation on his frequent absences from his desk. She felt sorry for him because it seemed a pity for an obviously gifted, intelligent man to have lost control over himself. She also became increasingly exasperated, because there was nothing she could do about it, and Polly did not like feeling powerless.

Towards the end of the afternoon before Jay's dinner party she had for the first time seen Brooks obviously drunk, when he returned from what was entered in his diary in his own hand simply as "Meeting, 2.45". That in itself was odd, since he rarely noted down any engagements himself, usually preferring to have her do it. When Polly went through the connecting door into his room she found him on his knees in front of the safe, closing its door and muttering to himself. His face was red and glistening with sweat, and he looked round at her with half-closed eyes, then lurched to his feet and staggered out of the door. There was a men's room not far away on the opposite side of the corridor, and it seemed fairly obvious to her that he was about to throw up.

It was not until Polly had closed the door behind him that it occurred to her that Brooks had not spun the dial on the safe door. The temptation was too much for her, and she pulled it open. The top shelf contained several squat, pint bottles of bourbon and two tumblers, one clean and one with a half-inch of whisky in it. In the lower half was a jumble of what looked like personal papers, including a cheque book, and underneath them a single regulation file cover.

Only a few seconds had passed, and with a quick and pointless glance back over her shoulder, Polly took the file out and looked at it. The cover bore no name, no serial number, no security marking. It contained only three sheets of paper on which were written a few hundred words in Brooks's crabby, pedantic writing, neatly laid out in note form, with main and sub-paragraphs numbered appropriately, under the title OPERATION HI-FLYER.

Polly scanned the sheets with mounting incredulity, alert for any sound from the corridor. Then her telephone rang. She hesitated for a moment, but then hurriedly put the file back and pushed the safe door to before going through to deal with the phone. It was Tom Berman offering her and Angie a ride to Jay Murakami's house, explaining that he'd already arranged to pick up Eleanor Curtis on the way. Polly managed to sound less distracted than she felt, but when she put the receiver down she realized that her throat was dry and her heart pounding.

Brooks had not yet returned. She went back into his room and ostentatiously leafed through the unclassified pending tray on his desk while wondering whether she dared sneak another look at the file. It was then that she noticed the scrap of paper on his blotter with three two-digit numbers written on it, and at the same moment heard Brooks in conversation with somebody just outside the door. The numbers just had to be the combination that opened the safe. Even if they weren't, nothing would be lost by memorizing them, and she mouthed them silently as she skipped back to her own desk and scribbled them down.

A minute later she heard the major return, and pretended to busy herself with some innocuous piece of work while listening hard for the sound of the safe door being opened again. It was, for a moment or two only, and when the door was slammed shut the twirl of the dial was distinctly audible. After that, to her mounting relief Polly heard nothing except the occasional squeak when Brooks moved in his chair, the rustle of papers and once something between a sigh and a groan.

After what seemed a very long time but was less than half an hour by her watch, Brooks appeared in the open doorway between their offices looking pale but otherwise normal. He made no reference to his earlier precipitate departure from his room, but said he wasn't feeling so good and was quitting early, going back to his quarters at the Imperial Hotel.

Left to herself at last, Polly relaxed. Brooks had obviously realized that the door of his safe had been unlocked while he was out of the room, and must have noticed that he had left his note of the combination – if it was that – on his blotter. All the same, it seemed he had persuaded himself that all was well, probably underestimating the length of time he had been gone. Sorely tempted as she was to try out the numbers, she thought it would be chancing her luck to risk it that day. It wasn't as though she hadn't quite enough to think about already.

With so much on her mind, dinner at Jay Murakami's was turning out to be something of an ordeal for her, and Polly realized she must seem tense and jumpy to the others. Fair enough. She was, and it was small wonder that the mere mention of Mike Brooks's name was enough to throw her off balance.

The upstairs bathroom had two doors, one from the landing and the other opening directly into the master bedroom. Momentarily disoriented, on leaving it Polly opened the wrong one, to find the housekeeper Fujiko-san bending over the bed.

"Oh. Hi. I guess I used the wrong door. Sorry." As Polly began to retreat into the bathroom again, the Japanese woman turned quickly but said nothing, and the expression on her face was unreadable. "Sorry," Polly faltered once more, and then closed the door and made her escape.

The encounter was curiously disconcerting, but at least it gave her something apart from the file in Major Brooks's safe to think about as she made her way back to the dining room, from which she could hear the sound of Angie's voice followed by a burst of general laughter. How interesting that Jay's bed was made up for two, with a crisp-looking pair of pyjamas on one side and a flimsy nightgown on the other!

Polly seemed to remember Jay mentioning that he had engaged a childless war widow as his housekeeper, and without really thinking about it she had visualized a drab, depressed, middle-aged woman. War widow she might well be, but Fujiko-san was certainly not yet thirty, and without the voluminous apron which she had been wearing over her kimono earlier, she looked slender and graceful. Moreover, she looked as though she belonged in that bedroom.

3

Jay Murakami whistled tunelessly as he contemplated his blurred reflection in the steamy surface of his shaving mirror, and continued while he finished towelling himself. He was sure everybody had meant it when they said on leaving that they'd enjoyed the party, even Polly Horvath who had seemed a little under the weather early on. Time of the month maybe. Fujiko had done a great job, needless to say. Must have been tired by the end of the evening, but she sure hadn't let it spoil things later; and now he could smell the coffee and bacon she'd have ready for him when he went downstairs. What a woman!

Their days now often began as that one had, when the amount of light filtering through the curtains meant it must be between six and six-thirty. Time to get up, really, but how could a man do it when his mistress slowly raised her head from his chest and gazed down at him like that? At such moments Jay soon became incapable of conscious thought; physical joy consumed his whole being. It wasn't until afterwards, when Fujiko had slipped out of bed and went down to her own room and he was showering and shaving, that his intellect awakened too. Then he often wondered coolly enough, as he was wondering this morning, how long his delight in her body could possibly be sustained at such a pitch.

Fujiko was a wonderful lover. Jay was enchanted by the childlike expression of grave concentration in her face when she explored his body with delicate fingers, soft lips and firm little tongue; and by her uninhibited reaction to his own caresses. Yet it was not, he thought, that he was after a mere few weeks in love with her. Nor did he seriously suppose that she was in love with him. His Japanese was fluent so there was no language barrier between them, but Fujiko kept her own counsel and seemed to have no inclination to talk about their relationship.

She had never asked him whether he had a wife in America. He hadn't, but in the case of a man of his age it would have been a reasonable supposition. So probably she had long ago checked him out by chatting to other Japanese employed as servants by the Americans in the neighbourhood. A good many of them spoke English after a fashion and could tune into the gossip they overheard. Since Fujiko seemed quite unconcerned about the possibility of becoming pregnant it was hardly cynical to speculate that she might welcome it, as opening up the possibility of marriage. Too level-headed to be trapped like that, Jay always took the necessary precautions.

He could well imagine that from Fujiko's point of view he must seem inconceivably rich, and that to her the American-style house in Washington Heights would represent the lap of luxury. It was hardly surprising that in those cold, dark days of deprivation plenty of Japanese women dreamed of marrying an American.

Even a temporary liaison was better than nothing. It offered the prospect of warmth, comfort and good food, and for the sake of these things many were more than willing to brave the hostile glances and barbed remarks they attracted when seen in the company of a western man. Jay knew that in one respect at least he would be a particularly good catch. His American upbringing had made him far more outgoing and free-spirited than either of his parents, but physically he was not obviously a foreigner, so no Japanese woman need fear ostracism or even unpleasantness by being seen with him.

Not that he had the slightest intention of taking Fujiko out, needless to say; and granted that she had already been enjoying all the material advantages of a liaison he wondered why, if it were not in the vague hope of marriage, she had offered herself to him in the first place. Out of simple gratitude for having found a safe haven? Hardly. Because he was sexually irresistible to her? Murakami dropped the towel, sucked in a deep breath and pummelled his skinny chest. Me Tarzan, you Jane? Come *on*, for chrissake! For all Fujiko's flatteringly enthusiastic behaviour in bed, the very idea was ludicrous. He was slightly built, his eyesight was so poor that he had to wear glasses all day, and he was after all not far short of forty. Yet there must be some reason, and seldom did a day go by without his teasing away at possible explanations. But that was no reason to put off getting dressed. He went back into the bedroom.

All Jay knew about Fujiko Ueda's background was what he had been told by the domestic employment agency who had sent her to see him in November. That she had been born in Omiya just north of Tokyo in 1920, and been married at nineteen to an executive of the Manchurian Railway Company who was commissioned into the Imperial Army in 1943 and was killed two years later in action in Okinawa. At that first interview Jay had asked the pale, quiet young woman in the plain kimono if she had any children. No, she had said, nor any surviving close relations. She had been repatriated from what had been Manchuria only a month or two earlier, with no more belongings than she could herself carry, and had been obliged to appeal for help to the welfare office of her late husband's regiment. Officials there, busy with what to them were the more pressing problems of resettling former servicemen, had been able to suggest only domestic service for an officer's widow with no particular skills or qualifications.

Fujiko's was a sadly commonplace story, and Jay had been impressed to see how quickly and effectively she adjusted to her new way of life. Her speech, manner and deportment made it obvious that she had had a privileged upbringing, and he guessed that in all probability until the surrender she had herself been waited on hand and foot. Yet once installed in the new house she scrubbed, dusted and polished with a will, washed and ironed, shopped in the black market to supplement what he brought home from the PX, and cooked for him more than adequately, although clearly happier when he asked for Japanese dishes.

An advance he gave her to buy clothes brought a transformation in Fujiko's appearance within a few days – beautiful, hardly worn kimonos, she coolly explained, were being offered for sale at bargain prices by upper-class women desperate for cash to spend on food for their families. Then Jay himself thought to cheer her up by persuading the ever-helpful Eleanor Curtis to put together a range of basic cosmetics for her from the shelves of the big PX in the Ginza. Fujiko received them with – for the first time – the tiniest of smiles as well as humble thanks. An hour later that same day, carefully made up and dressed in a kimono new to him, she served his evening meal. It was then that Jay first properly thought about his new housekeeper as a person: a hard-working woman only twenty-six years old who had suffered bereavement and deprivation, but with the composure and elegance of any lady of leisure.

Two evenings later Fujiko seduced him. Jay was pretty sure that had been the way of it. He was sitting in his living room after dinner, listening to *Mystery Playhouse* on the Armed Forces Radio and sipping bourbon and water when he heard a quickly stifled shriek from the kitchen where she was washing the dishes. He went to investigate.

It seemed that she had broken a glass and cut the side of her hand on a shard. Nothing serious: she was holding the hand under running cold water and Jay could see at once that the cut was a mere half-inch long and called for nothing more than antiseptic and a plaster strip. Fujiko seemed to be rooted to the spot and was visibly shaking, so Jay himself turned off the tap, pulled a fortunately clean handkerchief from his pocket and wrapped it tightly round the hand. Then he persuaded her to sit down, went quickly upstairs and fetched absorbent cotton, iodine and the flat tin of band-aids he kept in his bathroom cabinet.

Fujiko seemed not to have moved during his absence, and sat as if in a trance while he cleaned and dressed the unimpressive little wound. She winced and gasped at the sting of the iodine but otherwise remained silent until he had finished. Only then did she shudder, blink and seem to pull herself together, apologizing profusely for making such a fuss over so little. Jay was polite about it but Fujiko clearly thought that she had irritated him, and timidly explained that she had always experienced irrational terror at the sight of blood, particularly her own.

He brought her a little brandy which she at first refused, but he persuaded her to swallow a teaspoonful or so, and after a few moments she rose unsteadily to her feet. When Jay slipped his arm round her waist it was simply to support her, and he was astonished when Fujiko responded by clutching at him and burying her face in his chest.

He stood there in silence for what seemed like an eternity, supporting Fujiko's sagging body with one arm and patting her back almost absent-mindedly with his free hand. It felt so pleasant that only with some reluctance did he eventually mutter something about helping her to her room, and did so. There wasn't far to go: the house had been planned to accommodate a resident servant and Fujiko's small room with its own adjacent shower and toilet was on the ground floor just beyond the kitchen.

What happened after he lowered her to the bed seemed in retrospect to be inevitable. Fujiko's face was slightly flushed, her eyes closed and her lips were quivering almost imperceptibly until he kissed them; at once they opened greedily. Jay would never forget that kiss: the ridiculous thought which flashed through his mind that he ought to have helped Fujiko to take off her apron first, the smell of iodine from the dressing on her hand as she put her arms round his neck, the distant strains of the *Mystery Playhouse* closing signature tune, the visible pulsing at the base of her throat and then the shared fumbling at the complex fastenings of the stiff obi sash round her waist while their mouths remained joined. And after that, suddenly the unthinkable – unthinkable since his teenage years, at least – and he had been obliged to pull away from the panting woman with a blurted apology and rush out of the room to clean himself up.

Deeply embarrassed, he fled to his own bathroom where he stripped and showered, wondering what on earth to say to Fujiko and how to behave towards her after such an extraordinary episode. She had been married after all, and had presumably guessed what had happened. He need not have worried. When he went into the bedroom to put on clean clothes Fujiko was sitting up in his bed, smiling serenely. She opened her arms to him, the covers falling away to expose her breasts: small but pretty breasts with erect nipples which were unusually big even for a Japanese woman. Jay hesitated for no more than a second or two before going back to fetch the packet of condoms he kept (he had always told himself) more as an act of faith than of confidence.

Now fully dressed and with neatly brushed hair, Jay glanced round the bedroom, which had since that memorable evening been the setting for so much pleasure. Although it hadn't happened so very long ago, he could now smile at the recollection of the way his body had jumped the gun, and be thankful for the matter-of-fact way in which Fujiko restored his composure and led him into a relationship that seemed to become more magical every day. Whatever Fujiko's motives, she was, as many of his male colleagues would no doubt put it, one hell of a good lay and he was a very lucky guy.

John Prothero lived nearby and rated an official car with a Japanese chauffeur; so it was no trouble for him to give Jay a ride most days to the Forestry Building where SCAP's Labor Division was housed. When he heard the toot of the horn outside Jay swallowed the last of his third cup of coffee, went to the front door and smiled at Fujiko as she helped him into his top-coat and then handed him his brief-case with the same courteous dignity she had shown while serving his breakfast. Her formality never ceased to amaze Jay: it was as though his housekeeper and his inventive and enthusiastic mistress were two quite different people. He often wanted to kiss her on leaving and returning to the house, but had soon learned to accept that such a gesture would not be well received.

Fujiko Ueda bowed as Jay left the house, watched the car until it was out of sight, and then went back inside. In the kitchen she made toast for herself and drank a cup of coffee before picking up the telephone and dialling a number she had no need to look up. When the connection was made she listened to the voice at the other end for a moment but did not identify herself. When she spoke it was tersely and without honorifics.

"He'll probably be at the open-air rally in Hibiya Park the day after tomorrow. The Professor's driver heard them discussing it in the car on the way to the office yesterday. He rang a man called Sato yesterday evening before the guests arrived and arranged to meet him today at four. . . . No, I can't be certain, but probably the teachers' union Sato, I should think. . . . No, I don't know where. 'The usual place' was all he said. And he's going out to dinner tonight. Yes, of course I did, I always do. Nothing of interest, but I'll look through it again first thing tomorrow as usual while he's getting dressed."

After ringing off, Fujiko wandered into the dining room and stood there, unconsciously hugging herself as though cold. They had eaten a huge amount, those Americans. Especially the older woman, the noisy unfeminine one, but then she had a big body. So had the tall blonde, but hers was beautifully proportioned, even if she did seem to be too shy to flaunt it. The dark one who had strayed into the bedroom was much smaller, about her own age and around the same size, and worried about something. But she was sharp, the one they called Polly, and not so preoccupied as to have failed to put two and two together.

Fujiko hoped she wouldn't start rumours at the office about herself and Jay-san. The man she had just been reporting to on the telephone wouldn't like that to happen.

4

The heavy, brooding portico of the Dai-Ichi Building faced west, towards the moat surrounding the Imperial Palace. At that time of the year it was only briefly that the sunshine gave an illusion of warmth to the bleak stone cladding of the outer walls; but sometimes during the afternoon it illuminated a corner of the deeply recessed entrance. Then it threw into prominence the ugly concrete blocks hastily installed as part of the shoring-up process needed when the building – one of the few of any size still more or less intact at the end of the war – was being rehabilitated for the use of the Supreme Commander and his entourage.

Those responsible for the work had made no attempt to beautify the approach to the seat of power. At night a single electric light-bulb in a functional metal shade attached to a wire strung across the entrance at a height of about eight or nine feet cast its feeble glow on the steel helmet of the sentry on duty at the top of the one shallow and three ordinary stone steps from the sidewalk. All in all the public face of SCAP Headquarters was not so much forbidding as drab and unremarkable. Yet towards one o'clock every working day a crowd of ordinary Japanese assembled there. Its size varied with the weather, but there were never fewer than dozens of men, women and children on either side of the main entrance; and often hundreds turned up to watch the man they called the Blue-Eyed Shogun emerge to go home to the American Embassy Residence for lunch.

"Must be between three and four hundred rubberneckers here today," Noonan said to the American sailor standing beside him, a spotty-faced boy of eighteen or nineteen whose round white cap with its upturned brim was moving slightly to the rhythm of his jaws as he chewed gum. "Guy must be crazy taking this risk every day."

Noonan himself had a couple of uniforms somewhere among his belongings, very smart with the stripes and insignia of a master sergeant in the Counter-Intelligence Corps. They fitted him exceptionally well, having been done over for him by a Chinese tailor who had survived the destruction of Yokohama and set up business in a makeshift shack near the Atsugi air base within days of the arrival of the first Americans – hours, some said.

Nevertheless, Noonan would have had trouble recalling the last time he had been on the street in the guise of a military man. That day he was wearing an old brown suit with a flannel shirt and a greasy tie; the sort of shabby civilian clothes that were appropriate most of the time, for his work was largely clandestine and his sideline wholly so. There was certainly no call to dress up for the benefit of the Japanese girls at the bars where his contact had introduced him and where nobody ever presented him with a bill. An effort obviously had to be made whenever he felt like making a play for one of the American women working in Tokyo, but even on those occasions Noonan generally put on one of his sharp suits in preference to uniform. He didn't have a lot of luck in fooling people that way, but was sometimes taken for an officer.

The young sailor's silence irritated Noonan. "Right?" he demanded. "Some nut wants to take a shot at him, right? Just one guard at the top of the steps with a real gun, and a couple of sentries sashaying around with unloaded rifles. Big deal."

There was still no response, and the middle-aged Japanese woman standing on his other side shrank away uneasily as Noonan switched his attention from the uncommunicative sailor and glared around in exasperation. He had spotted the man he had come to meet standing about four rows back on the other side, and was disposed to be sociable with anybody handy during the few minutes before he could approach him.

"Hey, he's coming!" The sailor spoke at last, his voice strained, his eyes alight with something akin to religious awe. A collective silence fell over the crowd; not that many of the Japanese had in any case been talking to each other. Even the crop-headed small boys who normally cheekily demanded gum from any male westerner they encountered became subdued and gazed wide-eyed as the swing doors deep in the portico were opened from inside, the ceremonial guards smartly presented arms and General of the Army Douglas MacArthur emerged into the pale sunlight, pausing at the top of the steps to glance coldly to right and left.

The officer in attendance a pace behind him and to his left was in normal working uniform, the pale fawn of his trousers in contrast to the brown of the battledress tunic, the strip of medal ribbons above his left breast pocket a conspicuous touch of gaudy colour. MacArthur also wore battledress, but his trousers were of the same chocolate brown as his tunic. This, though beautifully cut, bore no decorations or insignia of any kind except for the five stars of his rank on each epaulette. The famous battered cap was set at an angle just a millimetre short of being jaunty, and the skin of his face was smoothly shaven and apparently unlined.

"Son of a bitch!" the sailor murmured admiringly as the tableau broke up and the Supreme Commander descended the steps and walked the few yards to the huge black car waiting at the sidewalk with its driver already at the wheel, the rear door held open by a soldier standing rigidly to attention. "I heard he's going on sixty-seven years old. That's older than my grandaddy, and he never stirs from his chair."

Noonan decided to be gracious to the boy. "Yup. It's the old poop's birthday at the end of the month. Look out for the write-up in *Stars and Stripes*." The car was pulling away and the crowd was beginning to disperse, though many of the Japanese seemed reluctant to move even when the military policeman at the top of the steps gestured dismissively and called out, "OK, folks, show's over!"

"You with *Stars and Stripes*?" Having earlier seemed to resent Noonan's friendly overtures, the sailor now looked relaxed and ready to chat.

"Me? Come on, kid! Do I look like a reporter?"

"I wouldn't know. Could be. You seem to know a lot about the big man."

"I know a lot about a whole bunch of things," Noonan said, and winked complacently. He had noticed that his man was turning away with the apparent intention of making off. "If I cared to I could make your hair stand on end, sailor. But I'm busy right now, I have to meet a guy. Nice talking to you. Have fun, but watch where you put it, huh?"

Noonan would have liked to preserve his dignity by sauntering nonchalantly after his quarry, but found that the other man's stride was deceptively long and that he had to move fast even to keep him in view, much less gain on him. He nearly lost him in the gloomy recesses of Shinbashi Station and was relieved to see him again on the other side of the elevated tracks, heading south-east towards the vast, sprawling complex of the Shiodome rail freight terminal. Noonan was breathing heavily when he eventually caught up with the Japanese.

"Matter with you? Trying to make me . . . look conspicuous, or what?" he complained. "Slow down there, will you?"

He was ignored until they had crossed several railway tracks and were in the shadow of a line of flatcars loaded with roughly finished lengths of timber which smelt clean and fresh in the still air. Then the Japanese stopped dead, took a pack of cigarettes from his pocket with a hand which lacked the top joints of two fingers, pulled a cigarette out with his lips and lit it. He did not offer the packet to Noonan, but did contrive to blow a great cloud of smoke into his face.

Though lithe and well-muscled, Masao Suekawa was not a handsome man. Across one cheek he bore a purplish scar which had evidently healed without the benefit of stitches, and he looked about thirty. Noonan had seen Suekawa looking a lot smarter, but that day he was dressed in a patched shirt and khaki trousers with down-at-heel shoes on his feet and an old Imperial Army fatigue cap on his head. When he did eventually speak it was in serviceable English with an accent not unlike Noonan's own.

"Who was the sailor?"

"Sailor? What sailor?"

"You know what sailor. You was supposed to meet me in the crowd, Noonan. Not get involved in a conversation with some guy gonna remember you for a bigmouth."

Noonan prepared to flare up, but something in Suekawa's eyes made him think again. "Damn half-assed place to meet anyway," he grumbled instead. "You wanted to come here after, why the Dai-Ichi first? All we know, they could have a guy with a camera up there behind a window above the entrance."

Suekawa dragged at his cigarette, inhaling the smoke, and then expelled it through his nostrils, one eyebrow raised as he looked at the American. "Why they want to do a thing like that?"

"Why not? Standing there, I was thinking some crazy could run out of one of these MacArthur fan-club crowds any time, pull a knife on Old Corn-Cob there. Could be the guys detailed to take care of him figure there'd be no harm in keeping a tab on just who does turn up every day."

"You have some imagination," Suekawa said. "August 1945 MacArthur flies in to Atsugi, right? OK, how many Yank soldiers in

Japan then? Couple hundred? And three *million* Japanese servicemen still holding on to their rifles. Nobody took a shot at him then, so why now? Come on, we'll take another little walk." He set off at a more moderate pace than before, continuing across the tracks in the same general direction. The freight terminal looked as shabby and run-down as almost everything else in Tokyo. Here and there in the huge marshalling yard a few trucks were being shunted, but it struck Noonan that there were hardly any workmen about.

"Strike committee called a meeting," Suekawa said, and pointed to a poster pasted to the ironwork of a nearby signal. It was as though he had read the American's mind. "Nobody gonna see us."

They reached the eastern boundary of the freight yard which was marked by a road, and the gangster waited for a decrepit charcoal-burning lorry loaded with small barrels of what smelt like pickled vegetables to lumber past before crossing it. There was little other traffic on the road, and for long periods no vehicle in sight.

On the far side was a pair of massive, metal-studded wooden gates set into a wall at least six feet high. The wall was of traditional construction, faced with plaster and capped with tiles. Most of it was still standing, but it was all in sad need of repair and in places there were gaps where it had crumbled to rubble.

"What is this, some kind of a temple?" Noonan enquired when they had walked a few yards and Suekawa paused by a particularly wide gap. Apart from his remark about the mass meeting called by the strike committee, his companion had said nothing since their brief exchange beside the timber wagons, ignoring two or three attempts by Noonan to make conversation. This time the Japanese did reply.

"No. Two hundred years ago it was a *daimyo*'s place. You know daimyo? Every part of Japan had its local lord. Some were small-time, some very big wheels indeed, but they all had to show up here once a year. The daimyo from Kofu province used this when he made his trips to Tokyo."

The road again looked deserted, and Suekawa's glance around seemed cursory. "OK. Through here," he said, and stepped neatly over the rubble. Noonan followed, and cursed as he twisted an ankle on a loose stone. There was much less light on the other side of the wall, and as he stumbled after the Japanese he suddenly became aware that it had become very chilly. There was also a different smell in the air; of seaweed, he thought.

From what he could see of the grounds they were laid out as a kind of compromise between a garden and a park, and were apparently being maintained after a fashion. Noonan found the going easier with gravel underfoot. Suekawa led the way along a path that skirted a sizeable ornamental lake with two small islands rearing up from the dark surface of the water; then up a slight rise, at the top of which he paused. Noonan found himself staring out over a low stone wall at a vast expanse of water, and was impressed.

"I'll be darned."

"Tokyo Bay," Suekawa said. "Five minutes' walk from Ginza and Tenth Street. Not too many Yanks ever think about it."

"These lords who fixed it up – family still own the place?"

"No. Belongs to City Hall now. Public park, or will be when they get around to it. Called the Hama Rikyu, remember that. The wall back there was knocked around pretty bad when the freight yards were firebombed. This whole place is off limits. As you can see, no problem getting in, night or day. But people are kind of used to doing what they're told, so nobody comes. Just the gardeners."

Suekawa moved off to the left, following the line of the sea wall. A great bank of purplish-grey cloud had obscured the sun, and though it was still early afternoon the effect was as though it were already twilight. Trailing behind, Noonan stared out across the bay and thought he could see a number of fishing boats in the far distance. When they reached the end of the wall he saw that they had come to another stretch of water, this looking much like a canal with what seemed to be warehouses on the far side.

"We call this Tsukiji River," Suekawa announced almost in the manner of a tour guide. "Over on the other side, central Tokyo fish market. GHQ motor pool beyond. Fishing boats come this way and offload there."

"Great," Noonan said. "So what?" He shivered and hugged himself against the chill breeze.

"So for a while we use this place as a pick-up point. OK, we control the labourers in the fish market, but they'd make a lot too many witnesses for an operation. We wouldn't want to pay to keep that many lips buttoned."

"So what's wrong with the way we're moving the stuff now?"

Noonan was puzzled. During the few months he had been working with Suekawa they had put together what he thought of as a very slick operation. The distribution of black-market cigarettes, whisky nylon stockings and other high-profit items to retailers was clearly the business of the gangster bosses who employed Suekawa as their intermediary because he spoke English. That went without saying, because it was their men who supervised, protected and effectively policed the street traders in the Tokyo area.

All Noonan had to do was to supply to Suekawa the bogus requisition documents on authentic SCAP forms which were in due course presented by the drivers of nondescript vans at certain military and PX warehouses where the goods were loaded and spirited away. One of his two key American collaborators was an army quartermaster captain, the other a senior PX manager, and how they tidied up their paperwork was their affair. Noonan prided himself on being a realist, and the two Americans received what he judged to be their fair cut of the profits.

He revelled in the irony of his own sweet situation. Master Sergeant Joseph Xavier Noonan was currently a member of the counter-intelligence team concerned with security checks on SCAP personnel. He was enjoying himself prying into other people's lives, but had yet to devise ways of turning the work to his financial advantage. That didn't bother him too much, because there seemed no reason why his existing operation shouldn't continue to prosper.

Until about a month earlier Noonan had been assigned to a group of special investigators analysing the operations of the black market at every level, in order to identify significant operators and where possible to accumulate sufficient evidence to build a legal case against them. In official circles it was generally agreed that the objective was to put large-scale black-marketeers out of business rather than into jail. The lieutenant to whom Noonan had been responsible went further, suggesting from time to time during their very occasional meetings that it might be as well to avoid bringing too much enthusiasm to the work.

There was really no need for the officer to resort to hints or ambiguities. Even if he had made the effort to read them Noonan would not have understood the analyses produced by the SCAP economists. All the same he knew as well as everybody else in GHQ that the black market in Japan could not possibly be suppressed so long as supplies of food and other essentials to the urban population could not be secured through legitimate channels. Or until it was no longer necessary for the Japanese government itself to use it in order to raise the money to satisfy

SCAP's peremptory demands for repayment of the costs of the Occupation.

So the open-air markets under the railway arches at Ueno and in innumerable other districts of Tokyo and other great cities flourished under the eyes of Japanese and military police alike, and American cigarettes in particular functioned as an essential if unorthodox medium of exchange at a time of roaring inflation.

One of the more elegant provisions of Noonan's original agreement with Suekawa's principals – whom he had never knowingly met – ensured that from time to time a cache of suitably unidentifiable black-market goods was "discovered" and confiscated by CIC agents. He had little doubt that since his reassignment reports of these seizures continued to keep the lieutenant and his superiors happy, and to constitute "evidence" that the Occupation authorities were not in the business of condoning illegal activities.

"Nothing wrong with it," Suekawa said, staring unseeingly over the bay. "But we're expanding, is why. We fixed up a deal with a guy down in Kobe. He has the docks there buttoned up, so we'll ship the stuff by boat. You know we can't truck it. The guards at the checkpoints on the routes out of Tokyo are too sharp."

"Now hold on there, bud! We're doing just fine as we are. Jesus, you got good business right here in Tokyo. You start straying into other territory, you're going to hit problems. Besides, there's a limit to the amount my guys can – "

Suekawa wheeled round and sneered at the American. "Getting nervous, Noonan? 'Fyou wanna quit, no sweat, our deal is off. You been kidding yourself you're the only guy in SCAP on the take? Or the biggest? Don't make me laugh. Last six months you made, what, twenty thousand bucks for yourself?"

"It's a lot of dough," Noonan said smugly, though he was almost as disconcerted by the accuracy of Suekawa's estimate as by his reference to the existence of competitors able and willing to supplant him. In fact his personal profits amounted to somewhat less than the figure mentioned: a little over seventeen thousand dollars. Suekawa shook his head slowly from side to side in the continuing gloom as he surveyed the American.

"It is small potatoes," he said. "And you don't call me bud, you call me Suekawa-san. Now listen while I explain what you have to do. You have twenty-four hours to think it over. Then you put up or get lost, *bud*."

5

"I wouldn't like to tell you how often I ask myself the same question, Polly." Lieutenant-Commander Arthur Reynolds of the Royal Australian Naval Volunteer Reserve took his lucky penny out of his pocket and twisted its edge in the groove provided at the side of the new two-ounce tin of Balkan Sobranie pipe tobacco, cocking his head to one side to listen for the sound of the brief hiss of air as the vacuum was broken. Polly watched him close his eyes momentarily to savour the unmistakable fragrance as he took the lid off.

Then he teased open the concertina folds of paper within, and took out and discarded the thinner, slightly stained paper disc which had protected the surface of the tobacco from direct contact with the metal lid. Catching Polly's eye, he beamed at her. "Ecstasy! Almost better than actually smoking the stuff. Rather like the moment just before you sink your teeth into a ripe strawberry."

"If you say so."

"Oh, I do, I do. I've been a half-ounce-a-day man for years, but I still get a kick out of opening a new tin. You know, Polly, the people who make this stuff are forever getting appreciative letters from explorers. So they claim in their ads, at least."

"Explorers? Why on earth?"

"You know, the chaps who always dress for dinner in the jungle. They return to a cache of provisions deposited years earlier in some rude hut, broach a rusty old tin of Sobranie and feel impelled to write to the company to let them know their unique blend was still in perfect smoking condition."

"You're kidding."

"*Somebody* may be kidding, but I swear they print tributes like that every month in *Lilliput*."

"Excuse me, Commander, should I have some idea what you're talking about?"

"Perhaps not, Sergeant Polly. I refer to a pocket-size monthly magazine for men which turns up now and then in the British Commonwealth officers' mess and from which the single decorous full-page nude photograph of the female form divine is invariably purloined within a day or two."

"Gee, that's really tough."

Reynolds filled his pipe, visualizing the ridiculous Sobranie advertisements. The ones for Rose's lime juice with their line drawings of deferential butlers bringing long drinks to upper-class young men lounging in deck-chairs on immaculate lawns were almost as enjoyable. The fantasy world of *Lilliput* was a far cry from the grubby realities with which he was concerned as one of the few non-Americans on MacArthur's intelligence staff.

He aimed his pipe at Polly like a revolver. "Want to know why I joined the reserve in the first place?"

She shrugged and grinned at the same time. "Sure. You're going to tell me anyway, but let me guess. What's that little song I've heard you sing to yourself – 'All the Nice Girls Love a Sailor'? That the reason?"

"That too, needless to say. But mainly because I enjoyed messing about in boats. I was young and fit in my youth, Polly, before I started living the soft life of an officer and a gentleman. Aged twenty-two in 1936, to be precise. I had my law degree but had to put in my time as an articled clerk."

"As a what?" Polly looked at him over the top of her coffee cup.

"Kind of apprentice, in a law firm in Melbourne. The snag was that they didn't pay you, you had to pay them, British style. I was due to be admitted as a fully fledged solicitor the following year, but money was tight even though my old man was more generous than he could really afford to be." The pipe was lit at last and Reynolds spoke through a veil of blue smoke.

"Well, the navy was ready to pay me – a pittance but none the less welcome for that – to spend my weekends and summer holidays doing the sort of thing I wanted to do anyway, so I signed up for the reserve. Foolish, impetuous lad that I was."

"You mean you're a *proper* sailor?"

"Don't push your luck, Sergeant." Reynolds scowled at Polly and then spoiled the effect by gazing pointedly at her knees. "Unless you're planning to cross those delectable legs again, that is."

"No use, Commander. Men are forever trying to make me blush. I don't. Seriously though, knowing you're a lawyer I just assumed you must have been in the legal branch before you got into this outfit."

"You assumed wrong. I was a man of action while you Yanks were still hoping for a quiet life. The mother country declared war on Germany in September 1939 and the Dominion of Australia was in from the start. I was a reserve lieutenant by then and naturally the powers that be realized at once that they couldn't do a thing without me. So by the time these lovely people dropped their visiting cards on Pearl Harbor I was skippering a fast patrol boat based in Darwin. Later in that same month of December I remember sounding the klaxon along with my mates to welcome the first American ships to arrive there."

Polly looked at the fair, wavy-haired, slightly built Australian with a new respect. She thought he was good looking, with more than a passing resemblance to the British film actor Leslie Howard, and liked his throwaway style. Being blessed with a sensitive ear Polly had also noticed that the broad Australian accent came and went, being replaced by much more clipped, British vowel sounds when he was talking shop. The revelation that he had actually commanded a naval vessel, even a little one, surprised her.

"There were American ships in Darwin as early as that? How come?"

"Yes indeedy, as your good Major Brooks is prone to remark. Two of them. We were rather disappointed not to see the big cruiser, the *Pensacola*. She'd been bound for Manila leading a convoy of ships stuffed with aircraft, artillery and ammunition. After Pearl Harbor they were diverted to Brisbane, except for the two we got. Mac was commanding in the Philippines, of course, and was still furious about it when he turned up in Australia the following March." Reynolds leant back in his chair and generated another cloud of smoke. There was a faraway look in his eyes.

"And I can vouch for that personally. I was among the first to be assigned to his liaison staff, and I heard him fuming often enough. As so often, His Nibs was the only one in step, because it was beginning to sink into most of us by then that Washington had made the right decision. Even with that colossal ego and any amount of material reinforcements the man hadn't a chance of shooing the Japs away from the Philippines with his ragtag and bobtail army at that stage in the game."

"Better not let him hear you say so."

"How right you are. Those were the days, Polly. Little did I imagine that Old Corn-Cob would give a nod of approval in my direction and that I'd still be with him nearly five years later. Must be my Christian name that appeals. His old man was an Arthur too, you know. Five years doesn't quite make me one of his Bataan Boy cronies, still, I must say I do sometimes feel like one of the oldest inhabitants in this place. But why am I telling you all this, as the *ingénue* invariably says in the better class of problem play? There's something worrying you, Polly. What is it?"

"Does it show?"

Reynolds leaned back in his chair and stretched his arms. "It's not like you to ask a silly question. Obviously it shows – to me at least – or I wouldn't have mentioned it. And there's no need to look around like a nervous kitten. To the best of my knowledge Willoughby the Prussian hasn't got around to having a microphone hidden in this room as yet. No doubt thinks I'm too handsome to be a Red."

Her lips firmly closed, Polly took a deep breath and exhaled through her nose. There was kindly concern in the Australian's hazel eyes, and she had to trust somebody. Somebody in a position of authority, but one who by reason of his nationality seemed to enjoy a certain independence of action. In spite of her relatively humble status Polly was in a good position to know in general terms who among the headquarters intelligence officers did what, and was aware that Lieutenant-Commander Reynolds was concerned with developments in Japanese domestic politics. His cheerfully disrespectful reference to their overlord General Willoughby helped Polly to overcome her hesitation, and she smiled.

"That must be the reason. Look, I think I need some advice."

"Legal advice? Go and see Tom Berman or one of the other prosecutors. They'll have time on their hands pretty soon. I don't believe you, though. You strike me as being essentially a law-abiding person, Polly."

"Not legal advice. At least, not in that sense. But you guessed almost right. Tom Berman could certainly answer my question, but I'd rather not ask him."

"Oh?" The reaction was casual enough, but it was as if Reynolds had turned to stone. Without quite understanding why, Polly felt apprehensive. "All right, you'd rather not ask him," Reynolds said when she hesitated. "No harm in trying me, then. Fire away."

"It's just . . . it's just that I heard that Admiral Nagano died of pneumonia the other day."

"He did indeed. Natural causes. I rather fancy I'd prefer that myself to being hanged as a war criminal."

"Sure. But it set me wondering why it is that only twenty-eight defendants were brought before the tribunal in the first place. What about all the others?"

"What others? Good grief, Polly, not you too!"

"What's that supposed to mean?"

"I assume you're referring to His Imperial Majesty. My esteemed compatriot Sir William Webb who presides over this expensive farce of ours isn't alone in thinking that Hirohito's the one they should be trying, not the diminished band of beauties still in the dock."

"Maybe he is, maybe he isn't, but that's not who I meant. I'm not totally uninformed, you know. I know quite well that immunity for the Emperor was the trade-off price for getting the new Constitution in place."

Reynolds noted the glint in Polly's eye and busied himself by tamping down and relighting his pipe.

"I'm sorry," she said after he had deliberately allowed the silence to become strained. "I meant the other Class A suspects who are still in Sugamo prison. Why aren't they on trial too?"

"Good question, Sergeant. Go to the top of the class. I don't quite see what your interest is in this, but I'll try to explain. We had a motley crew of candidates in jug when John Darsey began to draw up a short list – what, something over a year ago. December forty-five, I think. Darsey was fresh from Nuremberg, remember. He learned enough there to realize that if you want an effective show trial you shouldn't put too many villains in the dock together. As I say, Billy Webb thinks there's only one Japanese war criminal properly so called. At the other extreme, some maniacs would cheerfully slap the label on the entire adult population. But whichever way you look at it, we had hundreds of very naughty men behind bars and had to choose from them no more than a couple of dozen or so for exemplary punishment."

"Do you mean to say that Darsey picked them personally?"

"Hardly. He was just in charge of the horse-trading that went on while Sir Arthur Comyns Carr was drafting the indictment. That is one wily Brit, you know."

"Horse-trading?"

"Polly, Polly! Don't pretend to be naïve. Didn't you tell me yourself you'd trained as a legal stenographer after you left high school? And held down a responsible job in a law firm? And that they'd very sensibly put you in the Judge-Advocate General's branch when you volunteered as a WAC?"

If Polly had been prone to blushing, she would have done so then. She had indeed told Arthur Reynolds quite a lot about her background within an hour or two of first meeting him. The occasion was a farewell party for a junior G2 officer about to return to America and civilian life, held in the office no more than a few days after she went to work for Major Brooks. Beer and whisky flowed freely and distinctions of rank were increasingly disregarded as the party continued. Reynolds had in any case been in the civilian clothes he wore most of the time, and though much in demand herself as one of the very few women present Polly decided he was the most attractive man in the room. By the time the party began to break up her inhibitions had been lowered by several drinks and she made no attempt to disguise her enjoyment in being cornered by the Australian.

Unlike all the other men, Reynolds actually asked her about herself instead of expecting her to listen to him. By the time he had driven her in his jeep to the women's quarters at Hilltop House Reynolds knew that Polly's father was a Hungarian immigrant who had built up a modestly successful business as an electrical engineer; that her American-born mother had written two novels and failed to find a publisher for either, and that Polly had a younger sister who handled most of their father's paperwork, and a brother still in high school.

Having monopolized her at the party, Reynolds nevertheless made no serious attempt to pursue Polly subsequently. He was attracted by the slender, dark-haired woman with the intelligent brown eyes and usually made an excuse to chat to her for a minute or two when he happened to bump into her in a corridor of the Dai-Ichi Building. Once or twice too he had attended meetings at which she was present to take notes, and had been impressed by their quality when her drafts were circulated to him for comment. However, Reynolds was a senior officer and Polly a non-com, and she was therefore forbidden fruit. It was a pity, but he was not so smitten with her as to risk the consequences of trying to take the relationship further.

It had all the same been a pleasant surprise to spot her a little before Christmas sitting a few rows in front of him at a Nippon

Philharmonic Orchestra concert conducted by Joseph Rosenstock at the quaintly named Ernie Pyle Theater. There seemed to be no harm in seeking her out during the interval, especially as she was with Angie Brewster. Safe enough too to invite them both to go for a drink at the Press Club after the concert, for that was classless territory jealously preserved as such by the committee of American and other western correspondents who ran it. Unlike a good many other SCAP officers Reynolds was *persona grata* there, and the two women with him more than welcome, even if one of them was of a certain age. At least Angie was as cheery as she was heftily built.

That evening too ended with complete propriety outside the entrance of Hilltop House, and Reynolds felt refreshed and somehow cleansed as he drove back to his own quarters in the Yuraku Building. It was good to be reminded that even in the continuing sordid chaos of Tokyo there were people who cared enough about music to do something about it.

The musicians were almost certainly undernourished, their clothes shabby and ill-assorted. The sounds they made were brave rather than magnificent, their programme an unadventurous mix of the old Beethoven warhorses and other German works they had been permitted to play during the war, for where were they to get hold of orchestral parts for anything else? Yet now and then they created a tenderness, a yearning quality, that made Reynolds's eyes prickle, and feminine company afterwards had done even more to push his day-to-day preoccupations back for a few hours into a corner of his consciousness.

He had learned a little more about Polly's history, and something of Angie's. He knew Polly had left a good job with a Minneapolis law firm to volunteer as a WAC in 1942 and he suspected that she had done so as a result of some sort of personal crisis, probably of a romantic nature. She was a mature, lively-minded woman, and something in her eyes told him that she was not without sexual experience. Even now, when her expression was one of mingled puzzlement and concern, that hint of animal awareness was still evident.

"Yes," she said after shifting in her chair, clearly embarrassed. "You seem to have a talent for getting me to run on about the story of my life. I can't deny I did tell you all that. There's a world of difference between typing out contracts and wills and what they're doing in International Prosecution Section, though."

Reynolds knocked out the residue from his pipe and busied himself for a while with his smoker's penknife. Then he sat back and contemplated her.

"Curiouser and curiouser, as Alice put it," he said at last. "Sorry, Polly, you're going to have to come clean if you want this seminar to continue. I can understand you being interested in the tribunal. Any intelligent person working in this outfit can't help having a view about it. And your specific question as to why these particular guys are being tried and not others is fair enough. But you're obviously not just academically interested, are you?"

"I . . . I guess not."

"So? You came barging in here ostensibly in search of a file and kicked off by asking me whether there isn't a better way of making a living. As I recall, I confessed that I often put that very question to myself. Then I confided some of the sordid details of my naval career to you, after which I enquired what was really bothering you. Well, deliver."

Polly took a deep breath and seemed to come to a decision as Reynolds waited politely.

"You mentioned about horse-trading. You know, deciding which Class A suspects should be put on trial. Who exactly was this John Darsey – the Nuremberg man – horse-trading *with*, I wonder?"

"For heaven's sake, how should I know? All sorts of people would have wanted to get in on the act, I imagine. Pushing their particular candidate for the high jump."

"I guess so. And what about people who might have had reasons for ensuring that certain suspects were kept *out* of the dock? Apart from the special case of the Emperor himself, I mean."

The expression on Reynolds's face was no longer tolerantly indulgent. "Why would anybody on our side want to do that, Polly?"

She wanted to go on, but something still held her back. "Maybe because . . ." she began hesitantly. Then she glanced at her watch, pressed her lips together and expelled a breath through her nose. "Oh, Christ, it's already eleven-thirty. Commander, I'm really sorry – "

"You can call me Arthur when there's nobody around, Sergeant." He smiled. "No problem, sport, I don't want to rush you. Tell you what, if you're free this evening I'll buy you a drink at the Press Club. We'll find a quiet corner and you can tell me what's on your mind that you feel you can't discuss with Tom Berman. OK?"

Polly blinked a couple of times, then nodded and smiled as she stood up. "OK," she said. "Thank you. Arthur."

She arrived back at her office to find the connecting door open and peeped through. His glasses well down on his nose, Major Brooks was for once at his desk, rummaging in one of its open drawers.

"That you, Polly?"

"Yes. How are you today, Major?" She walked in and stood beside his desk. He was apparently sober, and seemed to have made more of an effort than usual to look smart. His sparse hair was neatly combed, and his battledress tunic was buttoned up. He still looked like a civilian in fancy dress rather than a military officer.

"I shall survive, with luck. A question, Polly. Yesterday afternoon after I got back here I left the room for a while. Did anybody drop in while I was gone?"

"Why, no. It was only a few minutes anyway."

"And you didn't slip out yourself during that time?"

"No, sir. Is something wrong?"

Brooks looked up at her, that attractive twisted smile on his lips. "In the sense in which I think you put the question, I don't know. And under the eye of eternity nothing much matters, does it? In between, Sergeant, we flounder in wrongness. For it's a mad world, my masters. Wouldn't you agree?"

Angry with herself for having broken off the conversation with Reynolds at such an unsatisfactory stage, Polly took a deep breath and came to a decision to clear at least some of the fog of confusion. "Major, I know you left your safe unlocked when you went out of the room in a hurry yesterday. I told the truth just now. Nobody came in while you were gone. But I was here, and . . . I looked inside. I also saw a scrap of paper with numbers on it on your blotter. I thought they were probably the combination and memorized them."

"Ah. Then I must change the combination, mustn't I?"

"Too late, sir, I'm afraid. I saw the file, you see, and I read what's in it."

"Close the door, Polly. Sit down."

She did so and they stared at each other in silence for some time. Once or twice Brooks opened his mouth to speak and then seemed to think better of it. Eventually he surprised her by rubbing a hand over his eyes and then sitting back and chuckling.

"Well, I guess you see plenty of confidential material in the line of duty. What did you make of it?"

Polly stared at him expressionlessly. "Major, I was appalled. I have to believe it's authentic material. Names, dates, places – God knows you're hardly likely to have made them up. I've been turning the whole thing over and over in my mind, asking myself why you compiled it – or maybe copied it from an official file. Hardly for fun."

Brooks no longer even pretended to be amused. "And?"

"And I'm still confused. I don't know how long it's been in your safe – "

"A somewhat academic question in the circumstances, don't you think? Two days."

"Two days too long, then. I figure you plan to pass that material to some interested party outside SCAP, and I wish to hell I knew who. Or why."

"Isn't that academic too, Sergeant? I presume you'll be reporting me to higher authority anyway?"

"Not necessarily, sir. I might decide to find an interested party of my own. Like a journalist, for example."

"Oh? May I ask why?"

"I'll tell you why, Major. Because if that project you've uncovered is for real, if there really is an Operation Hi-Flyer in the works, I think it stinks, that's why. And if – as I assume – you think so too, then I'm on your side."

Major Brooks hoisted himself out of his chair and went over to the window where he turned towards Polly again, his face now in shadow. "Well, thank you, Miss Valiant-For-Truth. I honour you. I can conceive of no good reason why you should believe me, but I do in fact share your opinion. It stinks."

Polly too was now on her feet. "Sir, I need to know. Is this just a personal thing of yours, or is anybody else in on it?"

"In on the project? Well, obviously. A very few people in SCAP are concerned with it. And of course the key people involved are outside. You've seen their names. But needless to say, they don't think it stinks. They think it's great. So far as I know I'm the only one who not only knows, but disapproves and proposes to alert the responsible press. And now it seems we are two."

The shrilling of the telephone on Brooks's desk made them both jump, but when the major picked up the receiver his manner was normal. Polly could make nothing of his brief responses, but noted the set of his mouth when the conversation was over.

"One of those in the know wants to see me urgently," he said quietly. "Before I go, let me thank you for believing an old drunk. And I'd better tell you exactly what I have it in mind to do with the file."

6

The painted sign outside said US ARMY XI CORPS STOCKADE NO 1, but everybody referred to the complex of buildings on the four-acre site in north-west Tokyo by the original name of Sugamo prison. Overnight, the poorly printed bills calling for support for the forthcoming general strike had been flyposted even on the formidable, barbed-wire-topped walls of the prison, but a working party of Japanese labourers under the supervision of an American military policeman was removing the last of them from the vicinity of the main gate as two civilians approached on foot.

The elder of them looked every inch the lawyer he was. He wore an old-fashioned wing collar with his black jacket and striped trousers, and was a familiar enough figure to the armed soldier on guard duty who greeted him by name but glanced at his official pass all the same before turning his attention to the man with him. For all his sober dark suit he seemed an odd sort of companion for the lawyer, and the American scrutinized him and his identification thoroughly before gesturing to the two men to wait where they were. Then he took both passes into the guardhouse; through the window they watched him making a telephone call.

"The young man probably doesn't know anything about General Arisue's organization," the lawyer said to Nakajima while they waited.

"I'd be astonished and rather disturbed if he did. My papers describe me as an official of the Demobilization Board War Data Department. There's a coded endorsement on them, though. It won't mean a lot to him except 'treat this man with courtesy', but in any case the duty officer has been warned I'm with you today. By the way, if you refer to my boss at all – and it's better not to – you ought to call him plain Arisue-san. No need to draw attention to the fact that he used to be head of our army intelligence."

Being over twenty years Nakajima's senior and a person of some consequence in his own right, the defence counsellor did not take kindly to the rebuke. "Such nonsense! It's no secret. The Americans know perfectly well what he was."

Nakajima looked at his companion in exasperation. "Of course they do. It's a matter of record that he flew to Manila to discuss the surrender arrangements with MacArthur's staff in August forty-five. That's where General Willoughby met him, took to him and probably decided to hire him. Arisue was on Willoughby's confidential payroll within weeks, anyway. But that's not the point. Obviously, senior Americans know about his wartime career. A very few of them know he works for Willoughby now. Others have already forgotten all about him, and the vast majority never heard of him in the first place. It's much better that way – " He broke off as the soldier emerged from the guardhouse accompanied by another who, without speaking, beckoned the two Japanese inside and went ahead of them, looking back from time to time to check that they were following.

At the entrance to one of the drab three-storey blocks their escort handed them over to another American soldier, who indicated that they should raise their arms. He then perfunctorily searched them both, humming tunelessly as he did so. He hesitated for a few seconds when he found a nearly full pack of Lucky Strikes and a lighter in Nakajima's jacket pocket, but then shrugged and passed them into the building. Nakajima had noticed that only the guard on duty at the gate seemed to be armed, and commented on the fact to the lawyer after they had been taken through a formidable barred gate and along a corridor with green and cream-painted walls and left to themselves in a cheerless ground-floor room furnished with a few hard upright chairs and a small table.

"There are between three and four hundred guards here," the old man snapped, still tetchy, "and to the best of my knowledge none of them goes about armed. A weapon might get into the wrong hands."

Nakajima lit one of the cigarettes he had been allowed to keep and, seeing a wistful look flicker over the lawyer's face, gave him one too. Amity was thereby restored.

"Though obviously they must have an armoury somewhere on the premises in case of emergency. Thank you, I'm most grateful to you. The prisoners are given a ration of five cigarettes a day each, which is two more than citizens outside get and three more than I can afford to smoke."

"How many prisoners are being held in this place?"

"Apart from the defendants, you mean?"

"Yes. Altogether."

"About a thousand, I'm told. At least half of them in single three-mat cells. Without doors, lights on permanently and guards patrolling twenty-four hours a day and looking into each one. They actually took me to see Kodama-san in his once, when he wasn't well. Or said he wasn't."

As he listened to this Nakajima expelled smoke through his nostrils, eyebrows raised in surprise. "No doors? I'd go mad."

"On the way out after the interview I said something of the kind to the officer who escorted me. A pleasant, intelligent sort of man, by no means unsympathetic. He smiled, and said he'd show me why they couldn't allow the prisoners any privacy." The elderly man's eyes were watering a little from the tobacco smoke. Before going on he dabbed at them with the liver-spotted back of a hand that shook slightly. "He took me to what they call the museum. A small room which certainly does have a door, kept locked. They have an extraordinary collection of things in there, all found in the possession of prisoners. Lengths of sharpened wire, bits of glass, paper impregnated with cyanide – "

"Ah. I used to keep some of that handy myself once," Nakajima cut in. "In Shanghai, when things were falling apart towards the end."

"Indeed? Hardly necessary in your case, I should have thought."

Nakajima smiled. "I *was* Kodama's naval liaison officer, you know. Openly and officially. And the top Chinese he dealt with certainly made it their business to keep tabs on me. Kodama gave me the cyanide paper himself. Didn't want me blabbing about any of his private business if I fell into the wrong hands and came under pressure."

"I see. I'm an innocent about such materials. In a way, the home-made things the officer showed me in the museum here were the more sobering to me anyway. It's one thing to swallow a fast-acting poison, I suppose, but imagine setting about killing yourself with a sharpened chopstick!" The sound of footsteps and conversation could be heard in the corridor outside, and he fell silent. A moment later the door was opened by a corporal who stood to one side as a Japanese entered the room followed by an American officer and another westerner, in civilian clothes.

Nakajima and the lawyer rose to their feet and bowed as the corporal withdrew, closing the door behind him. The officer spoke first, in English.

"I'm Captain Watkins, duty officer of the day. Good morning, Counsellor." He turned to Nakajima and nodded curtly. "Mr Nakajima, I assume." Nakajima inclined his head more politely.

"Good morning, sir."

"You're already acquainted with the prisoner Kodama, I believe."

"I . . . have met him, sir. A long time ago."

"So I am informed. Well, I suggest we all sit around this table."

Nakajima manoeuvred himself into a position from which he had a good view of the man he had last seen in Shanghai eighteen months earlier, wearing the uniform of a rear-admiral of the Imperial Japanese Navy. Yoshio Kodama's hair had been cropped short and there was patchy stubble on his chin. His civilian suit was shabby and the absence of both necktie and belt or braces ought to have made him look seedy and broken down. Yet unlike most men in such circumstances Kodama appeared neither crushed nor apathetic. His eyes were bright and he seemed both alert and, Nakajima thought, physically reasonably fit for a man of – good heavens, was it really possible that Kodama was still only thirty-six?

"You may smoke, gentlemen," Captain Watkins said, and offered his own cigarettes all round, beginning with the colleague he had not introduced and ending with Kodama. "Right. Mr Nakajima here has been asked to interpret as necessary. I know you speak good English too, Counsellor. The prisoner has been made aware of the purpose of this meeting, but in fairness to him I think I can allow you a brief preliminary conversation in Japanese if you wish."

The lawyer inclined his head. "Thank you, Captain," he said, and then turned to Kodama, switching to what Nakajima noticed at once was exceptionally rapid, complex and archaic Japanese. Kodama's replies were terse, but larded with the slang of the underworld and occasional phrases in Korean. It was an impressive performance on the part of both men, and Nakajima himself didn't find it too easy to keep up. It was obvious to Nakajima what they were about, and he did his best to follow their example when the time came for him to speak. While their coded conversation continued the American civilian made occasional notes on one of several loose sheets he had in a plain folder, but Nakajima was sure this was just to avoid losing face.

The captain's concession was an unexpected bonus, and after the briefest exchange of courtesies – during which Kodama expressed neither surprise nor pleasure at seeing Nakajima again after so long and eventful an interval – the three Japanese made the most of it. Kodama was hungry for news, and the lawyer told him about the latest purge order which had been promulgated by SCAP early in the new year. According to the press it might debar as many as a million Japanese from economic or political activity, for it was intended to apply to relatives of suspected individuals to the third degree. It had proved to be altogether too easy for previous "purgees" to continue to operate through nominees. Kodama simply smiled at this, though he scowled when the lawyer mentioned that it had been reported that the Grand Shrines at Ise were to be closed down and the buildings, among the holiest Shinto sanctuaries in the land, dismantled, their timbers to be used for firewood.

Nakajima scoffed at this idea. Now that the Emperor's personal position was safe, he argued, MacArthur would never allow such a thing. He had more sense than to invite civil war over an issue like that, and was already said to be regretting the Americans' haste in instigating the ultra-liberal 1945 Religious Bodies Law that had led within a matter of weeks to the establishment of any number of crackpot sects.

Kodama listened attentively to Nakajima, as he had usually done during their long association in Shanghai, and seemed satisfied by this argument. Then he changed the subject, referring to his senior fellow-prisoners Nobusuke Kishi and Ryoichi Sasakawa by nicknames. They were in good health and spirits, he said, and pleased to have been told the other day that Japanese could now send letters, albeit censored, in any of eight approved languages to any country. Communications within Japan had not been much of a problem for them, but it had been extremely difficult to keep in touch with important associates overseas. The cryptic remarks Kodama slipped from time to time into what was beginning to turn into a monologue meant a great deal more to Nakajima than they did to the lawyer.

By the time they had finished Nakajima was confident that even if the unidentified American observer was a Japanese speaker there to listen in on their exchanges, unless he was a linguist of rare versatility and skill he could have caught little of what had been said. He certainly wouldn't have understood any of the remarks Kodama intended for Nakajima's personal consumption.

Captain Watkins had been sitting quietly looking from one to another of the three Japanese during their conversation. Now the officer glanced at his watch, and immediately tapped the table-top with the knuckles of his left hand.

"Ten minutes gone," he said. "Now I wouldn't normally curtail your discussions with your client, Counsellor, but I'll remind you that today's arrangements are exceptional. I think this is the moment to introduce Mr Berman of the International Prosecution Section."

All three Japanese stared expressionlessly at the man in the expensive-looking grey suit. Berman's complexion was fresh and healthy, his expression seeming at first sight to be one of boyish enthusiasm, matching his tousled golden hair – until he began to speak. Then it was as if the menace in his well-modulated voice communicated itself to his eyes, coldly blue.

"Thank you, Captain. Counsellor. Mr Nakajima. I'll try to speak reasonably slowly and clearly for the benefit of Admiral Kodama here, but I'll be obliged if you'll interpret as necessary, Mr Nakajima. Right. Counsellor, as you well know, the prosecution is due to rest its case on Friday January twenty-fourth, and the defence is scheduled to open on the following Monday, the twenty-seventh. It may seem a little late in the day to be considering the situation of the other prisoners held as suspected Class A war criminals but not so far been indicted. From our point of view, however, it is absolutely the right time to do so. . . ."

Nakajima was a highly skilled interpreter, and was well able to convey the gist of Berman's statement to Kodama in Japanese while thinking fast about the implications of the unforeseen situation in which he found himself. He was both surprised and angry that Kodama's lawyer, who must have known what was in the wind, had not warned him that his client was to be confronted by one of the International Tribunal's prosecutors.

Nakajima had been given to understand that Kodama simply wanted to see him, and that strings had been pulled to enable him to visit Sugamo, ostensibly in his capacity as one of SCAP's locally engaged Japanese research assistants. This was a very different set-up, however. Far from being merely an anonymous language specialist present in order to listen in to their conversation, this was the formidable Tom Berman, about whom Nakajima had picked up quite a few snippets of information during recent months.

He knew that Berman was a Californian with a privileged background, who as a clever young Yale graduate with the right family connections had worked in General Courtney Whitney's law office in Manila for a couple of years in the thirties, before returning to the West Coast to become an assistant district attorney in Los Angeles. His appointment to the International Prosecution Section of SCAP was presumably due to General Whitney's continuing patronage, also thanks to which he now had a job any ambitious lawyer ought to be able to turn to great advantage. Nakajima concentrated even harder on what Berman was saying.

"In fact the cases of all Class A suspects have been under continuous review since the tribunal was constituted. I may as well make explicit what must certainly have occurred to you as well as to observers in the United States and elsewhere. Namely that there is no very logical explanation as to why several, perhaps as many as half, the defendants in the dock are there while others, notably Kishi, Sasakawa and you, Admiral Kodama, are conspicuous by your absence."

That was another thing that bothered Nakajima as he continued to translate. Twice now Berman had referred to Yoshio Kodama as "Admiral". This was ominous. The Americans – not to mention the Russians, the Chinese, the British and all the others represented on the Allied Council which MacArthur held in contempt and personally ignored – were well aware that high naval rank had been bestowed on Kodama as a matter of expediency only, in 1941. That was when the Naval Air Force commissioned him to set up a Shanghai-based network for the procurement of war materiel, and the "Kodama Organization" was born. Kodama had never in his life been on board a vessel of the Imperial Navy other than as a passenger or honoured guest. At that moment Kodama interrupted, speaking Japanese, to make the point for himself.

"I am not a naval man, sir," he said politely enough, though his eyes were like chips of ice. "Nor am I a prisoner of war. In order to undertake special assignments for His Majesty's government I have in the past been briefly attached to the Foreign Ministry and to the Imperial Army as well as to the Navy. You might just as well address me as Ambassador or Colonel – except that no Japanese today holds such a title. Here I am simply the civilian detainee Kodama."

"I think you may take it that we know very well what you are and have been. We know for example that as a teenager you claimed to be a socialist, before you found it more profitable to run errands for the ultra-nationalists."

"You insult me. I am in jail because I am a man of principle, Mr Prosecutor. Not for the first time, either." Kodama was using plain language now, and in interpreting Nakajima did the same, infusing contempt into his own voice and watching the expression on Berman's conventionally handsome, all-American face become angry, almost petulant. "I was sentenced to six months in 1929 for trying to hand a petition to His Majesty. I was eighteen. Again in 1934, for three years – "

"We know. That time, for trying to assassinate the prime minister. You'd come a long way in a few years, and in no time after they let you out you were a spy and dirty tricks specialist for the militarists running the Japanese government. That's when US Intelligence opened a file on you, *Admiral*. When you went to Manchuria in thirty-seven pretending to be a diplomat. It came as no surprise to us when you popped up again in Shanghai."

Nakajima began to feel personally vulnerable. He had long accepted the probability that immediately after Pearl Harbor American agents in Shanghai had kept a close eye on Kodama's activities there, but devoutly hoped that whatever papers had come Berman's way contained no references to himself. So far as General Willoughby and the other senior intelligence officers in SCAP were concerned, Eijiro Nakajima was a former regular officer of the Imperial Navy who had served for three years in the late thirties as assistant naval attaché at the Japanese Embassy in Washington. That much was certainly on the American record. There was little else, he liked to think, because the personnel archives of the Navy Ministry in Tokyo had all been destroyed on orders from above within days of the surrender. All the same, Berman was worrying him.

"The important fact for you to bear in mind is that when the cases presently before the tribunal have been disposed of, charges will in all probability be brought against you and others. In your particular case, let me make it perfectly plain that you haven't a hope of walking out of this place for a very long time to come. You, who extorted raw materials and armaments from Chinese dealers at ludicrous prices, financed the Shanghai organization of the Japanese secret police out of just part of the profits, dealt in drugs and minerals and built up a vast personal fortune in the process? Not a chance, Admiral. In fact I rather doubt if you'll *walk* out at all."

Conscious of his own unease, Nakajima was impressed by the calmness with which Kodama listened to Berman, who seemed to be increasingly consumed by righteous indignation. Everything he said about Kodama was true, of course, except the bit about not walking out of Sugamo in the foreseeable future. Nakajima knew that Kodama had every intention of doing just that, along with his friends Sasakawa and Kishi, and that he and others had plans for one in particular of these two. Nakajima also knew that Kodama's confidence was well founded, because a number of extremely influential people were working to ensure just such an outcome; and Nakajima knew that because he was one of those they most depended on to arrange it. He very much hoped their confidence wasn't misplaced, and made up his mind to find out more about the aggressive prosecutor Berman.

7

In the privacy of his cramped little office in the former headquarters of the NYK shipping line, ex-Colonel Tokushiro Hattori glared at Nakajima. "I've never been able to work out just how many people do pay you, and for what. But bear this in mind. Your only legitimate income is from the Americans. Not to mention the side-benefits like good rations and plenty of cigarettes and booze that make it worth a hundred times as much. It's simple common sense to keep them reasonably sweet by going through the motions expected of us."

"I agree, sir. But we're *working* for Japan."

"Don't pretend to be naïve. Of course we are. Why the hell else do you think I sought you out and recommended you for appointment?" Ostensibly a senior member of General Willoughby's team of Japanese "historical advisers" under former General Arisue, Hattori was in fact the principal organizer of the ghost general staff covertly designing a new Japanese army.

Most of the talented and experienced ex-officers he had located were now, with the connivance of the Japanese authorities, placed as civil servants in regional demobilization and ex-servicemen's welfare offices up and down the country. Between them these key organizers in the provinces could already raise in a matter of days a force of tens, if not hundreds, of thousands of seasoned men. That alone was a remarkable achievement, but Hattori had also set up an increasingly effective network of strategic planners. One of his most brilliant coups in this line was to have reassembled Arisue's wartime team of Russian specialists and arranged for them to work together in the northernmost island of Hokkaido. They were already supplying useful intelligence, and collaborating in drawing up outline plans for Japan's future defence by developing some interesting tactical ideas about ways of dislodging the Russians from Sakhalin and the smaller northern islands they had seized.

"Understood, sir. You know, I often wonder whether MacArthur himself knows Willoughby has people like us on the G2 payroll."

"That's not for you to speculate about, nor what passes between Arisue-san and General Willoughby when they meet. Suffice it to say that for the time being at least, our interests and Willoughby's coincide. Whether or not MacArthur himself knows we could raise an effective army again at short notice is neither here nor there. When the time comes – and it will – he'll be glad of it. Meantime it suits SCAP administration to think of us as a handful of middle-aged Japanese men who dress and behave unobtrusively and from time to time produce 'background papers'."

Nakajima smiled. "On such unexciting subjects as the measures taken to maintain wartime morale among Japanese servicemen or the former command structure in south-east Asia. Very few of the Americans in SCAP can even speak Japanese, let alone read it, and the official translators are hopelessly overworked. What if anything do you think happens to our efforts after they go to Miscellaneous and War Department Intelligence Division?"

"I haven't the remotest idea. Nevertheless, it's some clerk's job to make sure they keep coming, and you're late with your draft piece about the history of the Naval Academy. You're the only navy man we have here at present, and I want that draft soon."

Nakajima shrugged. "Very good, sir. But it'll take a lot of time that could be put to much better use on my other work for you."

"I'm aware of that. If you can farm the work out to a reliable former naval man, do so. But get it done within a month."

Nakajima bowed in acknowledgment, collected his coat and left the building at which he was seldom required to put in an appearance. He knew that he was viewed with some wariness by his colleagues who were all former soldiers. Whatever the prospects for the rebirth of a Japanese army, it would be out of the question to think in terms of a new navy for years to come, and his ideas on that subject were never sought.

Nakajima was content to let the others get on with their planning and to do what Hattori asked of him, which was to make use of his near-perfect English by cultivating Americans and others in and around the Allied Council and the war crimes tribunal and to feed back the snippets of information he picked up. He was well aware that though much of what Arisue and Hattori were doing was with the knowledge and connivance of Willoughby and his confidential aides on the American side, by no means everything was.

Nakajima's was a perfect assignment, which he could effectively carry out while also attending to his complex and confidential duties as one of Yoshio Kodama's key outside men. Hattori and Arisue certainly knew of his wartime association with Kodama in Shanghai, in spite of the fact that as a genuine serving naval officer in a desk job Nakajima himself had not been charged with war crimes. He had been assured that they did not know that he was one of the two or three people to whom, when defeat was imminent and arrest would surely follow, Kodama had entrusted the vast fortune he had made during the war. That being so, Nakajima had given Hattori only a carefully edited account of his visit to Kodama in Sugamo prison.

In choosing Nakajima to protect his financial interests Kodam had acted shrewdly. The suspected Class A war criminal's vast assets had largely disappeared from view, and SCAP's financial experts were having little luck in tracing them. Under Nakajima's secret stewardship, however, they had by no means diminished during the past eighteen months.

Indeed they were currently growing fast, having undergone some interesting transformations. At a time of rampant inflation, money as such was virtually valueless, and few other entrepreneurs were as cool-headed as Nakajima, or had his flair for taking calculated risks as he switched resources from gold and diamonds to land, property and stakes in the sort of enterprises likely to prosper in postwar Japan.

Some of these had been famous – often notorious – for generations. For a while in the early months of the Occupation it had looked as though the idealistic trust-busters among the SCAP economists might actually hurt the great industrial and financial conglomerates of Japan. Nakajima and the people he covertly dealt with watched and waited, and soon judged that the effects of the reforms SCAP did force the Japanese government to enact would prove to be more apparent than real. With impeccable timing he had secured for the imprisoned Kodama at comparatively modest cost a substantial piece of the explosive economic action soon to come.

Other business activities called for more than just seed money and a nose for investment. Hotels were being refurbished, rebuilt and newly established in the resort areas popular with free-spending GIs, and those who owned or developed them were doing well. The more imaginative were looking some years into the future, when the Japanese themselves would again have money to spend on tourism. They were encouraged when an official in Washington was quoted as predicting that by 1948 American vacationers would be venturing west of Hawaii in significant numbers.

These were only some of the reasons why construction companies were good things to own in the Japan of early 1947, even at a time when building materials could only be secured by devious means. In the process of establishing several under various names on Kodama's behalf, Nakajima made some interesting new friends. The people in the best position to lay their hands on the necessary supplies were the *yakuza* barons who controlled the black market, and who dealt with corrupt Americans at various levels in SCAP. He found that somehow or other Kodama had let the most senior of them know in advance that he would be in touch sooner or later. All the same the senior players in that high-stake game did not begin to trust him for some time, and then no more than they chose to. Nakajima enjoyed pitting his wits against theirs, and had no reason to be ashamed of his performance to date.

"Oh, it's absolutely fascinating, I can tell you," Jay Murakami said to Eleanor Curtis over coffee. They had met by chance, having arrived for lunch in the SCAP officers' club at the same time. It was towards the end of lunchtime, and they had a newly vacated table to themselves in a quiet corner. "Soon after I graduated and joined the FBI they put me on to a small research project looking at Japanese involvement in organized crime in Honolulu. I was born there, so I knew my way around."

"*Was* there Japanese involvement?"

"It didn't amount to an awful lot, but I picked up some interesting information. I even came here to Japan once, dressed up as a tourist. Moseyed round and met a few people. Back in thirty-seven, that was. There was a strange, unreal atmosphere here, Eleanor. People were hysterically patriotic, or pretended to be, but wild about Charlie Chaplin at the same time. Anyway, my project was of little more than academic interest in those days. But of course after Pearl Harbor the whole thing suddenly heated up. Every Japanese-American obviously had to be a spy, a traitor or a crook, and very possibly all three."

"It must have been awful." As usual, Eleanor looked both earnest and embarrassed. "I mean, even for you as an FBI man. And your family, of course."

Jay shrugged. "Yup. It was tough for a while. A lot tougher for others, though. Uncle Sam needed Japanese-speaking public servants like me, and I'd already been on the FBI payroll for nearly ten years, long enough for the powers that be to have decided I was probably OK, I suppose. So they had me searching for spies among the ethnic Japanese in Hawaii and on the West Coast. I even picked up one or two suspects. They could scarcely keep my own folks locked up after that."

"I do admire you, Jay. For not being bitter." Having blurted this out, Eleanor stared fiercely at her coffee cup, her face crimson. He looked at her profile with a half smile. Poor Eleanor. She could be a superb specimen of womanhood if only she would capitalize on her height and beautiful long blonde hair, straighten her shoulders to show off the breasts she tried to hide by her habitual hunched posture, and above all manage to overcome her crippling shyness. Poor Eleanor. He thought of her like that, and so did a lot of other people, he knew. Yet from another point of view she had everything. She was formidably qualified, a brilliant mathematical economist seconded from the Treasury Department. She was also privileged, the Washington-wise daughter of a wealthy Congressman from Kentucky. Poor Eleanor indeed!

"Thank you, I appreciate the compliment. If I may say so, maybe you should try admiring yourself a little more," he added gently as a white-jacketed Japanese mess boy approached bearing a coffee-pot and hovered timidly in the vicinity of their table. Probably a trainee, Jay thought, nodding to him and noticing the quivering dedication with which the young man refilled their cups. "But that's none of my business, of course. I was telling you about organized crime in Japan. Want me to go on?"

"Yes, do." She still didn't look at him, but her cheeks and neck were gradually returning to a more normal colour.

"Well, this could take hours, but I'll try to keep it brief. Essentially, there are three distinct kinds of gangster in Japan. Two of them have flourished – after a fashion – for centuries, and although a number of their activities were and are technically illegal it's hardly fair or accurate to think of them as criminals in our sense of the word. The first category comprises small-time street traders and hucksters. The Japanese call them *tekiya*. In the old days that kind of person had no rights. So if they wanted any sort of protection they had to organize their own. Above all, if they wanted to keep out of trouble with the authorities they had to police themselves, especially when they set up their stalls at the markets held in temple and shrine precincts at festival time. How to avoid squabbling over the best pitches? How to resolve the inevitable disputes when customers complained of being cheated?"

"I could try to guess, but you tell me."

"You've already figured it out, I'm sure. A beautifully subtle mechanism of social and economic control evolved over many generations. Individual tekiya families acquired hereditary rights to their locations in the markets or to local monopolies in particular types of merchandise. Guild organizations developed in cities and towns all over the country. Their leading lights arbitrated in disputes, prevented competition from outside the area from muscling in, employed suitably tough help to keep the peace, and thus usually managed to keep the regular authorities off the little men's backs. In return they of course exacted their own form of tax from the traders. Call it protection money by all means, but on the whole it seldom amounted to extortion."

"No. I can see that. Simple market forces would have excluded traders from areas where that kind of taxation was oppressive."

"Right. Now, any day, you can see the lineal descendants of those self-same tekiya operating under a system which has changed hardly at all. Just a block or two from here under the Shimbashi railway arches, across town by Ueno Station and in hundreds, more likely thousands, of other places all over Japan." Jay looked at his watch. "I'm sorry, I really have to go in a few minutes."

"At least tell me what the other two categories are. You can expand on them another day."

"Right, that's a date. The second category consists of the so-called *bakuto*, originally gamblers and conmen who made a living off simple souls breaking their journeys at post-towns. These are the original yakuza, involved in gambling of all kinds, the entertainment business both legitimate and otherwise, respectable and otherwise, and nowadays, for reasons I'll go into another time, the supply of unskilled labour – which is what principally concerns me right now. Over a period of several hundred years, these two groups evolved their own internal hierarchies, disciplines and traditions and achieved a very satisfactory mutual – what's the word – "

"Symbiotic relationship?"

"Eleanor, Eleanor, don't show up the poverty of my vocabulary. Yes, symbiotic relationship. And the important thing to bear in mind is that they've almost always operated with at least the tacit approval of the legitimate authorities. What's more, their leaders have usually – certainly in the twentieth century – been deeply conservative, even passionately patriotic men. They've become rich, and they want to hang on to what they have. They wield a lot of power, and have no wish to change a political system they know how to exploit."

Eleanor nodded, her full lower lip extended thoughtfully, and Jay in the glow of his own currently hyperactive sexuality found himself tempted to warn her not to do that around men. "And the third type?" she enquired, oblivious to his changed expression.

"Ah. Yes. The third type. In Japanese they're called *gurentai*, or hoodlums, and they're very much a postwar phenomenon. They're violent, they're anarchic, and they're very bad news for the proud, old-style Japanese gangsters." He stood up to go. "In fact lots of them aren't Japanese at all. They're Korean or Chinese, and often have very good reasons for their murderous hatred of Japanese. And that, Eleanor, is turning it into a whole new ball game."

8

When the sun shone, Tokyo could be pleasant enough by day even in January, but the sky was slate-grey that afternoon over Hibiya Park, and a chill wind made the crowd of two or three hundred poorly dressed people huddle into themselves as they listened to the speakers who one after another mounted the flimsy, improvised rostrum.

One of the fieriest of the orators was a young woman, dressed in the drab overalls provided for the women drafted to factory work during the war. She had a fine profile, and Jay Murakami thought she must at some stage have had some professional training in voice production, because though he was well to one side and near the back of the crowd he could hear every word she said. The same was not true of the other speakers. They were all men, as were nearly all the demonstrators gathered to listen to them.

The banners and placards that bedecked the platform and sprouted here and there above the heads of the crowd made a brave enough show with their slogans boldly lettered in black and red. So did the headbands worn by the organizers. From time to time a speaker would initiate and sustain for a while a rhythmic chanting of "Yoshida out!" or "Down with the Emperor system!", but to Jay's experienced eye and ear there was something half-hearted about the whole affair. Because he could pass for Japanese and was virtually bilingual, it was part of his job to mingle incognito with such crowds. By keeping his eyes and ears open he could sense such subtleties of mood, and discuss them subsequently with his boss John Prothero, "the Professor". The SCAP authorities were provided with plenty of statistics about the size, frequency and general nature of demonstrations, but with Jay's informed analyses to round out his written reports, Prothero was regarded as the top expert in the interpretation of the activities of trade unionists and their allies.

Jay suppressed a smile as he watched one youngish man with a pock-marked face and an unruly shock of hair leaping about in a frenzied but largely unsuccessful attempt to whip up greater enthusiasm among those near him. Jay decided he deserved an A for effort, at least. Then something made him unobtrusively edge closer so as to hear what he was actually saying. Interesting. Now that he could see him properly he detected in the agitator's face and eyes a certain calculation oddly inconsistent with his extravagant words and gestures, as though his frame of mind were in fact as detached and objective as Jay's own. Then he momentarily caught the man's eye and was sure.

With Prothero's approval and indeed at his behest, Jay himself moved among people involved at various levels in the labour movement, allowing most of them to take him for a Japanese and a sympathizer. More than once he had argued to Prothero that since SCAP regarded it as important for him to find out as much as he could from innocent and unguarded informants about key trade unionists, it was logical to assume that the Yoshida government would have gone further and planted agents close to them. That being so, shouldn't SCAP try to find out who they were?

The Professor seemed uncharacteristically obtuse about what was to Jay a matter of simple common sense. Prothero himself was SCAP's openly acknowledged expert on the left wing in Japan. He was officially encouraged to meet and talk to prominent opposition politicians and leaders of the labour movement about their objectives and programmes, many of which were entirely consonant with announced Occupation policies. His impeccable academic background, silver hair and old-world courtesy went down very well with his Japanese contacts. They came to see him as an enlightened and sympathetic man, an influential potential ally among the senior civilians in SCAP.

Jay knew him to be in reality much more critical of his contacts. He saw, at least in draft form, most of the confidential reports Prothero wrote about his conversations with the leading lights of the left wing, and had often smiled over Prothero's clear-eyed analyses of the muddled thinking and theatrical posturing which often passed for political activity. His acidly worded think-pieces mercilessly exposed emotions dressed up as arguments, stressed the unreality of the wilder expectations, and soberly assessed the likely prospects for success of current socialist tactics.

Although it would have compromised his own position, Jay rather wished his boss were there with him to observe the antics of the man he was now convinced was not only a government agent but very close to being an *agent provocateur*. As was usual at meetings and demonstrations, uniformed Japanese policemen were on duty, positioned in small groups of three or four at most, at some distance from the crowd and watching but in no way interfering with the proceedings. Some minutes previously a US Army jeep had pulled up and parked even further away, out of sight of the speakers. The driver and the man beside him both wore the white steel helmets of the military police, while the rear seats were occupied by an American officer and what looked like a senior Japanese police officer.

There was nothing so unusual about this either, and Jay continued to pay perfunctory attention to the oratory while keeping an eye on the particularly exuberant agitator in the crowd. The current speaker was enjoying himself by being rude about most members of the National Diet, who were idle and useless. Why shouldn't they be? he demanded rhetorically. They had plenty to eat themselves and were largely immune to the inflation that was making life a misery for ordinary workers. After a couple of minutes of this, someone – not the man Jay had marked – interrupted him, shouting that instead of wasting their breath, the organizers of the meeting should lead a march to the National Diet building there and then and confront the politicians face to face.

It might have been simply that many of those in the crowd were cold and tired of standing around, or perhaps the heckler had allies placed strategically here and there. Whatever the reason, his intervention had dramatic results. It was as though a charge of electricity transformed the assembly from a more or less apathetic collection of bystanders into a purposeful entity. The man's call for action was echoed almost at once by a few others, and became within a very short time a full-throated, angry chorus.

Jay was fairly sure that the development took the organizers of the meeting by surprise. One of them, a thick-set, middle-aged man who had already made a speech, leapt back up to the rostrum, hands raised in an attempt to get a hearing. But control had been lost, and Jay saw something of a mêlée developing as people grabbed for the bigger banners and placards and a few actually started off in the direction of the Diet building.

The pock-marked man Jay had been watching hesitated for a moment. Then he sprinted round the periphery of the crowd to the head of the embryonic procession, where Jay saw him apparently persuade its leaders to pause while he and a couple of others began to marshal people into some sort of order. Meantime, the speakers and organizers seemed to be arguing among themselves whether or not to accept the situation and join the march. The striking-looking young woman was the first to break away and take up a position near the head of the still ragged column. She was joined by two others who had addressed the crowd: a frail but determined-looking old man with a mane of white hair, and the one who had been speaking when the heckler intervened to such effect.

The situation was still confused, but it seemed clear to Jay that there was going to be trouble. The officers in the back of the jeep seemed to be of the same opinion, because both were now standing up in their seats, the man in police uniform with binoculars to his eyes. The MP beside the driver was cranking the handle of a field telephone, while two Japanese policemen had detached themselves from the group nearest the front of the growing column of demonstrators and were running towards the jeep.

Jay told himself that the prudent thing would be to make himself scarce and slip away anonymously into the busy streets around Yurakucho Station. At least twenty or thirty of the people in the original crowd had already made off and at least as many again were looking around apprehensively as though about to do the same. But that still left a hard core of a couple of hundred marchers, and Jay wanted very much to know what they would do. They were already decisively on the move along the thoroughfare the Occupation authorities had dubbed First Street. This followed the line of the moat round the grounds of the Imperial Palace, so that the massive but graceful curves of its centuries-old stone ramparts were to their right. Without further hesitation Jay joined them, slipping into the column as far forward as he could without making himself conspicuous.

Over his suit, far too good to be owned by a demonstrator, he was wearing an old Japanese army greatcoat he had bought from a sharp-faced pedlar in Ueno street market the previous week when night temperatures began to drop sharply. There were faded patches on the collar and sleeves where regimental insignia and badges of rank had been. Quite a few other men were wearing similar coats. The woollen muffler Jay wore with the greatcoat and kept with one or two other odds and ends of shabby clothing in a locker at the office had also once belonged to a Japanese soldier: knitted with more dedication than skill, no doubt by some idealistic schoolgirl, it had stretched in use to perhaps double its original length. The quality of his shoes could have given him away, but nobody had given him a second glance thus far. Someone near the front called out "*Jigu-jagu!*", zigzag: the march turned into a snake-dance, and soon those around him were in a state of such high excitement that Jay joined in the rhythmic yelling and stopped worrying about his camouflage.

The shouting, snake-dancing demonstrators had covered no more than two or three hundred yards and hadn't yet reached the junction of First Street and Mita Avenue when the slogans changed to screams and angry shouts as a solid phalanx of several dozen tough-looking men surged out from a side-street. Armed with lengths of wood and even occasional iron bars, they clubbed and kicked the marchers without distinction between old and young, men and women. Just in time Jay side-stepped and avoided a vicious blow to his head, and had just enough presence of mind to whip his glasses off and put them in his pocket. Then he turned on his attacker. His vision was blurred, but not so badly that he couldn't see that the thug was a Chinese. Jay managed to get in one kick before the Chinese thrust a hard fist into his windpipe. He fell back, choking for breath.

He was momentarily propped up by the pressure of the bodies of other marchers but then slid to his knees. Clutching at the clothing of the people around him he tried to pull himself up, but failed. Worse, he nearly fainted with agony when someone trod heavily on his awkwardly twisted ankle. Dimly aware of the sound of sirens and whistles, he finally managed to crawl to one side, away from the worst of the fighting, and saw a US Army jeep with a full complement of four military policemen squeal to a halt a few yards away. The men clambered out, batons at the ready, and to Jay's amazement stood there for several moments, *grinning*.

"Wowee! Now ain't this some party!" one exclaimed. "Hey, get a load of the broad over there!" He licked his lips and pointed at the young woman Jay had heard addressing the meeting earlier. She had managed to get hold of an improvised club and was using it not to attack anyone, but to defend herself from one of the hoodlums who was trying to grab at her. The MP made a revolting slurping sound with his lips. "I b'lieve I'll have myself a piece of that troublemaking bitch," he said, and launched himself into the crowd. Approaching the woman from behind, he grabbed her deliberately by the breasts and dragged her out, then shifted his hold and thrust his baton up between her thighs.

"Let her go, you bastard," Jay rasped as he lurched forward, blind with anger, his hands like claws going for the man's throat. He never reached it. Nor did he see the other white baton swinging towards the side of his head. He didn't even feel the blow until several minutes later when he came to and found himself in a crumpled heap by the side of the road, an anxious-looking elderly man at his side dabbing at the blood trickling down his cheek with his own scarf.

"Goddam it, John, the whole thing *must* have been a put-up job. There was no way they could have had those hoodlums ready and waiting for us otherwise."

Jay was mumbling anyway, and Prothero was leaning well forward in his chair, keeping his voice discreetly low. He had arrived half an hour earlier, had accepted and then ignored a glass of beer, and listened carefully to Jay's story.

"May I suggest, Jay, that if it proves necessary to discuss this unfortunate matter with anyone else in the office, it would probably be wise to refrain from identifying yourself too sympathetically with the participants in this afternoon's march?"

"I know, I know. But you weren't there. You didn't see the way those bastards laid into us. And the MPs and police didn't just stand by and let it go on for a hell of a long time before they finally broke it up. They looked like they were *enjoying* it, for chrissake. I saw some of them join in – sneakily, but they did it. I have this lump on my head to prove it. And some of them took the opportunity to rough up the women in a particularly filthy way. Specially a good-looking girl at the head of the march – I personally saw an MP indecently assault her. I'd like to scorch that guy's ass for him. God knows what happened to her when they got her and some of the other organizers into the paddy wagon."

Jay shifted uncomfortably, but at least it hurt in different places when he moved. Apart from the lump at the side of his head that hurt like hell, the ankle he had strapped up was sprained if not broken, and he was badly bruised and thought he might have a cracked rib. It was certainly painful to breathe, and although his teeth were intact and the split in his upper lip wasn't bad enough to need stitching it made talking something of an effort. He could hear Fujiko moving about in the kitchen, probably making him the savoury *chawan mushi* custard he had said he thought was all he would be able to manage for dinner. Sex with her was definitely off the programme for that night even if he had been capable of it. The behaviour of the brutish MP had made him feel ashamed to be a man.

Luckily, Fujiko had been out when he arrived at the Washington Heights house much earlier than his usual time. He had made no attempt to go back to his office but instead had taken a crowded streetcar as far as Aoyama and then hired a "welfare cab" or bicycle rickshaw man to pedal him the last mile. Before she returned there was time for him to bundle up the greatcoat and scarf and stow them away in an empty suitcase in the closet in the spare room, make a telephone call to Prothero and even clean up, soaking away a little of the pain and soreness with a prolonged and extra-hot shower. It was not Fujiko's style to ask questions, but her sharp intake of breath when she came in and saw his face, and the soft fingers feather-light at his cheek warmed Jay's heart. Her look of concern made it easier for him to inject a reasonably credible note of rueful self-pity into his voice as he made up a tale of an armful of files, a missed step and a tumble down a flight of stairs culminating in an encounter with a steel filing cabinet.

Prothero sighed and shook his head sorrowfully as he looked at Jay; almost as though his deputy's bad language upset him as much as his injuries. "That sort of thing is deeply, deeply distasteful, I agree. I can understand your sense of outrage. I can accept that having inferred reasonably enough that the man near you in the crowd was an *agent provocateur*, your decision to continue to keep him under observation by joining the march yourself was perhaps understandable. It was nevertheless extremely unwise, Jay, and not only because it had such unpleasant physical consequences for you. You of all people are well aware that on many occasions before today demonstrations have been broken up in regional centres as well as in Tokyo – "

"Yeah, and we know who by, don't we? By gangs of hoodlums. Directed by professional crooks in the pay of right-wing politicians. With the not-so-passive assistance of the police, and the complicity – "

"Don't say it, Jay. Whatever you may think, don't say something you would certainly have cause to regret. I think I should leave you now." Stony-faced, Prothero rose from his chair and looked down at Jay, watching the younger man wincing with pain as he too struggled laboriously to his feet. Prothero let him do it, and then briefly inclined his head in the direction of the kitchen. "How well does your housekeeper understand English?"

"Don't worry, John. Hardly at all. I'm not the totally indiscreet fool you seem to take me for. Right after I hired her, I took good care to test her comprehension thoroughly and over a period. Without her realizing it, of course." Though still angry and now additionally smarting under the impact of Prothero's rebuke, Jay managed a ghost of a smile. "Your mandarin style has us Americans tied up in knots often enough. It might as well be Arabic to Fujiko-san there."

Prothero made no reply until he was buttoning his overcoat just inside the front door. Then he stared directly at Jay, still hard-eyed. "Good. I'm reassured by your use of that phrase. 'Us Americans', I mean. It would worry others besides me if you were to imply even unconsciously that your loyalties might be divided."

Apparently oblivious of the furious expression which swept over Jay's face, Prothero reverted to his customary courtesy. "Do please feel free to rest at home for a day or two until you can get about more comfortably. I'll come by every morning as usual on my way to work, and your seat in the car will be ready for you when you are."

Then he was gone, leaving Jay fuming; meanwhile in the kitchen Fujiko carefully poured a warm, fragrant mixture of beaten egg and chicken broth into two cup-shaped bowls. They already contained small pieces of chicken breast, fish sausage, lily root, peeled prawns and previously soaked dried mushroom, and the improvised bain-marie in which they would go into the oven was filled in readiness with hot water.

Conversations which took place in the living room were clearly audible in the kitchen, and in view of Prothero's question about herself Fujiko had judged it wise not to put in an appearance at the door to help him into his coat when he left. Besides, it looked as though Jay-san was going to need a little time to himself before she could usefully begin to cheer him up, and she had plenty to think about anyway.

It was very encouraging to hear him confirm that he had deliberately tried to find out the extent of her knowledge of English and that she had come through the test with flying colours; and interesting of course to know what had really happened to him that afternoon. In fact Fujiko Ueda's command of English was excellent, and it had not been easy to pretend otherwise in the early days of her employment by Jay.

She had not told him the truth when claiming that she had no living relatives. She had one, by marriage: an uncle of her late husband, a member of the National Diet. After returning to Japan from Manchuria she had been too proud to seek his help, and still had no idea how he had traced her to the domestic employment agency that subsequently recommended her to Jay Murakami. Traced her he had, however, and persuaded her that she could be of service to her country in peace as her husband had been in war – provided that she never revealed to her employer that she understood English.

From girlhood Fujiko had been poised and undemonstrative in manner, so on moving into the Washington Heights house she had been able to look blank whenever, as if unthinkingly, Murakami put the occasional question to her in English. It had been much harder not to respond to his whispered endearments when they first became lovers, for her sexual drive was very strong and she had often come close to forgetting herself when those sweet spasms convulsed her being.

It was a relief to be able to feel that the danger was largely over. In bed she could safely excite him by using one or two of the vulgar English expressions he had amused himself and annoyed her by "teaching" her as though she were a cheap bar girl. But in ordinary conversation these days he used nothing but Japanese with her, and she sometimes had to remind herself that this gentle, kindly man really was an American: one of those dedicated to the destruction of all that had made Japan great and that must be preserved if greatness was to return.

9

"Hi."

Eleanor Curtis looked up at the sharp-featured man with the crew-cut hair and snappy brown suit who was standing in the open doorway of her office. He was grinning and chewing gum with his mouth half open, and he was looking not into her eyes but at the front of her blouse.

"I didn't hear you knock." Eleanor's often incapacitating shyness in social situations didn't extend to encounters with ill-mannered creeps who interrupted her work.

"I guess not. I didn't is why. I want to talk to you, lady."

"Indeed? And who may you be?"

"Noonan. Special investigator, CIC."

"The Counter-Intelligence Corps? I think you must be in the wrong office, Mr Noonan."

"Nope. This is the right office, and the view's great from where I'm standing."

"Let me see your identification, please. No, hand it to . . . I see. Well, Sergeant, state your business."

"*Master* sergeant. But you can call me Joe."

"Really? Well, you can call me Miss Curtis. Or ma'am."

Noonan goggled at her for several seconds before closing the door behind him with exaggerated care. "Well, par'me for breathin' . . . ma'am. Do I have the lady's permission to take a seat?" Eleanor wordlessly gestured to the upright chair in front of her desk. His jaw still rotating, Noonan lowered himself into it and adjusted his trousers at the knee to preserve their knife-edge creases.

"Oh, boy. Guess I got off to a bad start there," he said at last. Eleanor found his assumption of an ingratiating manner even more offensive than his original crassness, and continued to stare at him in silence as Noonan took a slender notebook from an inside pocket and thumbed through it. "Yeah. Right. State your business, the lady says. OK. We've been going through the lists of names of non-SCAP contacts filed by US-based civilian personnel. You've been here what, three, four months?"

"Nearly five."

Noonan nodded judiciously, as though he had been expecting her to lie and was both pleased and slightly surprised that she had come clean. "Correct. And since you arrived you've filed around two, three dozen names, mostly Jap professors and stuff like that. Couple of Bank of Japan officials."

"Yes. University economists and 'stuff like that' are the sort of experts I need to talk to in connection with my work."

"'Fyou say so. We'll get around to them in a while. But twenty, thirty at most in five months? OK, nobody's asking you to report the name of the guy who mends your shoes or the woman who takes care of your laundry, but gee whiz, I'd have thought you'd meet that many new faces in a *week*."

"Then you'd have thought wrong."

"Uh huh. Maybe. OK, these names we do have. Which ones are Reds?"

"*Reds*? For heaven's sake, I haven't the slightest idea. I don't discuss politics with them."

"Come on, come on, you're a very smart lady with a college education. You know about economics and I don't. But I do know it has an awful lot to do with politics. And I don't see how you can talk turkey with these guys and not get a pretty damn good idea which ones are Reds."

Eleanor glared at him, momentarily at a loss because though Noonan expressed himself crudely she knew he was perfectly right. Then she seized the initiative before he could follow up. "These 'Reds' you're talking about. How do you define them? Active members of the Japan Communist Party? Passive sympathizers? Socialists? Marxist theorists? You admit you're not a specialist, so you may not be aware that a number of the economic and social policies we in SCAP are urging on the Japanese government can quite accurately be described as broadly socialist. Not to mention the fact that there's a Soviet representative on the Allied Council. Does all that make the Supreme Commander a Red? Or your General Willoughby?"

"Heck no! But it might mean there are Reds right here in SCAP two-timing them. And making deals with Jap Reds outside." A dull flush had crept into Noonan's previously sallow face. He was obviously ready to lose his temper. So was Eleanor.

"That is an outrageous insinuation! You know perfectly well that all civilian specialists in SCAP have security clearance. It's entirely natural – essential indeed – that we should have contacts with people across the whole range of political opinion. I think you owe me an apology."

Noonan extended a hand towards her palm downwards and made a patting motion as though pacifying a dog. Eleanor looked at the grubby nails and thickets of black hair on the backs of the fingers with distaste. "OK. Sorry. Calm down, lady. You got a job to do, I got a job to do."

"Then I suggest you leave me to get on with mine."

"I'm not through yet. You know Prothero in Labor Division, don't you? One they call the Professor?"

"Everybody knows of Mr Prothero. He's a very senior official."

"I meant know personally."

"I've participated in discussion meetings from time to time at which he has been present. Economic Division's concerns often overlap with those of Labor Division."

"Ever see him off duty?"

For the first time during the conversation Eleanor's poise momentarily deserted her and she began to flounder. "I've . . . I've met him socially once or twice, yes."

"You mean he's dated you?"

The anger surged up again, to Eleanor's conscious relief. It was much easier to handle than embarrassment. "That question is as ridiculous as it is impertinent, Mr Noonan. My personal life is no concern of yours. But since you have asked it, the answer is no. I have met Mr Prothero outside the office context precisely twice. Once at a cocktail party given by General Marquat for some visiting Congressmen, one of whom happened to be my father, and once just a few days ago at Mr Murakami's house."

Eleanor had expected the reference to her father's status to have a chastening effect, but Noonan seemed in no way abashed. "That's Jay Murakami. He works for Prothero, right? And lives right along the same street. Washington Heights. Pretty fancy. That where you met Berman too? International Prosecution Section? He says he knows you."

Eleanor picked up her fountain pen, slipped its cap off the wrong end of the barrel and screwed it into place. Then she looked at her wrist-watch. "Mr Noonan. I have a job to do, as you acknowledged a few minutes ago. And right now it calls for my presence elsewhere in this building. I have no idea what the real purport of your questions may be, but if you have any further official business with me maybe you – or one of your superiors – should make an appointment." She stood up, but Noonan made no immediate move to do the same. His eyes were once more assessing her breasts, his lips slack, wet and ugly.

"First she pulls rank," he murmured loudly enough for her to hear, but as if to himself, "then she points out her daddy's a Congressman. Then she acts all offended because they sent old Joe Noonan to talk to her instead of an officer. Oh my, if she wasn't such a good-lookin' dame I'd lose interest real fast." He eased himself up from the chair and made a slight adjustment to the knot of his garish tie before turning and going to the door. Then, his hand on the handle, he wheeled round to face her again.

"Impertinent, am I? Ignorant? Don't know the difference between a Red and a hole in the ground? Listen, before I got into this crappy outfit I was a New York cop. I've heard it all already. Including horse manure from high-class dames that started out looking down on Joseph Xavier Noonan who never got to college because he was helping out in his old man's corner grocery. And you know what? After a while some of those dames got to know Joe Noonan a little better. Found themselves looking *up* at him instead. In bed, begging for more." The foxy smile was back in place. "See you around, Eleanor."

"But Polly, wasn't it out of order to do it like that anyway? Shouldn't Noonan have been accompanied by another CIC man as a witness, or to take notes or something?"

Polly forced a smile but Eleanor was staring down at the untouched food on her plate and didn't notice. "Not necessarily. You've been seeing too many British movies, where police detectives go around in pairs. One kind of aristocratic and the other one dumb."

Eleanor refused to be cheered up. "But that obnoxious man could make up all sorts of lies about what I said or didn't say. And then there was the crude, vulgar way he was staring at me, chewing gum with his mouth open, and his filthy innuendoes. God, I feel *soiled* by him. I keep wishing I'd had more presence of mind and got rid of him right after he burst in on me."

"Look, Eleanor, so the CIC is part of G2, and I work for G2 as well. But that doesn't mean I've ever come across this Noonan, and

I certainly don't know a thing about whatever internal rules their investigators are supposed to operate under. Even so, I'd imagine they have a good deal of latitude when they're just sniffing around speculatively as he seems to be doing. Whatever, though, you don't have to put up with insolent behaviour. Why not file a complaint about him? I could probably find out who his officer is."

"Could you, Polly? That's really why I asked you to meet me. I know very little about how to go through military channels, and wouldn't know where to start. So I'd be grateful if you could let me know who I should approach. . . . He was just *horrible*. It's not just that Noonan was so offensive, though. The whole thing's degrading, poking around trying to get people to gossip about their friends. All this wild talk about Reds, implying that I might be a communist, for God's sake, or John Prothero – and why should he have been asking Tom Berman of all people about me?"

Polly shrugged. "Sure, it's unpleasant. But I wouldn't let it get under your skin, Eleanor. This Noonan's probably being over-zealous, but I'd guess he's authorized to snoop around. It's no secret that Willoughby sees himself as some sort of anti-communist crusader. And for heaven's sake, you're in a better position than most to know that SCAP policy started out pretty liberal and has gotten a lot more cautious in the past few months. The Professor is one of the old-time academic Far East experts with State Department links, after all. What do they call them?"

"The China Crowd."

"Right. The ones who want permanent demilitarization and American-style democracy. They're not too popular right now. How do you know Prothero's *not* a Red? Some of the China Crowd are pretty far left. And then, take Tom Berman. He obviously thinks he's terrific, but who knows what his political opinions are? Do you? If it comes to that, how the hell do I know where *you* stand, politically?"

Belatedly it appeared to dawn on Eleanor that she was not the only one with troubles. "Do Tom's or my private opinions matter to you, Polly?"

"They might."

"Why? What exactly are you getting at?"

Polly passed a hand over her eyes and then sighed. "I suppose what I'm trying to say is that I'm beginning to wonder if there's anyone around here who isn't a phoney of some sort."

"Well, I don't think Tom's a phoney, for a start. He's an ambitious man, certainly, but he isn't afraid to say what he thinks." Eleanor drew herself up a little. "Neither am I, Polly." Then she relaxed again, and spoke less stiffly. "Has somebody let you down? Is that it?"

"Not . . . not exactly." Polly stopped staring at her plate and looked up with a wry little smile. "It isn't what you're thinking, Eleanor. Not man trouble. It's just that I'm in need of somebody to trust."

10

Being sufficiently senior in rank, if he had troubled to pull strings, Tom Berman could probably have arranged to have a house allotted to him in Washington Heights or one of the other new residential complexes, as Jay Murakami had. He had little taste for the practicalities of housekeeping, though, and the room he had been allotted in the Shufunotomo Building billet for male civilian officials was comfortable enough. It suited him for other reasons, too.

Some of the residents brought women in from time to time, accepting the high risk of being spotted and becoming as a consequence the butt of coarse wisecracks. Since these came almost inevitably from men who were behaving in the same way it didn't bother the offenders much. Those who were disinclined to parade their peccadilloes and amused themselves off the premises, or were chaste as a matter of principle or prudence, might purse their lips censoriously, but they rarely voiced their opinions.

Nobody had ever seen a bar girl or a *pan-pan* entering or leaving Berman's end-of-corridor room, even though he was not yet forty and with his mop of unruly hair and fresh complexion looked not much over thirty. He dressed well, was rumoured to have a substantial private income, and made no secret of the fact that he was divorced. It was hardly surprising in the circumstances that once in a while envious acquaintances surmised aloud in his presence that a man with so many desirable qualifications probably had to beat the women off with a club. Berman greeted such sallies with a tired, practised smile, pointing out that given the workload of each and every lawyer on the staff of the International Prosecution Section it was tough enough to make time to eat and catch a few hours' sleep a night. Any sort of social life was out of the question.

Few really believed him, and it was generally thought that he guarded his reputation because he had political ambitions, a reasonable enough assumption on the part of those who were aware of his professional background. Even had he simply continued for a while as an assistant district attorney in Los Angeles, Berman would have been well placed to run for local or state office. Now, with the continuing goodwill of his old Manila employer General Whitney smoothing his way in Tokyo, and priceless experience at the war crimes tribunal to exploit, there seemed no reason why he should not sooner or later aim at Washington.

The object of all the speculation picked up the open bottle of bourbon and pointed a finger of his other hand at his guest's glass, his eyebrows raised enquiringly. "Thank you, Tom," the Professor said. "Just a little, please." Berman refreshed his own drink as well and took a sip before sitting back with a sigh.

"To recapitulate, then, whatever the British, the Russians or anybody else on the Allied Council may argue, it's not going to be easy to get agreement to a second round of prosecutions. The Allied Council has become a joke anyway. The Chief ignores it, and as long as his wishes are made known to the Japanese government orally rather than in writing he doesn't have to report what he's up to. Either to the Council, or to Washington, for that matter."

"As I am well aware," Prothero said, putting his glass down and joining his hands at the fingertips almost as though in prayer. "You are drafting a submission to him, though, are you not? Recommending putting the remaining fifty Class A detainees on trial?"

"I don't know how you come by your information, John. You never cease to surprise me. Yes, some of us are doing just that. Not only at the insistence of the Allied prosecutors, but because we believe it's in the long-term interests of this country to put the old guard out of circulation once and for all. But it'll probably be months before our submission lands on the great man's desk. If it ever does. Joe Keenan's dragging his feet, and he is the chief prosecutor, after all. Keep it under your hat, but I gather that he and one or two of the brighter sparks on his personal staff figure that the smart thing would be to reclassify the fifty as Class B or even C. That idea would almost certainly appeal to MacArthur, because if it were to happen they could be prosecuted before an all-American military tribunal instead of this international circus. The old man wants the whole crew of us off the premises the day before yesterday, needless to say."

"Ingenious. Some of us may have been underestimating Mr Keenan's capacity for guile, it seems."

"In his day he was very good indeed. That's why he got the job. And even pickled in alcohol as he is now, he's still capable of pulling a few rabbits out of the hat. Incidentally, talking of alcoholics, did you hear about Mike Brooks?"

"Major Brooks? Polly Horvath's officer?"

"The same. It's been known within G2 for some time that he hits the bottle very hard. A lot more discreetly than Keenan, but word gets around. To the point I gather that it was brought to the attention of General Willoughby himself. Brooks is close to the inner circle, after all. Could well be thought a security risk. Willoughby likes him, though, and wanted to keep him in place. Well, somebody must have persuaded the Prussian that enough is enough. I heard today that Brooks has been hospitalized, and the scuttlebutt is that he'll be shipped home as soon as they get him more or less dried out. So Polly will probably get a new boss."

"I see. Interesting. Polly Horvath strikes me as being a highly intelligent young woman. Being in daily contact with Brooks, no doubt she knew about his weakness. Good heavens, I seem to have drunk all that whisky. Perhaps just a little more . . . thank you. I must be on my way shortly, but before I leave you, let me just confirm one thing. I infer from what you have said that not only you but a number of your colleagues would be in favour of further Class A prosecutions. Is that correct?"

"It is. Not all fifty of them. The passage of time gives a certain perspective, and it's agreed that a good many of them are much smaller fry than they seemed to be back in forty-five. But there are still some prime specimens who ought to be in that dock. I went to see one of them in Sugamo just yesterday. Kodama."

"The Kodama Organization. Shanghai. Yes. One has often wondered why he wasn't included. The same applies to Kishi, of course. The man was the effective political dictator of Manchuria, after all, with all that implies. Tell me, what was your impression of Kodama?"

"I don't quite know how to express this, but he . . . *angered* me, John. I knew from his record that he must be both shrewd and tough, or he could never have pulled himself up by the bootstraps and achieved so much so young. I must admit that I'd expected him after nearly eighteen months in jail to be at least, well, apprehensive. But the bastard was so arrogant you'd have thought he was granting me an audience rather than expecting to have to answer for his actions."

"Perhaps you shouldn't have been surprised, Tom. Years of imprisonment before the war didn't chasten him, after all. And in the course of Japanese history a good many thugs have risen from humble origins to positions of great political power."

"Yes, but there's nothing specially Japanese about that. You could say the same thing about almost any country in the world. So far as I'm concerned, if Tojo and any of the others on trial deserve to hang, then so does Kodama. And he must know that, but you'd never guess it from his manner."

Prothero brushed the usual stray lock of hair away from his forehead but seemed not to notice that it flopped down again when he looked at his wrist-watch. "It's after ten. I really should go. You're right, of course. Japanese society is not unique in having thrown up powerful individuals from its lower levels. Nevertheless, Kodama is an example of a kind much more common here than in the West, though we and the French both have names for it. The *éminence grise* or power behind the throne. In Japanese *kuromaki*, literally 'black curtain'. He is a political power broker."

"Was, perhaps, but not now. Now he's in jail, where he belongs."

"No, Tom. Kodama is still a power to be reckoned with, and I fear will continue to be. I too would like to see him tried and convicted, but I don't expect it to happen. I am quite sure that the arrogance you saw in him springs from a conviction that he has not only a future, but a national role to play. A man like Kodama can work surprisingly effectively from jail, through his many friends and clients outside. I wish you well in your endeavours, but frankly I'm not sanguine about your prospects of success."

After bidding Prothero good-night in the lobby Berman went back to his room and sat for some time doing nothing. Then he stood up, pulled off his tie and smoothed out the creases in it before putting it with the other half-dozen on the rack fixed to the inside of the door of his clothes closet. His jacket and trousers were next, tidily arranged on a hanger and stowed away, and his shirt and socks went into the laundry bag in a corner of the closet.

The bathrobe he put on over his undershirt and shorts was a good one, of heavy silk, but beginning to show its age. It was the only garment he still had which dated from the days of his marriage, a birthday present from Julie in fact, and a more powerful reminder of her than any photograph would have been. He thought about her while cleaning his teeth at the wash-hand basin in his room. The ritual had long since become automatic: twenty strokes each side and in front inside *and* out and the same for the lower jaw, two hundred and forty in all.

No wonder you wreck several toothbrushes a month, she would say, dentists must hate people like you. And all the time the anxious love in her face making everything worse and worse until she found those damned pictures in a drawer of the desk in his study. From that moment on her pathetic attempts to please and the cloying, tender concern were replaced by horror and revulsion, as though he were some kind of evil monster instead of . . . oh, to hell with it, Julie had no business going through his personal papers in the first place.

The Colgate tingle vying not unpleasingly with the residual taste of the bourbon, Berman sat down again, this time at his desk. Nobody would ever find anything compromising here, he reflected. Certainly not that jerk from counter-intelligence. Noonan. He shook his head in disbelief that internal security investigations could be entrusted to such an unsubtle, stupid, but cocky and self-satisfied ignoramus. All those heavily suggestive questions about poor Eleanor Curtis – it was perfectly obvious that Noonan had seen her somewhere and decided to use the access his job gave him to make a play for her. Huh! Fat chance.

Noonan had asked about John Prothero too: dumb, shallow political questions. Berman wouldn't have minded being a fly on the wall if Noonan dared to approach the Professor personally. John would – politely of course – shred him into little pieces and puff him away in minutes. He reviewed in his mind their own recent conversation. John was inclined to lecture, even in conversation with someone he must surely recognize as an intellectual equal, but he had some interesting ideas. And he had obviously given thought to Kodama.

Berman leafed through the notes he had made following his visit to Sugamo prison and decided that nothing Prothero had said made it necessary for him to revise his conclusions. If anything could put a noose round Kodama's neck it would be verifiable facts, not guesswork; and Prothero's estimates of Kodama's present and possible future political influence had been based on pure speculation. Unless, of course, there was anything in this extraordinary notion that Arthur Reynolds the Australian had got into his head and sought him out earlier that day to raise in private. Reynolds was no fool, but surely it was preposterous to imagine that Kodama, Kishi or indeed any of the other unindicted Class A detainees could have an *American* protector somewhere high up in SCAP? How in the world could Reynolds have dreamed up such a crazy idea?

Berman was shaking his head over his notes when he heard what he had been waiting for. The scratching at the door had hardly begun before he was on his feet and striding towards it. He needed to open it only an inch or two to see the shy but reassuring smile, and it took less than a second to admit a slender young Japanese in dark trousers and a white cotton jacket, who giggled as he held out the bogus telephone message slip he had been carrying. Berman took it, crumpled it in his hand and tossed it on to his desk. Then he put one hand on each of the boy's shoulders, drew him towards him and held him close for a moment.

"You smell so good! Off duty now, Kiyoshi?"

"Off duty, Tom-san. All OK. Nobody see me."

"Good." Berman took him by the hand and led him over to the bed. Then, while they were both still standing, he placed a hand under the young man's chin, tilted his head up and kissed him gently on the lips. After a moment Berman disengaged himself, reached down and removed the slim hand already groping at the front of his bathrobe. "Not yet, Kiyoshi. We're in no hurry, my dear."

Berman took his time unbuttoning the white cotton jacket, breaking off now and then to plant delicate kisses on the smooth, pale olive skin. Brow, cheeks, neck, hands . . . and only then the slow, protracted, humble uncovering and approach to the regions of special delight.

11

Confused and perturbed as she was, Polly slept badly. One of the results was that she missed her usual chance to take a shower before the other women crowded the washroom out, and had to catch the late instead of the early special SCAP bus from Hilltop House to the Dai-Ichi Building. All the military buses had slogans painted on their sides and in the ordinary way she never noticed them, but this one seemed to jeer at her: PLAN YOUR FUTURE – ENLIST IN THE REGULAR ARMY NOW.

Her mood was not improved when she went to the security office window giving on to the inner lobby, to pick up and sign for her office keys.

"Already been checked out, Sergeant," the duty corporal said.

"Checked out? Who by?" Polly stared at him coldly. The man looked somehow shifty, avoiding her eye.

"The duty officer of the day signed for them."

"Why would he do a thing like that? What's going on, Corporal?"

He shrugged. "How would I know? They don't tell me nothing. You better go find out for yourself."

Without another word Polly headed for the stairs and her office. The door was closed but unlocked, and she flung it open to find a stranger inside: a sergeant, standing at her open filing cabinet going through the contents of the top drawer. He turned and smiled at her without speaking as she marched straight past him to the open connecting door and looked into Major Brooks's room. A captain was sitting at his desk. Polly's first instinct was to ask him what the hell he thought he was doing, but her military conditioning brought her to attention and her right hand rose in a half-hearted salute to which the officer responded with a casual gesture.

"At ease, Sergeant. May I ask what you're doing here?"

"I was about to ask you the same question, sir."

"Oh, oh. Somebody must have goofed. Didn't you get a message to report to personnel admin?"

"No, Captain, I didn't. And I'd still like to know what you're doing in Major Brooks's office, what that sergeant out there is doing in mine and how come he has the key to my filing cabinet."

"Don't tell me you hadn't heard the major's in hospital?"

"Yes, sir, I heard yesterday afternoon, and that's another thing that's bothering me. Major Brooks was just fine when I was talking to him in the morning, then no more than a couple of hours later he's supposed to be sick enough to be sent straight to hospital in Yokohama. He wasn't in an accident, just sick is what they told me when I checked with the adjutant's office."

"Sick is what I've heard, too, Sergeant, and don't take that tone with me. I've been assigned to stand in for Major Brooks, and Sergeant Hawkins out there is going to be assisting me. If you have questions go ask personnel admin. Like I said, they're expecting you. Dismissed. No, wait. You have a note of the combination for that safe over there, I presume?"

"That's Major Brooks's personal safe. He sets the combination himself and changes it whenever he thinks fit."

The captain sighed. "Sergeant, your attitude is beginning to bug me. I ask again, do you have a note of the combination?"

"Captain, if Major Brooks wishes to authorize you to open that safe in his absence no doubt he will tell you the combination. He has never told it to me."

"Noted. Report to personnel admin immediately. Dismissed."

"But this is ridiculous, Lieutenant! I never applied for a furlough."

The bespectacled lieutenant in charge of the personnel administration office sat back in his chair, stretched and then yawned. "Pardon me. I'm still a couple of cups of coffee below par." He looked again at the paper in front of him. "OK, so you say you never asked for one. You got one anyway, duly authorized, so what are you beefing about?"

"Who authorized it?"

"Why, the guy we've just been talking about. Major Brooks, who else? His signature's right here in front of me. Dated last week. Look, I don't understand why you're all het up at the prospect of a vacation, but so far as this office is concerned you're off duty as of now for ten days, Sergeant. I sure wish I was, too. Have a great time anyway."

Flinging herself out of the officer's glassed-in cubicle, Polly went over to the corner of the big general office where Angie Brewster sat, half-concealed behind bulwarks of files. "Welcome back," Angie said equably. "I cleared a chair for you. Want some coffee?"

"No thanks. I'm half-way up the wall as it is. Angie, why in the world would anybody want to go on ten days' vacation in *January*, for God's sake? And do they seriously expect me to believe that Major Brooks signed a leave authorization form a week ago without telling me? I couldn't see the signature, but sure as hell it isn't genuine. What *is* going on?"

"Search me, honey. I'm as mystified as you are. What did the lieutenant say? About Mike Brooks?"

"He seemed pretty confused himself. Said he understood the major collapsed, and that the medical officer who looked at him ordered up an ambulance right away. I kept asking what's actually *wrong* with him and why Yokohama when there's a perfectly good military hospital right on Kuramae Avenue a mile or so away. And also why I was given the runaround when I called the hospital yesterday evening. He just shrugged. Everybody seems to be doing that around me today." Polly turned her head to glare at the closed door of the lieutenant's office. Several other clerks worked near Angie, but the clatter of typewriters and the several other conversations going on in the room at the same time paradoxically gave them a degree of privacy.

"Well, believe me, I didn't hear a word about any of this until I got in this morning and found the file copy of your authorization in my tray. I was going to call you, but then you came steaming in here like a bat out of hell anyway. At least I can tell you who the captain in your office is. Name of Henderson, from Army Security Agency Tech Intelligence Detachment out there in Icky Buckeroo, near Sugamo prison. And his sergeant's called Charlie Hawkins."

Polly suddenly felt sick to her stomach, and closed her eyes momentarily. Thank God she had taken the Operation Hi-Flyer folder out of the safe the previous afternoon, the moment she heard Mike Brooks had been sent to hospital. Combination or no combination, it wouldn't take a technical intelligence expert long to open that door.

"You all right, Polly? You look kind of pale."

"What? No. No, I'm OK. Just angry. And confused."

"I don't blame you. Can't see what the hurry is myself, assigning a new man overnight like that while the poor guy's seat's still warm. Looks like they don't expect him back, doesn't it? And it looks to me as if this furlough they've dropped in your lap could be to give them time to figure out what to do about you. Hey, I have an idea! Why don't I organize a few days for myself too, and we'll take a little trip next week? Get out of this crazy town for a while. Go to Nikko maybe, stay by the lake and do the tourist bit. I'm the gal that knows how to fix travel orders and reserve accommodations, after all. How about it?"

"I . . . I'll think about it, Angie. Sure. Give me a little while to get my head straightened out first, will you?"

Three minutes later, in the privacy of the women's room, Polly felt her heart miss a beat as a new idea occurred to her, prompted perhaps by Angie's use of the word "overnight". Suppose Henderson and Hawkins had *already* opened the safe, and that the captain's question had been designed to trap her? That the existence of the incriminating notes was known, and the search for them was on? What she had said was literally true: Brooks had never *told* her the combination, but would they believe that? This Captain Henderson was a security specialist. He'd surely have the wit to realize that she hadn't denied *knowing* it. Why the hell wasn't she a better liar?

The empty file cover was no problem. After taking the three pages of notes out and checking carefully that there was nothing whatever written on it, even in the faintest pencil, she had put it with the stack of identical ones in plain view in her stationery cupboard. The papers were something else again. They were in an envelope, still in her shoulder-bag where she had stowed them the previous day to look after until Major Brooks returned. It *must* have been a premonition that made her do that.

It was hard to take it in, but everything pointed to the likelihood that Angie Brewster was right, and that people in authority in G2 were not expecting Brooks back. Had quite possibly removed him deliberately. In which case she had to go to the hospital in Yokohama to see him. Take the papers with her? For God's sake, pull yourself together, of course not. Stash them away somewhere, but where? No, keep them with her at all times, safe enough for the time being, unless, oh Jesus, *unless they suspected her and searched her*. Dear God, was there *anyone* she could trust?

"Liver failure, I imagine, but I'm no medical man, Polly. Let's not beat about the bush, though. You must have known as well as any of us that Mike Brooks is an alcoholic. People like that can keep functioning apparently normally for a surprisingly long time. Then one fine day their systems decide to go on strike. I don't want to be gloomy and believe me, I think a lot of Mike. But face it, he's brought it on himself, the damn fool. I'm not in the least surprised the medics decided he needs specialist treatment they can't provide in the 361st Station Hospital here in town. And frankly, I think the powers that be have acted reasonably enough in replacing him right away. Willoughby probably gave the order personally. He wouldn't want even a temporary vacancy in his retinue with so much going on at the moment." Arthur Reynolds leant back in his chair and surveyed Polly's troubled face.

"I'm sorry for you though, Polly. I don't know this new man – Henderson? Anderson? – but I don't think you should take it personally. If he's had the same sergeant working with him for some time it's natural enough he should want to bring him here. If I were you I'd make the best of things. Enjoy your unexpected leave bonus. Rest and recreate yourself, my dear. Who knows, maybe I could pull some strings and get you reassigned to work with me. Does the idea have any appeal? It certainly does for me. Think about it. Meantime you're off duty, it seems. I have to go out now, for a ride in my jeep to see a man about a problem. Can I drop you off at Hilltop House, or wherever?"

"Oh. Would you do that? I'd be really grateful. If it's not out of your way." In her relief Polly could have hugged him and very nearly did. Maybe she was imagining things, maybe Arthur was right and there was a reasonable explanation for what was happening and nothing necessarily sinister in Captain Henderson's question about the safe. On the other hand if anybody *did* know about those notes and suspected her, they would hardly want to cause a furore by having her stopped and searched when she left the building in the company of a senior officer.

The sense of relief she experienced on finding herself safely outside the Dai-Ichi Building again and bowling along beside Reynolds in his jeep was so great that she put a hand on his forearm and timidly smiled at him. He glanced at her.

"Well, that's more like it! You looked like a dying duck in a thunderstorm half an hour ago."

"Were you serious, Arthur? About trying to get me assigned to help you?"

"Serious, absolutely. And only too glad to try. It doesn't necessarily follow that I'd succeed, of course."

"Listen, could you stop somewhere out of the way for a few minutes? There's something I have to tell you in private."

"I'd never have guessed. I can listen and drive at the same time, you know. Shoot."

The fact that she didn't have to look him in the eye while talking made it much easier for Polly to take the plunge and, for good or ill, let everything tumble out. Nearly everything, anyway. Reynolds said little, beyond assuring her that he had never heard of Operation Hi-Flyer but was not altogether surprised to learn that General Willoughby and a few others were involved in top-secret clandestine negotiations with right-wing Japanese politicians. He nodded in silence when Polly described the terms of the bargain that had been arrived at, as pieced together by Mike Brooks and described in his notes. Namely, that the detainees Kodama and Kishi at least would not only be guaranteed immunity from prosecution as war criminals, but that their early release would be arranged. That, with Kodama's financial and political support, Kishi would be groomed for high office on the understanding that he would push for the suppression of communism in Japan, for rearmament and for a long-term security treaty with the United States.

Reynolds finally stopped the jeep outside Hilltop House. "That's four or five times around the block, Polly, and I really have to go now. Thank you for confiding in me at last. I'd suspected something of the kind, from what little you let slip the other day. And it might help you to know that I've tried out a hypothesis of my own on Tom Berman. You say you've personally seen documentary evidence of all this, Polly? In the form of Mike Brooks's handwritten notes?"

"Yes. And everything that's happened to me this morning makes me certain that Willoughby's people suspect that they exist, and want very much to get their hands on them. That's why the major's been shipped out of town, and why they want me out of the way too. I'm scared, Arthur."

He reached for her hand and squeezed it. "I'm not surprised. But a trouble shared is a trouble halved, Polly. I won't let you down, I promise. But I must do some hard thinking. Try to relax now, and come and have drinks with me at the Press Club this evening. By then I may know how best to advise you. I'll come and pick you up from here. Around eight? Splendid. Cheer up, it isn't the end of the world."

Polly clambered out and Reynolds drove off with a cheery wave. She did feel better after their conversation. The sun was shining, and she thought she might go out for a walk after changing out of her uniform. It was odd to be at leisure at this hour on a working day, a little like being let out of school early on the last day before a vacation, and she might as well make the best of it while deciding what to do about the damned papers in her bag.

It was warm enough for a stroll round the second-hand bookshops in the Kanda district, perhaps. Her mother had written to say how happy she and Dad were with their Christmas present: the woodblock prints an acquaintance arrived back in the States on demobilization leave had mailed for her. Obviously they didn't look as lurid in Minneapolis as they had in Tokyo. Oh boy, if only her parents knew how cheap they had been! But they didn't, and with Mother's birthday coming up in April it would obviously be worth picking up some more.

There was nobody at the reception desk in the former hotel; only one of the cleaners mopping the linoleum floor. The whole place seemed a little forlorn without the sound of footsteps on the stairs, doors being opened and closed and women's voices. No fun sitting around in a mausoleum: she'd definitely go out for that walk. In her room on the third floor Polly hung up her uniform, took off her slip and tossed it on the bed and then pulled on a pair of slacks. Then she stood indecisively, wondering whether she needed anything between brassière and sweater. Probably not. Not if she wore the thick brown one with the cable-stitch design. She bent down and opened the bottom drawer in the right of the closet where she kept it. She stared inside and then snatched open the one above. Then the one above that, and finally the small one at the top where she kept stockings and underwear.

It was not the practice for the residents at Hilltop House to lock their rooms, but they did each have a metal locker in which to keep anything valuable or very personal. Polly tried the door of hers before unlocking it and looking inside. Then, leaving it open, she backed away and slowly sat down on the edge of the bed to think, and it wasn't until nearly fifteen minutes later when she became conscious of the goose-pimples on her bare arms and shoulders that she stood up again with a shudder, finally took the sweater from the drawer and pulled it on.

It was true, then. She hadn't been making a fuss about nothing. Someone had searched her room. Not the woman who came in to clean. Not one of the other girls. A man almost certainly, because surely no woman would have done so poor a job of refolding garments and putting them back where they belonged? A man from Technical Intelligence maybe, to whom her locker would have presented about as much of a problem as a paper sack; and a man who had been through her letters, photographs and other few treasures, but had not found what he was looking for because it wasn't there.

It was foul, like a kind of mental rape, but did it mean that he or they – whoever they were – would now leave her in peace? Or would they be back? Polly fidgeted around her room in an agony of indecision. Wouldn't the most sensible thing be to memorize the essential names, dates and places if possible and then tear the papers into shreds and put a match to them? Then whoever was so interested could search till they were blue in the face and get nowhere, while she could still carry out the plan Mike Brooks had confided to her, on his behalf.

If the poor man was indeed seriously ill, unlikely to recover, conceivably about to die, it would be her tribute to a person she admired whatever his failings, as well as something that should be done for its own sake. But then again, would anybody believe such an extraordinary story without written evidence, evidence made credible because in the identifiable handwriting of one of General Willoughby's senior aides? Arthur Reynolds had seemed to, but had immediately asked if she'd seen written evidence. Why hadn't she wanted to tell him she had the notes on her? Simple caution, of course. He wasn't named, but suppose after all he was himself one of the conspirators? No, the notes were the only tangible evidence she had, and she *had* to hang on to them, at least until she could talk to the major. And study them properly too, because from them she might at least be able to work out who *not* to trust; and that meant hiding them somewhere.

Angie Brewster! Angie would look after them for her, Polly was sure of it. So sure that with no further hesitation she closed the locker door and turned the key, pushed the drawers back into place in the closet and went out of her room and down the stairs to the floor below. The corridor there was also deserted, and she slipped quickly into Angie's room. There she looked around, satisfying herself that the cleaner had set it to rights for the day. Then she transferred the envelope from her own bag to one of Angie's she found at the back of the closet, and hurried out again.

12

"Come in! Oh, hi. How's the vacation gal?"

"Hi, Angie. OK, thanks. Listen, I'm just on my way downstairs. I'm meeting Commander Reynolds, but there's something I have to ask you. A favour."

Angie Brewster had opened her mouth to react in a suitably jocular way to Polly's announcement, but something in the younger woman's face made her close it again and nod.

"Look, after what happened today you must have been wondering what's going on."

"You can say that again."

"Sure. Well, I don't know for sure myself, but I mean to find out. Because . . . listen, Angie, when I got back here this morning I discovered that somebody's searched my room."

"You're kidding!"

"I am not. My stuff was mussed up. Not all that much, but I know the way I fold my things, and they'd definitely been moved."

There was concern in Angie's big, homely face. "Polly honey, you seem to have an awful lot on your mind right now. Even I can see something darn peculiar's going on. But are you sure you aren't imagining things?"

"I was afraid you might say that. No, I'm not being neurotic. Because I know what he – I feel sure it was a man – was looking for. Angie, it's some confidential notes Major Brooks wrote. He . . . he discussed them with me before they took him to hospital. Fortunately I had them with me this morning. When I realized what had happened, well, I suppose I panicked a little. I just have to keep those notes safe, at least until I get to see the major. So I brought them here to your room and hid them, Angie. Excuse me."

Polly went to the closet, reached for the handbag and took the sealed envelope from it. She held it out. "I hate to drag you into this mess, but would you keep this for me for a couple of days?"

"Why, sure I will, Polly."

"Do you – would you like to open it and see what's inside?"

Angie's smile transformed her. "If you trust me enough to hand this over, that's good enough for me."

"It's a, well, political matter. And it's hot."

"If it's that important, then no thank you, I'd rather not know the details. Not right now, anyway. I'll take good care of this, I promise. You better go. Don't keep that handsome commander waiting."

"Bless you, Angie."

After Polly had gone Angie Brewster sat looking at the envelope for a long time, one hand to the cheek Polly had kissed. Then she put it back in the handbag and returned it to the closet. It would be safe enough there overnight.

The Press Club bar was busy as usual, and Polly wondered not only why Arthur Reynolds had taken her there, but also why he had wasted the time they had been alone together in his jeep on the way in bright, social chitchat. "Time enough for shop-talk later," was all he said when she tried to turn the conversation. And now that they had arrived he continued in the same way, as though neither of them had a care in the world, interrupting himself to hail and exchange a few words with acquaintances. He did keep glancing towards the entrance, however, and Polly got the impression that he was waiting for someone.

She was right. "Ah, there he is," he said a few minutes later, and raised an arm in greeting to a man who was threading his way between the tables towards them.

"You made it. Good. Polly, I'd like you to meet a SCAP colleague, Jerry Nakajima. Polly Horvath."

"Hello. Pleased to meet you." The hand that took hers and shook it was warm, the pressure firm.

"Sit down, Jerry. I'll buy you a drink." Reynolds beckoned a waiter while Nakajima sat down. Polly assumed that he must be an American of Japanese ancestry like Jay Murakami, and wondered why she'd never come across him before.

"Which division do you work in, Mr Nakajima?"

"I'm attached to G2."

"Is that right?" There were an awful lot of people "attached" to G2 in one way or another, and no particular reason why she should have come across him before. All the same, Polly wondered about him, until his drink arrived and Reynolds enlightened her.

"Don't be fooled by his perfect English, Polly. Jerry's real name is Eijiro. He's Japanese and works as a researcher in the War Data Department over there in the NYK shipping office building."

Polly did her best to conceal her astonishment and her almost instinctive tendency to shrink away from Nakajima. It was the first time since she had arrived in Tokyo that she found herself on equal human and social terms with a former enemy. The Japanese either didn't notice her reaction or pretended not to, and as the three of them chatted the sense of strangeness soon wore off.

Jerry Nakajima was so different from the handful of other Japanese white-collar SCAP employees she had encountered. Most of them were interpreters or translators, and Polly could understand that the nature of their work put them in a tricky personal situation. Perhaps this was why they all seemed so much alike, relating to the Americans with an uneasy blend of unctuous obsequiousness and pushy over-familiarity that made her take against them.

This man was not in the least like that. He looked self-contained and confident, but his manner towards her was courteously considerate. Moreover, he was *very* good-looking and she was acutely conscious of the physical contact and the momentary locking of eyes when it was time to go and they shook hands in farewell.

"I apologize for not warning you I'd invited Nakajima, but I wanted you to form your own impression of him," Reynolds said when they were on their own again. "What do you think?"

"He's – well, he's certainly impressive."

"I'll tell you more about him outside. You have eaten, by the way?"

"Yes, ages ago."

"So you won't mind if I take you back pretty soon?"

"No. Today has left me completely shot."

Some two hours later, Polly Horvath lay in bed staring at the ceiling. Her bedside lamp was still on, the chair back over which she had flung her clothes was in shadow in the corner, and she was trying to decide whether on top of everything else she now had to be frightened of Arthur Reynolds. In spite of his having said some nice things and kissed her a few times while saying good-night. The last two were French kisses and, even given her distracted state of mind, unexpectedly enjoyable. He would obviously be quite happy to take her to bed if she were to give him the green light.

Yet it was as if nothing was now what it seemed to be. From innocently stumbling upon evidence of a conspiracy, she had within a matter of days been sucked into it, and it seemed that from now on it was to stain even her emotional life. If only she hadn't been tempted to look inside the safe in the first place and seen that damned file! Or stupidly approached Reynolds with questions that went far beyond everyday office chatter and cynical speculation about SCAP policies, and on top of that telling him about the existence of Mike Brooks's Operation Hi-Flyer file!

The ridiculous thing was that she was physically attracted to him. If only the calendar could have been put back a week, those kisses might have opened up intriguing possibilities. An affair between a senior officer and a non-com would have had to be handled discreetly, but such relationships could and did develop. Especially if the two people concerned worked alongside each other as Arthur Reynolds was still suggesting they might, in spite of the fact that she was clearly under suspicion in certain G2 quarters. Even before this evening she would have been unlikely to lose her head over Arthur, but they could have had a pretty good time all the same.

Not now, though. Not after he had deliberately set up the encounter with Jerry Nakajima, who could easily have been the unnamed man Reynolds had been going to see "to discuss a problem" that morning. And might not the problem for discussion have been the sudden disappearance of Major Brooks and his instant replacement by two army security agency men, coupled with her own effective suspension from duty?

She had held back from telling him so, but Reynolds must either suspect or know that Polly had the Brooks papers in her possession. He could have suspected after her earlier approach to him that something serious was bothering her, and have worked out some devious plan to find out what it was. Maybe it was some such motive rather than straightforward sexual attraction that accounted for his new attentiveness, and for his suggestion about working together; he had already gained much of her confidence and could hope to find out everything in the natural course of a developing affair.

If not that, then what the hell was Reynolds up to? He was a colleague of Brooks, after all. He could be pretending ignorance while all the time knowing all about Operation Hi-Flyer, could even be involved in it himself. Maybe with this mysterious Jerry Nakajima. Reynolds had, seemingly, been frank about him on the way back to Hilltop House.

A one-time naval officer who had served at the Japanese Embassy in Washington before the war, a man not only cleared by American security but actually hired by them. A man, Reynolds had told her, who had extensive contacts in political circles in Japan and was one of his own most valuable informants about the developments it was his job to study and report on. Why had Reynolds wanted him to meet her? Presumably because they had already discussed her between themselves, and Reynolds was interested to know Jerry Nakajima's personal impressions of her. Why, if not in the context of Operation Hi-Flyer?

Polly turned on to her side to reach for the light switch. Then she hesitated as a different idea occurred to her and made her feel angry as well as even more confused. Turn it around. Suppose that, rather than wanting Nakajima to meet her, Reynolds had deliberately planned to have her meet Nakajima? Suppose he had cynically predicted that she would be bowled over by his Japanese friend and would become putty in his hands – a lot quicker than she was likely to in his own?

Then again, how come a man hired as a local employee of SCAP was on such friendly personal terms with an Australian naval officer, had access to the Press Club and could afford to dress so well? His whole style breathed authority and assurance, and it wasn't easy to acquire a polish like his without a classy upbringing, so maybe he came from a wealthy family. Even so, plenty of former Japanese aristocrats were having to swallow their pride and scrape a living by selling off their kimonos, scroll paintings and other heirlooms. Somehow she doubted he was doing anything like that. Jerry Nakajima had to be on the take from somebody.

Back to Arthur Reynolds, who was no fool and had been around MacArthur and his intimate circle of Bataan Boys for several years. He and others had known all along that Major Brooks was an alcoholic, and everybody knew that a lush was liable to be careless; careless enough perhaps for his personal assistant to hear and see things she was not supposed to.

Flat on her back again, the light still on and her hands behind her head, Polly tried hard to recall in detail her first serious conversation with Reynolds and everything she had said to him subsequently, but it was Jerry Nakajima's face that kept swimming into focus in her mind's eye. After a few minutes she flung herself over on to her side, switched off the light and buried her face in the pillow. It was no use trying to think straight. She still felt wide awake, and was experienced enough to realize that she was more than a little sexually frustrated. For God's sake, even at a time like this she was wondering what it would be like to be kissed by Nakajima! As good as by Arthur or better? She must be going out of her mind.

Polly was telling herself that there was a fat chance of getting any sleep that night even as she sank effortlessly into the welcoming, dreamless darkness.

"Interesting, I agree, if perhaps naïve. Though perhaps I shouldn't make that kind of judgment on the strength of one conversation about nothing much," Nakajima said. "You omitted to mention that she's also a very attractive woman. Reasons of your own for that, were there?"

"Mind your own business, sport. The thing to bear in mind about Polly Horvath is that Brooks had a high opinion of her abilities. Told me once he thought she ought to have been commissioned."

"*Had* a high opinion?"

"Past tense because I doubt if he'll be back, but don't jump to conclusions. So far as I've been able to find out without being obviously nosy, it was a perfectly genuine collapse. I'm sure he's seriously ill, and for all I know the man could be at death's door. If he pulls through it's a safe bet they'll keep him in dock until he's fit to travel. Then he'll be shipped home and invalided out."

"Convenient enough for somebody to have arranged it?"

"I've wondered, of course. It seems to have been spectacular, anyway. I'm told Brooks passed out in Willoughby's office, before the general's own startled eyes. So it wasn't possible to keep it from the old man or to twist the information that reached him. That's why I'm so sure he'll be sent home. Seems Willoughby liked Brooks a lot, insisted on talking personally to the specialist in Yokohama by phone after they'd checked him out there. Hence the great show of military efficiency and the immediate transfer of a fellow called Henderson from Army Security to take Brooks's place. Again Willoughby's personal *diktat*, but it seems logical enough. After all, his work, if you can call it that, is concerned with security at bases up and down the country. The theory is that Henderson may have done one or two little technical jobs for the general personally and made a good impression. Have you ever come across him?"

"Not to my knowledge. Go on about this woman Brooks thought so highly of. This morning you implied she might have been in his confidence."

"Yes. Though whether he positively *took* her into his confidence about anything above and beyond their legitimate official concerns remains to be discovered. Having met her now, you'll probably agree that she's obviously quite clever enough to have found out a good deal for herself by simply working with and for a man who was never completely sober even if seldom obviously drunk."

"I agree. I find it hard to understand how a man like that could have been allowed to stay so close to the general. You people are remarkably casual about security, aren't you?"

"Oh, now, come *on*! The war's over. SCAP's full of gossipy amateurs anyway and a new rumour starts the rounds every five minutes. Amounts to rather effective if unorthodox security as a matter of fact. Who'd be in a position to recognize it if something really important did leak out?"

"You don't really believe that, Arthur. If you did you wouldn't be so worried about this Sergeant Horvath. You people have secrets you want kept, and so do my friends."

Reynolds sighed and nodded slightly. After driving Polly back to her billet he had picked up Nakajima as arranged not far from the British Embassy. Now they were driving slowly round the three-mile circumference of the Imperial Palace precincts, the mighty stone ramparts beyond the black water of the moat on their left as they passed the National Diet building for the third time.

"You're right, of course. She knows a surprising amount."

"Any idea where she stands politically?"

"No. It was quite perceptive on your part to guess she might be naïve. Idealistic, I'd say, and therefore probably liberal. She takes a reasonably informed interest in the war crimes tribunal, and I know she has one or two civilian friends in Economic Section."

"Does she indeed? Who in particular?"

"Jay Murakami in Labor Division, for one. As you observed, she's attractive, personable and a woman. That's not too common a combination around here, so she gets invited out a lot, in circles a sergeant wouldn't normally reckon to move in."

"Murakami. Professor Prothero's deputy. He's a spy you know, Arthur. And he has far too many friends in the trade unions."

"Good God, don't make me laugh, you'll have me off the road even at this speed. A spy, is he? Because he goes around in shabby clothes keeping his ears and eyes open and lets people think he's Japanese? Be your age. If Murakami's a spy, what does that make you, pray?"

Nakajima ignored the jibe. "He also got beaten up the other day. Not far from here, as a matter of fact. He stupidly joined in a demo that turned into a march. A snake-dance, heading from Hibiya Park towards the Diet building. Some hoodlums broke it up with a little discreet help from your MPs and the police. Did you know that?"

Reynolds stopped the jeep suddenly and turned to look squarely at his passenger. "No. No, I must admit I did not know that. But you did, didn't you? And I find that interesting. Was it by any chance because it was friends of yours who paid those hoodlums? We work with each other, Jerry, but that doesn't mean I like you. Sometimes I begin to think I do, then you come out with something like that and I remember the sort of people you work for. The *other* people, I mean."

Nakajima returned his glare coolly. "Who's being naïve now? Listen to me, friend. You know perfectly well that SCAP's biggest mistake from the beginning was to install a military government without teeth and try to work through the Japanese authorities. But on the few significant occasions the Americans have flexed their muscles and simply imposed a course of action we Japanese have crumpled, socialists and conservatives alike, right? Like when they railroaded the new Constitution through the National Diet. And the way they maintain effective press censorship by sitting on newspaper owners and editors, whatever the fancy new liberal laws say. But they haven't learned the lesson, and neither have you, that the Japanese as a people are essentially obedient by nature, and will almost always knuckle under when they know who's boss. Just now they don't, though. Think what's been happening for the past few weeks, since about last November. Just because he can't stand the thought of even reporting to the Allied Council, much less answering to it, MacArthur's even stopped indicating his wishes to Prime Minister Yoshida in writing. What good does he imagine a word in the ear's going to do?"

"Can you blame him?"

"Yes I can, and I do. He's popular among the Japanese, damn it, and he's stuck his neck out before and got away with it. Why not now? When there's drift and chaos all around? Some people – and I include both Japanese and Americans – realize that for the good of the country this national strike the left are planning *must not happen*. Is it so surprising that they're taking whatever steps are available to them to make sure it doesn't?"

"Such as hiring thugs to beat up people whose only crime is to get mad because they're cold and hungry? Your well-fed political friends are revolting, you know that?"

"It may surprise you to know I agree, Commander Bleeding Heart. There are some repulsive specimens among them. But unfortunately you don't have to be nice to be right. Besides, why only Japanese politicians? Is the US Congress full of saints? Or SCAP? Who do you think you're trying to kid? You know what Willoughby thinks, and he's got plenty of support right down the line. There are people in the military police only too happy to lend a hand, here and down in Osaka; anywhere else the unions need to be discouraged."

"Intimidated."

"If that's the word you prefer. Anyway, you know it, I know it and General Willoughby knows it. The Yoshida government *must not fall*. If it does there could be civil war here, and people I know are prepared to get very rough to stop that happening. But it doesn't have to be handled this way. MacArthur can pick up his pen any time and stop demonstrators getting beaten up simply by unilaterally banning the strike."

"Just like that."

"Yes. Just like that. Meantime we can do without starry-eyed crusaders like Brooks and Murakami making trouble, or your girlfriend if that's what she has in mind. Stop and let me out here, will you? Thanks. Think about it, Arthur. Good-night."

13

"You look great, Major!" Polly said with an aching heart after the nurse had with obvious reluctance finally left the room.

"Polly, Polly. We haven't time . . . for such nonsense."

"No, sir. We haven't. Five minutes and not a second more, the doctor said." She bent down over the pallid, sunken face and lowered her voice. "Don't worry about the Operation Hi-Flyer notes. They're searching for them but I have them safe."

"Thank God." Polly thought the look of relief on Mike Brooks's face would alone have been enough to justify her tedious journey to Yokohama in an unheated stopping train and the difficulties she had experienced in talking her way past the formidable army nurse at the front desk and the doctor in the lieutenant-colonel's uniform. What with them and the run-in with Captain Henderson when she'd been booted out of her own office, she had begun to think she might pretty soon come face to face with a prosecuting officer at a court martial, but she suppressed the idea. She might indeed yet do so, but there was no point in assuming it was inevitable.

The faint words were still coming, punctuated by harsh breathing. "And thank you . . . for coming . . . in uniform. I told . . . told the doctor you . . . were on urgent . . . official business. Did they . . . check you out?"

"I had to show my ID, but I don't think anybody called Tokyo to check my current status. If they had, I don't think they'd have let me anywhere near you."

"Are you . . . in trouble, my dear?"

Polly shook her head. "Nothing I can't handle. Major, I know you're very sick, but they'll get you on your feet again pretty soon." She knew it wasn't so. The lieutenant-colonel had been professionally protective of his patient whose condition, he said, had sharply deteriorated the previous day and was now critical. It was a mercy that Brooks was conscious: he looked dreadful and his voice was almost inaudible.

"No they won't. I'm . . . on the way out. A man embarked . . . on a protracted suicide . . . mustn't start complaining when he's . . . on the point of succeeding. Polly, I was planning to . . . ask Jay . . . Murakami to help me."

"I know. You told me. I'll do it for you. I promise."

"Still Miss . . . Valiant-For-Truth. Thank you."

There was little more to say, and Polly sat quietly holding his hand until the nurse returned and she had to leave.

On the train back to Tokyo she tried to get used to the idea that she wasn't going to see Mike Brooks again. It was something to have been able to comfort him a little, and leave him to die in the hope that something would result from his work. Out of respect as well as conviction she had to try to carry it forward, but the sense of loneliness and inadequacy that now afflicted her was all but crippling. Still, she could at least hope it might all work out. It was hard to believe that, having checked her out so thoroughly, Henderson and whoever else had been taking an interest in her would continue to bother with a mere sergeant. And whether or not Arthur Reynolds was really on her side, there was time to think about others she might be able to trust enough to try to recruit as allies.

The Japanese janitor at Hilltop House waylaid her when she walked in and handed her a note he fetched from behind the front desk: a single sheet of poor-quality paper folded twice and sealed with a couple of staples. Polly ripped it open as she went upstairs, paused in surprise and then hurried to her room, where she read the message through a second time.

Dear Miss Horvath,

I hope you are taking care of yourself in this cold weather, and will not think me impertinent in writing this letter to you. It was a very great pleasure for me when Commander Reynolds kindly introduced me to you at the Press Club yesterday evening.

Frankly speaking, it is not often that a Japanese like me can have a chance to meet an American lady and speak as international friends about the real Japan. I think you are very interested about Japan. How about traditional Japanese music? If you would like, I shall be happy to take you to a performance on Saturday evening so I will come to Hilltop House at eighteen hundred hours.

Yours truly,

Eijiro Nakajima (Jerry)

Depressed as she was, Polly couldn't help smiling. He certainly had a nerve, but darn it, why not? It was the disarmingly stilted yet jaunty English that tipped the balance for her. The contrast it made with the fluent, idiomatic way in which Jerry Nakajima had talked to her in the Press Club bar was startling, and the effect of his letter was to make him seem much less formidably self-possessed than he had impressed her as being when they met. She felt physically and mentally drained, and the prospect of a little diversion the following day did something to lift the feeling of listlessness. She even found herself wondering what to wear, and that had to be a positive sign.

Though he still had reservations about the idea of expanding his black-market operations to the extent the gangster Masao Suekawa said his principals wanted him to do, Joe Noonan was experiencing fewer difficulties than he had expected in setting up the first major shipment of black-market goods destined for Kobe. The five thousand dollars he had received in cash from Suekawa by way of down payment on agreeing to do so had helped a great deal, both to stiffen his own resolve and to encourage his two American partners to co-operate. Noonan had given them a thousand dollars each, with the promise of a similar sum approximately a week after the consignments had been picked up. There was no need for them to know that this was when the fishing boat or boats could be expected to arrive in Kobe. There was indeed no need for them to know the destination of the goods at all, or the method of transportation to be used.

In fact it slightly bothered Noonan that he knew himself. Since the afternoon Suekawa had taken him to the deserted park called Hama Rikyu, shown him the inlet where the boats came in to unload at the fish market and treated him to a detailed account of what was proposed he had been wondering why the gangster had done it. It surely wasn't because he regarded yours truly as a partner with whom it was reasonable to exchange confidences, no, sir. Noonan was still smarting over Suekawa's high and mighty attitude that day, and the contemptuous way he had made it clear that if Noonan didn't want the business, he knew of plenty of other Americans who'd jump at it.

The ugly s.o.b. could have been bluffing, of course, but probably wasn't. It would be worth a lot to know what other contacts Suekawa and the guys behind him had in Tokyo. It was one thing to know from his previous work with the CIC black-market investigation squad that amateur American operators were being identified all the time. They were small fry; hardly worth the bother of hauling in except to be turned into statistics to please the brass. Suekawa wouldn't bother with them.

When you thought about it, it was too much to hope he was the only significant supplier of imported goods diverted from military or PX supplies. And obviously it didn't only happen in Tokyo. There was a whole bunch of British stationed around Kure down there by Hiroshima with their own procurement arrangements, for a start. More limeys and Commonwealth people in Tokyo itself, along with Russians, Chinese, all manner of military liaison staff. And the lawyers attached to the war crimes tribunal. They all had privileges, and any of them could be on the make. Problem was, the CIC team were supposed to lay off everybody except American military personnel and the civilians working in SCAP.

What the hell. He'd provided his own men with the details of the goods they were to supply to Suekawa's drivers, and with the signed and stamped official requisition forms they'd need to doctor, and they could get on with it. Right now he had money to burn and was enjoying his new job.

Imagine getting paid to snoop around some of those characters! That Berman, for a start. He had to be a fairy. Not for nothing had Joseph Xavier Noonan served in the New York Police Department vice squad for a while in forty-two and forty-three – until that bastard of a lieutenant figured out the sweet little deal he wasn't getting a piece of. Then it was a case of handing in his badge and volunteering for the army or having the book thrown at him, and what kind of a choice was that? No regrets, though. The life of a corporal in the provost branch wasn't great but it hadn't been all that bad either, not in Hawaii anyway. Or in Australia later on. New Guinea was so-so but he'd made sergeant there, and the all-important switch to counter-intelligence and another promotion with the surrender and the move to Japan.

The smart thing would be to keep his thoughts about Berman to himself for the time being and look for the hard evidence himself. It would be too bad if some other snoop were to get the credit for nailing a security risk right there in the tribunal itself. In fact, if it was true Berman had some idea of going into politics, it might be smarter still to find that evidence and then sit on it. The way things were shaping up on the deal with Suekawa's people, a guy might be finding himself getting out of the army in a year or so with enough dough to think about politics himself.

It would need working out, but it could be that one of those Senators beginning to make a noise about Reds in government would be interested to hire an aide with a bucketful of dirt about some of these characters in SCAP . . . and after that, why not aim higher? Wouldn't that be something? To ride the wave, get right in among the action in Washington, and one day see the look on that broad's face when she had to be polite to her daddy's colleague, go-getting *Congressman Joe Noonan*? Oh boy!

Second thoughts, no need to wait that long, not if he was right about Miss Ice Cold Tin Pants too. She was a pinko, no doubt about it, like her nisei buddy Murakami sitting there in his fancy house in Washington Heights. Maybe she'd decide to be a little more co-operative when he'd shown her he was no dummy by putting together enough to get her security clearance revoked. Specially when he went on to tell her he was a nice guy all the same who could be persuaded to give her another chance by forgetting to report it. Of course, she was too high and mighty to room at Hilltop House. She was at the Shiba Park Hotel, and it would be sort of nice to try out a bed there.

As he passed the comb one more time through his hair and flicked a speck of dust from his lapel, Noonan winked at his reflection in the mottled mirror attached to the wall of the room he occupied in the senior NCO quarters at Ebisu Camp. The girls at Suekawa's club would be ready and willing whatever time he showed up, but what with one thing and another he felt *horny*, so let's get going, buster.

14

Angie Brewster fumbled unseeingly in her handbag and found a handkerchief, embarrassed to realize that a drop of moisture was about to form on the end of her nose. She dealt with it just in time and pulled her collar more closely round her neck. Angie always hated to breathe the stale air of the confessional, having since girlhood been unable to rid herself of the notion that such places must be permeated by the miasma of discarded sins. The petty and pathetic ones probably sank with time to floor level and became part of a layer of neutralized and inoffensive detritus, much as physical death and corruption at or near the surface of the ocean became cleansed and inert by the time they reached the sea bed.

What about huge, terrifying sins, though? No matter what the penance imposed, no matter how many Hail Marys or Acts of Contrition were to follow, how could even the lovely words of absolution purify the moral stench left by someone who had done something *really* awful? Could evil be deprived of its power to corrupt as easily as all that? Might it not hang about like tobacco smoke, getting into the clothes, the hair, even the *soul* of one who entered the cubicle after a desperate sinner?

Quite apart from all that, it was just as cold in there that drab Saturday afternoon as in the main body of the little makeshift chapel attached to the Benedictine mission in Roppongi, and Angie's feet were like ice.

"I'm sorry, Father. I didn't catch that."

"I said it isn't so much absolution you need as some friendly conversation, I suppose." Although he was over seventy and had once told Angie that he had not been back to his native Holland in thirty years, Father Pieter Leydekkers spoke English with a strong Dutch accent and used some quaint turns of phrase. "So you have unclean thoughts, temptations. Heavens, child, you think that is a bit special? When the person in your mind hasn't no idea anyway?

And you're so ashamed even to dream such things, much less do anything? You get your absolution all right, that's for sure. And the other thing, not betraying a confidence, I can't advise you. It depends on the confidence. For you, anyway. The rules are different for priests in the confessional, you know that. If you're not in a hurry after this, wait in the church a minute or two for me. We'll go over to the house and have a cup of nice coffee, and talk just like friends, eh? Father Morelli will be here to take over in a little while."

Still perturbed and confused, but pleased by the invitation, Angie waited by the outer door of the church and watched the priest emerge from his side of the confessional, his purple stole now neatly folded and held with his breviary in one capacious hand. After kneeling for a moment in prayer before the altar and crossing himself, Father Leydekkers took his time over getting up and then approached her with a broad smile on his red face. He was a big old man, and Angie could easily picture him in one of those group paintings of gourmandizing Renaissance cardinals at table. There was a twinkle in his eye, too, and about him still an aura of masculine awareness which in his younger days must have given rise to sinful fantasies on the part of many a good Catholic wife and mother.

Father Morelli was just leaving the rectory adjoining the church when they arrived there. He shook his head at them in mock outrage, a faint smile on the thin lips below the huge Roman nose.

"Another date, Father? Good afternoon, Miss Brewster. Don't pay attention to a word he says. Blarney, Father Flynn calls it."

"Father Morelli is simply jealous, Miss Brewster. Just because an American chaplain from Yokohama brought me two pounds of coffee from the PX. Off you go, Father. Customers waiting, no doubt. I'll give you a cup too when you get back."

"You mustn't mind our nonsense, Miss Brewster," Father Leydekkers said as he took Angie's coat and hung it on a peg just inside the door. "Come in here and get warm. Half a dozen men sharing a house – better to make jokes than quarrel, I suppose."

The little parlour into which he ushered her was gloomy and poorly furnished; a far cry from the splendours of the Vatican apartments or archiepiscopal palaces which were the setting for the extravagant jollifications in the paintings Angie remembered. A battered kerosene stove made the room blessedly warm, though, more than enough to make up for the horrible smell it produced.

The old Dutchman sniffed the reek with apparent appreciation. "We're very lucky. We get a special allocation of kerosene, you know. For the cooker in the kitchen and this one stove. There is an electric fire somewhere but there are so many cuts, and even when the current is connected each other day it behaves funny and the fuse pops. Sit here for a minute, now, while I make the coffee and upset Kobayashi-san. She's a good old soul but it's better for her to stick to tea, I suppose." He opened the door. "And her cabbage soup is a little bit nice," he added as he disappeared.

Angie's thoughts were all over the place during the next ten minutes, and when Father Leydekkers bustled back with the coffee she looked with surprise at an almost finished cigarette she had no recollection of having lit, stubbed it out and blinked at her host. He had brought a little jar of powdered milk with him but seemed pleased when Angie said she preferred hers black. In fact he was so proud of his brew that she told herself to try to remember to keep the fathers supplied with treats from the PX in the future, ashamed that the idea hadn't occurred to her before.

"In Groningen when I was a boy, an uncle of mine came home on leave from Surabaja in the East Indies and brought us some extra-special Java coffee as a present. Oh dear, I used to dream about that delicious coffee sometimes in the war, when Surabaja was mentioned in the newspaper, you know."

"Were you and the others interned, Father?" It was something Angie had been meaning to find out for some time but hadn't got round to checking.

"No, the authorities left most of us gaijin priests alone. Even Americans. Of course, we weren't allowed to travel." He chuckled fatly. "But Benedictines mostly live under kind of house arrest anyway, no? So it wasn't so bad. Some Protestant missionaries were interned or had bad experiences, especially lay people. Not the famous Miss Florence Denton of Kyoto, though. You know, the police down there were told to take her in as an enemy alien. She was such a celebrity that the police chief went personally to her house full of apologies. He had been a student of hers at Doshisha University, and they had a nice talk before he managed to get down to business. They say she corrected his English, told him not to be so silly and that she hadn't got no intention of allowing herself to be arrested. So he bowed and went away, and Miss Denton carried on as usual for the rest of the war."

Angie sighed, and Father Leydekkers fell silent. When he spoke again it was gently, not jovially.

"So, my child. You are not amused."

"You're wrong, Father. It's a very funny story, and this Miss Denton sounds like a brave and . . . happy lady. It's just that I'm neither one. I envy her a lot."

"A strange thing to say. I don't know how brave you are, but why shouldn't you be happy? You have an interesting job, and many, many friends. They all want you to go to their parties – "

"*Goddam it!* Oh gosh, I'm sorry. . . ."

"Go ahead. Be angry. I'm not offended, and He isn't either, I suppose. May I have one of those, please?" He looked hopefully at the pack of cigarettes she had grabbed from her bag and now held in a hand that trembled slightly.

"What? Oh, sure. Sure." By the time they both had cigarettes alight the silence had become a little less charged.

"Thank you. Now, you can tell an old man what's really on your mind, besides the temptations you can't do nothing about except pray for strength to resist. You said about drinking too much too. I don't think you are seriously worried about that?"

"I guess not. I know it makes me aggressive and boring, but everybody around is usually a little high too. They don't seem to get mad with me the way I do with myself. And beer makes me fat, but I'm nearly forty-nine years old so it's a little late to start worrying about my figure."

Father Leydekkers glanced down at his own considerable bulk and patted his midriff. "Me too, but I have a better excuse. Twenty-five years better!" He sat quietly, openly watching Angie fiddling with her cigarette lighter until she coloured with embarrassment.

"I know. I *am* ashamed, and I will try harder. But one of the reasons I joined the army in the first place was for friendship, Father. After I graduated from high school I just assumed I'd get married like most girls. Figured that my stenographer's diploma would help me get a job in a smart office for a few years and catch me a good-looking young executive. Well, there weren't too many of those around the Acme Insurance Company of Seattle, and the few that were soon went off to France. By the time World War I ended I was twenty-one or two, and . . . well, fellows needing wives never seemed to think of a big noisy girl like me in that way. I guess I worked at it too hard. Story of my life."

"So you have been nearly thirty years feeling sorry for yourself? Shame on you!" The rebuke stung, and Angie avoided the old man's eyes.

"No, of course not. I've had . . . a lot of fun. The Acme Insurance people let me go during the depression, but I managed to get a job as a civilian clerk at a big army base outside Seattle. And I guess that was when I began to realize that even if marriage and kids were out I could be popular. As one of the boys . . . good ole unshockable Angie, cussin' an boozin' with the best of them, life and soul of the party." Tears had begun to well out of her eyes and trickle down her cheeks, but she made no attempt to check them. "Friends? I'll say I made friends. So many that they fixed things so I could enlist as a WAC even though I was well over the age limit. And then I began to wonder about myself, when the other girls obviously took me for a – you know, I don't have to spell it out, do I? And living with the idea they might be right? Oh, you bet, I've had a lot of fun – " She broke down completely, sobbing and snorting in ungainly abandonment.

Father Leydekkers reached into the pocket of his threadbare habit and produced a handkerchief, scrutinizing it dubiously and refolding it to expose a reasonably clean section before holding it out to her. Angie took it mechanically and dabbed at her face, but it took her a long time to regain a semblance of control of herself. When eventually she sat back in her chair exhausted, her eyes closed, the priest began to talk quietly, almost to himself.

"It is very hard to do without love. Human love, I mean, expressed in physical ways, like being hugged, kissed, the other things. Harder still not to have some special person to love. Men and women who choose to live the kind of life I do, we know that very well, and my heart aches for those who do not have that choice."

"I'm sorry, Father. Don't know what got into me. You were right before. I have no right to feel sorry for myself, so don't encourage me."

"Sure, it's so. I'm ashamed too, of this warm room and my so nice coffee. Even in *Stars and Stripes* – Father Flynn gets it – they write that people all over Tokyo are sleeping in burned-out buildings with newspaper for blankets. Tonight in the tunnel at Ueno Station two thousand poor wretches will be huddled together. Repatriated from Manchuria, Korea, Taiwan, with no homes to go to. At least half a dozen die every week there from malnutrition, pneumonia. You know the only way they can get a little bit warm? Not with a fine kerosene stove like us, no, no. Public bathhouse is the only way. One yen to get in. The manager says some go four and five times a day, instead of buying food. The police want to send these people away – to Hokkaido, the snow country! They think they get warm in Hokkaido? You have a good camera, Miss Brewster?"

"I did have. It got stolen."

"Good. Why do you think *Stars and Stripes* has so many small ads – camera mislaid, wallet mislaid, such and such, has anyone found? Because a person can sell a camera for enough to build a small *house* is why! Which is better, you take pictures to put in an album, or a Japanese family has a little house to live in again?"

"Stealing's stealing, Father, whoever does it."

"Poof! You're feeling better, that's good, but now you are silly instead. This American colonel who got away with the Bank of Japan diamonds what, two hundred thousand dollars, hah! *That* is stealing. All right, enough. You have been to see the doctor?"

"No, I'm not sick."

"Depressed, though. And forty-nine years old. So?"

"Father, you can call a spade a spade with me. No, believe me, I shall be the first to know when the change of life hits me. I'm sorry I cracked up on you, but I'm OK now. Thanks for the coffee. And for telling me where I get off."

Angie gathered her things together and stood up to go. She knew she must look a sight. Her eyes felt puffy and her nose was probably red as well as congested, but for no very good reason that she could think of her heart was somewhat lighter. As to the other thing, the questions Captain Henderson had put to her about Polly, she would have to think about it, and felt more able to do so after her outburst. And to continue playing dumb if security got at her again. OK, Father Leydekkers was bound by the seal of the confessional, so *he* wouldn't betray a confidence whispered in that frightening box full of leftover sins. But even if Angie could be sure of that – and she was – and used it as an excuse to share her burden it wouldn't lessen her guilt over blabbing. And if she'd blurted it out in the stuffy little parlour or asked the old priest to take care of Polly's envelope, he would have been just as free to pass it on as anybody else.

"Angie? You there?" It was Polly's voice that accompanied the tap on her door, and Angie was glad that she had had time to wash and fix her face. It was about six-thirty and Hilltop House was alive with the warm bustle of early Saturday evening, when many of the women who lived there were getting ready to meet their dates. All the toing and froing helped to blur the edges of Angie's uncomfortable recollection of the dark, cheerless clergy house in which a group of Benedictine monks softened the austerity of their lives by teasing each other like prematurely aged schoolboys.

Though she was now physically much nearer to Ueno Station with its night population of the cold, the hungry and the dispossessed, their image too had become shadowy. She might not have left anything much in the way of sins in the confessional, but Father Leydekkers had somehow loosened the cold grip of fear. Also, Hilltop House wasn't exactly the Waldorf Astoria, but like all the other buildings commandeered by SCAP it had electricity all the time, not just every other day, and hot water in abundance.

"Yeah. Come on in!" When Polly opened the door Angie could hear quite a babble of voices in the corridor. The atmosphere in the former hotel was always strongly feminine, spiced on Friday and Saturday evenings in particular by a generous sisterly camaraderie. Girls lent each other bobby pins, lipsticks and perfume; traded nylons for the loan of a particular brooch or bracelet and speculated openly about what the evening might offer in the way of romance. "You look a hundred per cent better."

"You're a good friend, Angie, but you're a lousy liar. After what happened on Thursday and seeing poor Major Brooks in the hospital yesterday I know I look a hundred years old."

Angie sighed. "A lot short of that, but you do have a way to go before you get that cover-girl look back, I guess. My, aren't we all gussied up, though! I can't think why, but I have this weird notion you're planning on going out." She waved her friend to the single easy chair but Polly sat on the bed as usual, slipped her shoes off and tucked her legs up to one side. Angie stood over her, hands on hips, and scrutinized her with some care.

Polly always took care of her appearance, but the puzzling and disturbing events of the past few days had left her looking strained, almost haggard. She had, however, clearly made an effort to make herself attractive, not with complete success. She had probably applied no more than her usual make-up, but the underlying pallor made it seem that she had overdone it. Then again, though there was no need to make a public parade of concern over the condition of Major Brooks, the crimson woollen dress Angie hadn't seen before struck her as being unnecessarily bright in the circumstances. Polly had had her hair done, and painted her nails. She very nearly looked tarty.

"Can't keep a thing from you, can I? Yes, I am. Life goes on, I guess. Are you going out yourself, Angie?"

"Me? Nope. I'm planning on eating downstairs and taking my old bones to bed early. You need something, Polly? I mean, you don't want your envelope back?"

Polly quickly raised a finger to her lips and shook her head. "Not yet. No, please bear with me on that till after the weekend, will you? I just called in to say hello. I stopped by this afternoon, as a matter of fact, but you were out."

Angie sat on the bed beside her and took her hand, worried by the forced, brittle note in her voice. "Take it easy, won't you, Polly? All this must have left you pretty shook up, kid. Mind if I ask who the lucky guy is?"

"Sure you can ask, but you don't know him. A friend of Arthur Reynolds."

"A *friend* of the Aussie? I kind of had the idea it was the commander himself that might interest you."

Polly pulled a face. "Mm. He does, sort of. But come on, how many places can a commander take a non-com? Even if he wants to?"

"But you have been out with him? Since that time we ran into him at the concert?"

"Yes. He's given me lunch a couple of times, and just the other evening drinks at the Press Club, where he took us both after the concert. That's where I met his friend. Oh, and he – Arthur, that is – wants me to go see *The Best Years of Our Lives* with him. Of course, he asked me before all this mess, and I'm not sure I want to compete with Myrna Loy right now."

"Just the other evening? And the friend's taking you out tonight? Boy, he's some fast mover. Well, come on, give!"

"Angie, I hardly know the guy. Don't really know why I said yes, except it's Saturday, I've been feeling down and I'd kind of like some male company. I'll tell you more about him after tonight. He's good-looking, late thirties I'd guess, charming, courteous, obviously been around."

"Sounds great. So go on out and have yourself a good time. Or is there a problem? He married or something?"

"I don't know. Could be, I suppose, but somehow I don't think so. No, that isn't it, Angie. There is one thing though. He's . . . as a matter of fact he's Japanese."

Polly eased herself off the bed with a flash of thigh, and stood up, ready to go. Angie looked up at her, aghast. "He's *what*? Are you crazy or something?"

"Of course not. The war's over, Angie. And in any case, he's what you might call a colleague. Works as a locally hired researcher, attached to G2. Maybe I'll introduce you some time. You'd like him."

15

Six o'clock on a Saturday evening was early for a date, and Polly had rather hoped there would be nobody else around when Jerry Nakajima called for her. She was out of luck. She went down to the lobby a couple of minutes early so as to be able to make a rapid getaway the moment he arrived, only to find that he was already there, looking positively elegant in a dark suit and overcoat, hat in hand and perfectly at ease as he chatted to old Ishii-san the janitor. As soon as he spotted her he broke off the conversation neatly, and the old man bowed and disappeared into the little office behind the reception desk while Polly descended the last few stairs and Nakajima smiled up at her.

"Hello, Mr Nakajima."

"Miss Horvath! I'm so happy you could spare the time." The hand that enfolded hers was warm and welcoming, like the deep, friendly voice.

"Thank you for the invitation."

"Let me help you with your coat. Just as well the janitor went away, it would give him a heart attack."

"What would? Oh, thank you."

"Seeing a Japanese man help a lady put her coat on. I'll admit it took me a long time to learn to do it, when I was living in Washington before the war. I hope you won't be cold. I have a cab right outside. A proper taxi, I mean, not a welfare cab."

Polly had shivered briefly, not on account of the cold but because his hand had brushed the back of her neck. Then, before she could say anything else, her heart sank as Estelle Yarwood came bustling in through the door. There was nothing for it but to introduce Nakajima to her as briefly but nonchalantly as possible and escape, in the depressing certainty that she would gossip happily to all and sundry about the encounter. Polly was still disconcerted when they left the building and she sat back in the ancient car without at first registering that it was the first time since arriving in Japan that she had been in a motor vehicle of any kind which didn't belong to the army. Then she pulled herself together.

"This is really nice of you. It can't be too easy to find a cab in Tokyo. Except a welfare cab like you said, and we'd have needed two of those."

"Proper taxis are certainly few and far between. And I can't imagine who thought of calling those contraptions built on to bike frames *welfare* cabs. Quite the reverse from the passenger's point of view, I'd say. Have you ever ridden in one?"

"No. I've been in an old-fashioned rickshaw, though." Polly had seen plenty of the bicycle cabs with the open-fronted sidecars, but had never been tempted to hail one. People said they overturned pretty easily, especially when going downhill.

"Ah, a *jinrikisha*, yes. Did you like it?"

"It can be fun on a sunny afternoon, but the idea of being dragged around by another human being who probably doesn't get half as much to eat as I do takes a lot of adjusting to."

"I wish a lot more foreigners were as sensitive as you, Miss Horvath." His tone didn't seem quite as friendly as before, and Polly decided to change the subject.

"Tell me about the concert you're taking me to."

"Well, it isn't exactly a concert. It's what you might call a special performance. You'll see in a little while, and I can explain better then."

The taxi driver had taken them down to Fifth Street and turned left, then left again just beyond the Bank of Japan. The streets through which they were now passing were dark and unfamiliar to Polly, who was beginning to feel apprehensive.

"Where are we, exactly?"

"In the Nihonbashi district, just a few blocks east of downtown. This is one of the oldest parts of Tokyo, especially right here in what everybody used to call Yanagibashi. Willow Bridge. Nihonbashi itself means Japan Bridge: it was the beginning of the highway to Kyoto where the emperors used to live. And here we are."

Apprehensiveness turned to something not far short of panic when the taxi stopped outside what looked to Polly like an old-fashioned two-storey private house made of wood, its façade blank and secretive. It was with great reluctance that she got out when the driver opened the passenger door on her side.

"Listen, I'm not sure. . . ."

"Don't be nervous, Miss Horvath. You're perfectly safe, I assure you."

With the taxi disappearing round a corner Polly was unconvinced, but then Nakajima opened a sliding latticed gate and she saw a little garden with a short stone-flagged path illuminated by the candlelight glimmering from tiny ankle-high paper lanterns ranked on either side. Beyond was an open front door, and inside a woman in a kimono, kneeling in welcome on a kind of raised platform set about a yard back from the entrance.

"Go ahead. This place is what we call a *machiai*. A teahouse."

Whatever it was, the approach was certainly pretty, and though Polly hadn't the slightest idea what to expect inside she was reassured by the motherly appearance of the lady as she raised her head from the tatami matting and with a flood of incomprehensible words urged them both to enter.

"Just step up out of your shoes," Nakajima said after interjecting a phrase or two himself. He bent down to unlace his own. "They'll take care of them for you. And our coats. I'm afraid it would be very bad manners to keep them on inside."

The hostess rose from her knees, and Polly saw that she wore what looked like thick, tailored cotton ankle socks of a curious design, with a separate compartment for the big toe. Polly stepped up on to the yielding matting, golden in the subdued light. It felt surprisingly good to walk on in stockinged feet, and she was reluctant to put on the pair of backless slippers the woman pressed upon her after she had led the way to a corridor of highly polished wood beyond. Made of bright blue felt, they flopped about, were practically impossible for her to keep on when going up a flight of equally shiny wooden stairs at the end of the corridor, and were startlingly ugly.

When she glanced behind she saw that Nakajima was shuffling along in almost as ungainly a fashion as herself, but it was still a relief when their little procession arrived outside a sliding screen door. Its surface seemed to be made of canvas or some other tough material, and was decorated with a beautiful, impressionistic ink painting of a long-legged crane standing in a rocky pool. The Japanese woman again knelt, and slid it open with a movement of extraordinary grace. Polly watched with interest. At least she wasn't scared any more; well, not very. She heard Nakajima's deep voice again from just behind her.

"You leave the slippers out here in the corridor."

"Thank the Lord for that. You might as well tell the lady I shall never get down those stairs again with them on. Oh, this is so pretty! It's like being in a doll's house."

The room they entered was indeed small, barely big enough to accommodate a low table with stubby, slightly curved legs placed directly on the tatami, a plump cushion covered with rich brocade in subdued colours at either side. The table was lacquered and its surface gleamed like a sheet of black ice in moonlight.

"You sit there," Nakajima said, "with your back to the alcove."

"Oh, can't I sit the other side, please? I want to admire the flowers. I haven't seen real flowers for so long."

"Sorry. You're the guest of honour, you see. So I get to admire *you* and the flower arrangement too. It's early plum blossom, actually, must have come from somewhere very sheltered. In this kind of place they go to a lot of trouble over flower arrangements. This is intended to suggest that spring's not too far away. We'll only be in here ten minutes or so, just long enough to drink a cup of green tea. Then we'll be taken to a much bigger room. I'm sorry it's not very warm, but if you put your hand over the *hibachi* there you'll find it'll help."

After a brief conference in Japanese with Nakajima, the woman had departed with another kindly smile in Polly's direction. Polly looked at the cushion. "Do I have to kneel on that?"

"You could try, but I don't think you'd be very comfortable. Western ladies generally prefer to sit, and kind of tuck up their legs beside them."

Obscurely offended by the implication that she was by no means the first western woman Nakajima had entertained in traditional Japanese style, Polly sat down and fidgeted about until she felt reasonably secure, then stretched out a hand as suggested over the huge, heavy earthenware pot beside her. It seemed to be nearly full of sand, on top of which were a few pieces of charcoal, more powdery grey ash than anything else. The gentle warmth that rose from it was nevertheless extremely welcome, and after a minute or two she began to feel less cold all over. She ventured a timid smile at Nakajima who had settled himself cross-legged on the opposite side of the table.

"What happens now?"

"Well, as I said, any moment now a maid will bring us green tea and a Japanese cake, more like a piece of sugar candy, really. We shall see the other lady again later. She's the *okami-san*, the owner of this place. I can see you're still a little – *ohairi!*"

He turned towards the door and raised his voice on the last word in response to something said softly outside; and as he had predicted a much younger woman, hardly more than a girl, came in with a tray. She too bowed humbly before setting in front of each of them a small blue and white cup without handles on a brown lacquered saucer, and an irregularly shaped flat piece of ceramic on which was a little dumpling-like cake decorated with a sprig of pine, and beside it a piece of wood shaped like a flattened, oversized toothpick. Then the maid, who was also wearing a kimono, poured green tea into each cup from a pot with a sideways spout, bowed again and withdrew.

"You cut a piece off the cake with the little stick and pick it up with it. There's no need to eat it if you don't like it."

"I'm still a little what?"

"I beg your pardon? Oh, I see. I was going to say that you're still a little nervous, aren't you?"

"No, I'm not, not now. All this is quite interesting. But I think you have a little explaining to do. Don't you?"

"Oh? Like what?"

"Like, a performance of traditional Japanese music? And how it happens that you speak English a whole lot better than you write it?"

Before replying, Nakajima dealt with his own cake in the way he had described, and drank some tea with a distinct slurping noise. "Ah. I'm very sorry if you think I've misled you, Miss Horvath, but I promise you will be hearing the Japanese music very soon now, and I hope you'll like it. About the letter, there were some mistakes, I know. I deliberately used what some people call 'Japlish'. That was because I didn't want you to think I was . . . overconfident, but I did want to see you again, very much."

Polly sighed. "I enjoyed meeting you too, Nakajima-san. I'd very likely have said yes if you'd simply asked me for a date, without trying to be cute. Now I suggest we begin again. You're welcome to call me Polly, by the way."

He nodded slowly. "Thank you. Thank you, Polly. Please call me Jerry. Using my real first name would make me feel awkward. It's a thing we hardly ever do in Japan."

"OK. Why 'Jerry', particularly?"

"Over twenty years ago when I was a kid in school, one of the teachers was an old Englishman. A surprising number of them worked in Japan in those days. For English conversation practice he gave us all English names, and he figured that Jerry was near enough to Eijiro for the others to remember. And they could pronounce it, more or less. The letter R is no problem. Not like L. Most Japanese would have trouble with your name and pronounce it 'Porry', as you know. Anyway, later on when I lived in the States I used to introduce myself to people as Jerry. It was easier for them and not in the least embarrassing for me."

Polly was about to reply when the young maid returned and stood in the open doorway, murmuring politely.

"Ah, they're ready for us now. Let's go, shall we?"

The next two hours were magical for Polly. She and Nakajima were escorted to another room, similar in general appearance to the one they had just left but more brightly lit, three or four times larger and with a much higher ceiling. As before there were cushions to sit on, but instead of sharing a table they were provided with small individual ones, like lacquer trays on legs. Polly was again made to sit with her back to the alcove. This time instead of a flower arrangement there was a scroll hanging in the recess, its central panel a marvel of calligraphy. The flowing brush-strokes of the Chinese characters, incomprehensible of course to Polly, again made her feel coarse and uncivilized. Nakajima smiled gently at her, as though reading her mind.

The middle-aged woman Nakajima had said was the proprietor had been waiting to welcome them all over again, and as soon as they were seated she clapped her hands softly and two other women entered the room. They too were wearing silk kimonos, one a delicate green with the edge of a deep purple undergarment showing at the neckline; the other a soft crimson that had Polly glancing at the strident colour of her own dress and briefly wanting to die of embarrassment as Nakajima contrived introductions of a kind.

"These women are geisha, Polly, and they apologize very much for not being able to speak English."

"I'm the one who should be apologizing. I feel a complete idiot just sitting here smiling and nodding."

"Don't worry, they're enjoying the experience. Now we're going to eat, and then they'll sing and play for us."

They were served a meal the like of which Polly had never in her life experienced before. The two geisha sat with them, taking nothing themselves except now and then at Nakajima's insistence a sip or two of *sake* from his cup. Nakajima did describe the various dishes as they were brought in by the young maid, but afterwards Polly could hardly recall what they had been; only that each had looked much too beautiful to eat and had consisted of not much more than a mouthful anyway. She had no idea what some of the things she tasted were, but did notice that the flavours had a fragility and delicacy that made the allegedly authentic Japanese food she had tried in restaurants popular with SCAP staff seem over-seasoned and vulgar.

The geisha changed places now and then, and Nakajima went to a lot of trouble to interpret for her, but most of the time Polly was content just to look at their two exotic companions and wonder. They were both obviously well into their thirties and neither was in any conventional sense of the word beautiful. She would have expected expensively dressed women of their profession working in such exquisite surroundings to be not only young and stunningly attractive but also demure and remote to a degree. Yet these mature geisha seemed unfazed by the language barrier, and had plenty to say for themselves. The only Japanese women Polly had come across before were either humbly self-effacing like those who cleaned the rooms at Hilltop House, or occasionally brassy, like some of the waitresses in noisy sukiyaki restaurants. It was hard for her to credit that their present companions, who managed so perfectly to be warm, friendly, sensitive and delicate all at the same time, belonged to the same race. She said as much to Nakajima.

"You think so? Well, I have a surprise for you. Towards the end of the war all these places were ordered to close. The geisha – literally thousands of them – were drafted to work in factories. So a couple of years ago these ladies could have been working on an assembly line, wearing coveralls. Excuse me." He turned to the woman currently at his side and exchanged a few sentences with her before looking at Polly again and winking. "Well, I was only partly right. Some geisha really did. But it seems an awful lot managed to get themselves put on the company payrolls of their patrons instead. As so-called 'clerks'. Anyway, you're about to see that they're not here this evening just to sit beside us and encourage us to eat and drink."

He spoke to the geisha again and she and her colleague at once rose from their knees in a single movement without the least apparent effort. They went to the other end of the room, where a three-fold screen with a cherry-blossom design painted on it had been placed. There they made music.

One of them sang, to her own *shamisen* accompaniment. The plaintive twanging she produced from its strings with a huge ivory plectrum provided a perfect background for what sounded to Polly like a wild, desolate lament. According to Nakajima it was in fact quite cheerful, a folk song from the north. Her colleague conjured a miraculous cascade of bright points of sound from an instrument that looked a little like a zither laid flat on the tatami matting: a *koto*, she was told. Songs and koto pieces alternated with each other, and as Polly listened the strange progressions and harmonies began to seem less alien; compellingly mysterious still, but eloquent and beautiful.

Nakajima kept asking her if she was bored, and each time Polly shook her head impatiently, wanting to hear more. Eventually, however, at the end of a piece he said something to the two geisha which made them nod in understanding, bow low in their kneeling position, and then rise to their feet. Polly realized that it must be the end of the performance, and time to leave.

"Please tell them . . . oh, how can I possibly put it into words? Tell them it was fantastic, and that I feel honoured."

After speaking at some length in Japanese to the geisha Nakajima turned to Polly. "You really did like it, didn't you? I was watching your face."

"Yes, it was marvellous. And the food, and . . . oh, everything. At last I feel as if I'm in Japan. The real Japan people talk about."

He shook his head slowly from side to side. "I'm very glad you enjoyed it, Polly. And I hate to disillusion you. But I'm afraid this isn't the real Japan, not any more."

"Whatever do you mean?"

"It would take too long to explain now. Some other time, maybe. We ought to leave now."

The business of leaving the teahouse was if anything even more complicated than arriving had been, and after Polly had bowed for what seemed the hundredth time to the proprietor and the two geisha who assembled at the downstairs entrance to see them off the premises, her facial muscles ached with smiling. Turning away at last from the chorus of farewells, she saw that the outer gate stood open, and that the taxi had miraculously reappeared.

16

"Come on in, Polly, have a seat. Good to see you." Having stood to greet her, Jay Murakami gingerly lowered himself back into his chair.

"Sure you're not too busy, Jay?"

"Never too busy for you. Sorry, I guess all the guys say that. I mean it, though."

"But on the phone you said you'd been off work for a couple of days last week. You must have a stack of things piled up. You OK now? That must have been some tumble you took."

"I'm fine. If I knew you better I could show you some glorious technicolour bruises, but I'm just about mobile. I don't often have a whole lot of paperwork to do anyway, so I'm not exactly snowed under." He took off his glasses and polished them. Polly had never seen him without them before and he looked to her immediately younger and somehow vulnerable, almost as though half expecting to be attacked. "So, what's on your mind, Polly?"

"It's hard to know how to put this. You heard that I'm out of a job just now?"

"I know you're on leave, you told me when you called. Out of a job, though? Aren't you planning on going back to work next week?"

"Good question. I imagine so, but exactly where I can't say. It's because Major Brooks is seriously ill. Critically, they say. Anyhow, he's not expected to be able to come back to *his* job. So they've assigned another officer in his place, a Captain Henderson, and he brought his own sergeant with him. So I get an unexpected vacation, and a change of job as soon as they've figured out what to do with me."

"I heard about Mike Brooks of course. Pity. He's a good guy."

"I'm glad you said that, Jay. Because I visited him in the hospital in Yokohama just before the weekend. He's why I asked to see you today."

"He is?" His eyes once more defended by his glasses, Murakami looked cool and self-possessed again.

"Yes. Look, Jay, this isn't easy for me to explain, but there isn't time to beat about the bush. Not too long ago I found out that the major uncovered something, something that ought to be stopped. A . . . well, a conspiracy."

"You don't say? This had better be good, Polly, conspiracies are a dime a dozen around here."

"Don't laugh at me. *Please*."

"I'm sorry. Go ahead."

"The thing is, the major put together a detailed dossier with the intention of blowing this scheme right out of the water, but then he collapsed and was hauled off to hospital before he could do what he had planned. He *is* a good man, Jay. He'll probably . . . he isn't expected to live, but even so, when I saw him the thing worrying him most was the fear that his notes would get into the wrong hands and be destroyed. Well, I was able to reassure him, by telling him that I have them. In a safe place. He'd told me roughly what he had in mind before he got sick, but in the hospital last week I asked him again what to do, and he said to confide in you. He believed you would agree with us, and because you're from the FBI you'd know what to do."

"Us? Who's us?"

"Just the major and me. I know what's in the notes, you see, and I'm sure too. That this thing has to be stopped."

"Polly, Mike Brooks has been a sick man for a long time, and I'm sure you know what's wrong with him as well as I do. It could easily have affected his brain, you know. Are you sure the poor guy isn't off his head?"

"He has always struck me as a totally rational, extremely astute man, but I've considered the possibility, certainly. And I might have gone on wondering, except that I'm convinced somebody somewhere either knows of or suspects the existence of the dossier, and thinks I may have it. Whoever it is wants it badly enough to have searched my room at Hilltop House. The search is *fact*. I also have a feeling, no hard evidence but a lot of little things adding up, a feeling that the reason I was removed from my job the very day after the major was taken to hospital is connected."

"Uh huh. There's a hole in your logic, but it can wait. If what you say's so, I can understand your being jittery. Well, I'm listening. Tell me about this conspiracy. Come on, woman, don't sit there clearly wondering if I'm in it too. Mike obviously doesn't think so or he wouldn't have sent you to me."

"Yes. I'm sorry, I'm getting neurotic. First, have you ever heard of Operation Hi-Flyer?"

"Hi-Flyer? No."

"That's what he called it, but maybe its real name is something else. Well, basically, it's a plan to subvert the democratic process here in Japan, to frustrate the Peace Constitution and to rearm the country."

"So?"

"*So*? For crying out loud, is that all you have to say?"

"For the moment, yes. I have a great deal of respect for your intelligence and I don't want to sound condescending, but I have to point out that all sorts of people both in this country and elsewhere are busily pursuing those very objectives quite openly. In other words, you're telling me what every reasonably well-informed observer of the Japanese scene already knows. Forgive me if I don't sound amazed."

"Listen to me, Jay. Do these well-informed people also know that a detailed timetable has been drawn up to get two, maybe three prominent war criminals out of Sugamo, rehabilitate them and put one of them into the legislature within five years from now? And into the prime minister's office within ten?"

"No, I don't believe they do. And I have to say that if Mike Brooks claims to have evidence of such a scheme then I'm afraid he really is out of his mind. Put General Tojo and those other beauties back in charge? Oh, come *on*!"

"I didn't say anything about Tojo. The people concerned are called Kodama, Kishi and Sasakawa." Polly had the satisfaction of seeing Murakami's eyebrows shoot up. "Class A detainees, but they aren't in the dock yet. They can be put there, if the major's information is handled the right way. Jay, it's detailed and it's specific. Names, dates and places of clandestine meetings between high-ranking Americans and Japanese politicians and financiers – and former military leaders – it's all there, noted in manuscript by a senior G2 staff officer whose writing can easily be verified. That's why I didn't simply memorize the whole document – it's only three pages – and destroy it. It's vital to have the original. I've made a copy of it. Will you at least look at it before you decide Major Brooks invented it all?"

Murakami sat back and surveyed her for a long moment. Then leaned forward, propping himself on his elbows. "All right. I'll look at it."

"Good. Here's the copy." Polly took an envelope from her shoulder-bag and handed it across the desk.

"Why a copy? Why not show me the real thing?" He looked at her quizzically as he tore the flap and took out the single sheet of paper covered on both sides with her own handwriting.

"Because you might decide not to help. Might even feel you ought to report all this to higher authority. Turn the papers in."

"You're a very determined lady, Polly, I give you that. . . ." His voice trailed away as he began to read, and before he turned the paper over his lips had pursed and he was whistling tunelessly.

"Wow. I begin to see what you mean. May I keep this copy to study more carefully? I'll burn it when I'm through, I promise."

"Well . . . OK. If you're convinced the information's genuine. Are you?"

"Not quite. It takes a lot to convince an old FBI man. But I'm sufficiently impressed to hunt around quietly for something which could corroborate this material. If and when I find it, *then* I'll be convinced. I'll say this much: if those statements are true, then I'm in sympathy with you and Mike Brooks, and I'm inclined to agree that something ought to be done to throw a monkey wrench into their scheme. What have you done with the original?"

"It's in a safe place." Polly had barely hesitated before replying, but Murakami had noticed.

"Fair enough. Keep it to yourself for the moment. Brooks told you to confide in me and you have done. Up to a prudent point. Let me point out one thing, though. Sooner or later you must tell somebody – not necessarily me, but somebody you trust completely – where the papers are. So that they won't be lost if something were to happen to you too. Don't look so horrified, I'm not suggesting anybody may be thinking of arranging an accident for you, but you *could* take a nasty tumble, like I did last week."

"Sure I will, Polly," Angie said. "If that's what you want. You've made me a little nervous myself about keeping it in my room, I must admit. Whatever it is."

"Angie, I'd like to tell you more and I probably will be able to very soon. Thank you for bearing with me."

"OK, tell you what I'll do, I'll take it over to church tomorrow morning, and ask old Father Leydekkers to take care of it for me and not to hand it over to anybody but you or me. You can be absolutely confident he won't peek or let another living soul know he has it. He'll be surprised to see me again so soon. I'll tell him it's on account of the delicious coffee he gave me last time. Tell you the truth, it tasted of kerosene."

"Angie, you're great."

"You're looking quite a lot brighter yourself today, kid. Hey, how did the date go Saturday? The Japanese boyfriend? Was he the one put the sparkle in your eye? He certainly charmed the pants off Estelle Yarwood, according to her."

"Oh, God, I was afraid she'd tell the world. He's just an acquaintance, Angie. Really. It was a fascinating evening, all the same. I met a couple of real-life geisha girls. Well, they were hardly girls and he said we're wrong to call them that in English anyway. Geisha means 'art person'.."

"Yeah, and I've heard a thing or two about their art."

"It isn't like that at all, Angie. They're totally different from B-girls. They sing, play classical music . . . oh, I can't possibly explain, you have to experience it."

"And did the Aussie's friend behave himself?"

"The perfect gentleman throughout, Angie. It must have cost him a packet, but he didn't sneak so much as a peck on the cheek at the end of the evening."

"Disappointed?"

Polly laughed, and thought that it was probably the first time she had since the day she first set eyes on the Operation Hi-Flyer file. "A little, perhaps. I admit it. Are you shocked?"

"*Me*? Shocked? The Brewsters of Seattle don't shock that easy. I begin to suspect why you're not enthusiastic about the idea of that trip to Nikko any more, though. Did he ask for another date?"

"It really wasn't a date in any normal sense, Angie. It was an education. But yes, he asked me if I'd like to see a Noh play some time and I said I would."

At different moments during the rest of the day Jay Murakami gave a lot of thought to what Polly Horvath had told him and what he had gathered from a very quick reading of the notes she said she had copied from Brooks's original. There was no opportunity for him to study them properly, though, and the envelope stayed in his breast pocket until after the ride home in John Prothero's car. Prothero had been in chatty mood; he had been struck by the news that the Empress had tiptoed back into public life by agreeing to become honorary president of the Japan Red Cross, and he had also tried to interest Jay in a meeting of the Asiatic Society of Japan to be held at the Canadian legation towards the end of the month.

Jay read the document with care over his pre-dinner bourbon, and again after he had eaten. If the story it told was a fabrication by a man whose mental processes had been distorted by long addiction to alcohol, it was a remarkable achievement. He tried to put it out of his mind long enough to concentrate on some routine papers he had brought home in his brief-case; but he failed, and looked through the description of Operation Hi-Flyer one more time before putting it back in the breast pocket of his jacket. A final glance through it in the morning when he felt more alert ought to fix the details in his mind, then he would put a match to it.

It would be safe enough in his jacket upstairs in the bedroom closet overnight. Nice that he was quite recovered enough to enjoy Fujiko's attentions again.

17

"I'm sorry to have to convey disturbing news," the old lawyer said to Yoshio Kodama in an interview room at Sugamo prison after greeting his client respectfully. It was the room in which they had last met, in the company of Nakajima, Tom Berman and the American officer Captain Watkins. This time they could speak freely, since this was a routine meeting between a detainee and his legal adviser. The only other person present was a bored American corporal who whiled away the time by rereading a number of creased letters he produced from the pocket of his tunic.

"Well?" Kodama sat very still but as usual seemed to be overflowing with barely suppressed energy.

"It seems that an unexpected and, shall we say, disconcertingly informed interest is being taken in your case by persons who should not be in any way involved."

"Who?"

"There is a civilian employed in the SCAP Labor Division - in quite a senior capacity. A Japanese-American called Murakami. He is unmarried, and lives in one of the new houses built for the Americans in the so-called Washington Heights development at Yoyogi."

"Why should I care about his domestic arrangements?"

The old lawyer sniffed haughtily. "If you will hear me out you will see that they are of particular interest. Because one of our friends in the National Diet has a niece who is employed by this Murakami as housekeeper. She, the niece, is the widow of an army officer. A patriotic young woman who has apparently from time to time been able to come by useful information and pass it to her uncle."

"So? Don't beat about the bush, we haven't all that much time."

The old man declined to be hurried, even by Kodama. "There is good reason to suppose that Murakami is a leftist; or at least a sympathizer."

"What of it? SCAP is full of them."

"Not so many as there were a few months ago. The mood is changing. MacArthur's three top men are still at daggers drawn with each other, but the indications are that Willoughby's views are beginning to prevail."

"All to the good. In what way does this nisei constitute a problem, then?"

"As you point out, Murakami isn't the only leftist sympathizer in SCAP by any means. But we know of no other who is of senior rank and also bilingual in Japanese. Indeed he frequently passes as a Japanese and has contacts at all levels in the public service and teachers' unions. Perhaps even more important, he is on secondment from the FBI, and is something of an expert on the subject of organized crime here. That is why the young woman's help has been so valuable, and never more so than now."

"Come to the point."

The lawyer sniffed again, and deliberately took his time over replying. "We are advised that this senior SCAP official has in his possession a document which purports to give in note form specific details of highly confidential negotiations between our side and certain of Willoughby's representatives. Also of our strategy and plans for you and the other two."

"I see. What's the provenance of this document, and how did he come by it?"

"Our informant has no idea. She had only a brief opportunity to look at it, and it does her credit that she was immediately able to conclude that it could be of great importance. It is handwritten. We surmise that it, or its content at least, must have emanated from G2. And in view of its subject matter, from someone close to General Willoughby's personal staff. I have consulted Nakajima, who is almost certain that it must have been a major called Brooks. Brooks is currently critically ill in hospital in Yokohama. Advanced alcoholism."

"Have you got a cigarette?"

"I'm sorry, no. Shall I ask the guard?"

"No. Leave him to his girlfriend's letters. It doesn't matter. This woman, the housekeeper. Reliable, is she? Couldn't have been imagining things? Telling her - uncle, did you say? Telling her uncle what she thinks might interest him?"

"Most unlikely, I'm told. She understands English very well and like most of us reads it more easily than she speaks it."

"I see. And what's our friend the Dietman so specially worried about? There are all manner of rumours current about us, after all. Even if he's got hold of some sensitive information, what's this Murakami supposed to do with his document, show it to a journalist? No paper in Japan would dare to take a chance on printing it. Send it back to America? Not much point. People there would treat it as idle speculation, ignore it more probably. And he's certainly not going to get it on to MacArthur's desk. Not if Willoughby has anything to do with it, and General Arisue can make sure he's briefed if necessary. Tell our friend that."

"I will, certainly. As a matter of fact, word of this might already have reached Willoughby. After Brooks was sent to hospital, another intelligence officer was put into his job extraordinarily quickly, and Brooks's assistant has also been reassigned. There remains one specific cause for concern, though. Murakami is on friendly personal terms with the prosecutor Berman, the man who sat in when I brought Nakajima here recently, and who took such an aggressive line with you."

Kodama scowled. "He was grossly impertinent."

"I agree. And he is also obviously hostile, to the point where he made no secret of wishing to see you indicted. That's why it's disturbing to know that Berman is a fairly frequent guest at Murakami's house, and that the two men often talk to each other on the telephone. Innocuously enough, I'm told, but that's only to be expected. The point is that if Murakami were to pass whatever information he has to Berman, it could do you great damage. That is what worries us most. Berman carries some weight in International Prosecution Section, I know that from my personal and professional experience in recent months. And he is also close to General Courtney Whitney. In fact he used to work for him in Manila before the war."

Kodama's smile was infinitely more chilling than his scowl had been. "Then it seems that the man Murakami is a present danger and the man Berman potentially so. In that case you and our friends will have to get busy, won't you?"

"Yes, but what do you suggest we should do?"

"Do? Oh, I leave that up to my friends outside. I'm sure they can think of some way of . . . *discrediting* this precious pair. And perhaps silencing the man Brooks as a precautionary measure." Kodama's face darkened. "If you want to go on getting the sort of fees and perks you do, get that disapproving look off your face. And another thing. Tell them to keep Nakajima right out of it. He isn't to know of these instructions. I have plans for Nakajima's future, and I don't want him compromised."

A few hours later, and as a consequence of a number of carefully coded telephone calls, a middle-aged man with a stethoscope protruding from one of the pockets of his white coat slipped out of the room where Mike Brooks lay, and made his way along the corridor. His shoes must have been new, because they squeaked on the highly polished linoleum of the floor. Turning a corner, he went into a nearby men's room where a Japanese orderly was mopping the floor, and nodded to him. Then he slipped out of the coat, hung it with the stethoscope still in its pocket on one of the hooks beside the wash-basins, and left without having spoken.

After he had gone, the orderly bundled up the coat and put it in a basket underneath a pile of used towels. Then he returned to his mopping. He could return the stethoscope to where it belonged at leisure.

When Jay Murakami called the hospital in Yokohama late the same afternoon with the idea of arranging to go to talk to Brooks himself, he was kept waiting for a considerable time before being brusquely informed that Major Michael Brooks had died earlier that day. He sighed as he put the phone down. The news was hardly surprising, but the timing was, to say the least of it, unfortunate.

He sat back and pondered the situation. Apart from Polly herself he had no acquaintances in G2 with whom he was on close enough terms to ask even very oblique questions touching on Operation Hi-Flyer. John Prothero was a wily old bird who knew a lot, but ever since he had reacted so critically to the business of Jay's joining the march and getting beaten up for his pains there had been a distancing in their personal relationship. The Professor talked freely enough in his affably urbane way about their current official concerns, but the former warmth seemed to Jay to be lacking. No, he couldn't possibly raise the subject with Prothero.

Tom Berman was a pretty good friend who – when the two of them were on their own, at least – seemed to be on the side of the angels in terms of his opinions about the way he'd like to see Japan shape up. And he was a clever man with powerful connections, not least General Courtney Whitney who had the ear of MacArthur himself.

On the other hand Tom had political ambitions of his own, and would hardly be likely to relish the idea of taking hold of a hot potato at this stage in his career.

Eleanor Curtis was a possibility. Not only was she highly intelligent but her father was an influential Congressman. This fact was well known to General Marquat, the cheery but not very bright ex-cavalryman and former small-time journalist whom General MacArthur liked well enough to have chosen as one of his three heads of sections. Jay knew that for this reason the general from time to time included Eleanor among his party and dinner guests, and there was a good chance she had heard plenty of indiscreet high-level gossip. Yes, it might be worth taking a chance with Eleanor, especially since she had made him promise to take up their conversation about the Japanese underworld at some future date.

If she had heard anything which tended to support the – well, call it hypothesis – that Brooks had set out in his notes, Eleanor might well be the right person to do something about the situation. Always provided, of course, that he and Polly felt sure enough of her to admit her to their confidence, and Jay didn't think it likely that her in particular would make a fundamental error of judgment in that context. Eleanor was the sort of person who would unhesitatingly stick her neck out, do almost anything in fact, if she felt strongly about a point of principle. Yes, Eleanor could be immensely helpful.

She could alert her father to what was going on, for a start. And he in turn could, if necessary, probably get confidential access to the right people in the White House and a private message to MacArthur. The "Peace" Constitution was *his* baby, after all. However paradoxical people professed to find the much-decorated old warrior's loudly trumpeted attitudes, nobody doubted that it was his personal, pig-headed insistence that Japan should for ever renounce war as an instrument of policy that had carried the day. He had in fact personally drafted the relevant clause and overcome a lot of very determined opposition in getting it duly enshrined as the cornerstone of the postwar Japanese Constitution. The fiercely anti-communist General Willoughby might have the odd man's confidence, but nothing would budge MacArthur's determination to keep Japan unarmed and democratic, of that Jay was sure. However high up the conspiracy – if it was one – went inside or outside SCAP, it certainly didn't include the Blue-Eyed Shogun.

It looked then as if the first sensible step would be to have a word with Eleanor. Just as well he hadn't yet burned Polly's copy of the notes. The conversation might go well enough for him to risk giving her a quick look at it. Economic Division's offices were also in the Forestry Building, and it would only take a few minutes to go along and see if she was in her room.

He was too late: Eleanor had gone to Tokyo University and was not expected to return to the office that day. Her secretary was helpful. Miss Curtis was, she was pretty sure, planning to go straight back to the Shiba Park Hotel to change before going to a party at General Marquat's house at six. If it was urgent, Mr Murakami could almost surely reach her there by phone, say between four-thirty and five.

"Thanks. Maybe I'll try that. In case I don't catch her, ask her to give me a call some time tomorrow morning, would you?"

Jay had no occasion to speak to anybody else during the remainder of the day, and made his way out of the building alone. Prothero had already warned him that he had an engagement that evening and wouldn't be able to offer the usual ride to Washington Heights. That suited Jay just fine, because he also had other plans.

Once clear of the building he paused in a deserted alleyway to put on the shabby ex-army greatcoat he had carried over his arm, and then headed towards Shinbashi railway station. It was nearly dark, and he planned to arrive after the Korean moonshiners had set up their ramshackle stalls and men were buying their rough, fiery *kasutori*. The trade unionist friend Jay intended to meet actually professed to like the illicit spirit, insisting on referring to it as "Japanese calvados", but one small sip months earlier had been more than enough for Jay. Thereafter he just held the cracked little cup in which it came until he could surreptitiously pour the contents on to the ground. That evening he intended to avoid embarrassment by persuading his contact to go with him into one of the shanty "restaurants" for a crude meal of black-market corned beef hash, potato rice and pumpkin, washed down with the weakest of green tea.

Emerging from the alleyway and still hobbling because of his painful, strapped-up ankle, he merged with the flow of people walking towards the station. A man apparently in a hurry came up behind him and jostled past, and Jay glanced irritably at him as he was obliged to step off the sidewalk for a moment. Then came the sickening realization that it was no accident, when he felt the violent shove and, arms flailing in an attempt to keep his balance, was sent staggering into the doorway, a few yards in front of a charcoal-burning truck that was coming up fast. Then it was upon him. Jay gestured wildly, as if he could stop it with his bare hands. And then there was only a red wave of agony, pressure, choking and final nothingness. The truck vanished into the darkness as quickly as it had emerged from it, leaving a crumpled, bloody heap in the road.

The man who had pushed Murakami into the path of the vehicle rushed to his side, knelt and fumbled at the body. As he expected, the envelope he had been told to retrieve was in an inside jacket pocket. So it was simplicity itself to whip it into the sleeve of his own coat while pretending to be feeling for a heartbeat, and transfer it to his pocket after he rose to his feet, shaking his head sadly.

"He's a gonner," he said to the little knot of passers-by who had stopped to see what was happening. "Where's the nearest police box?"

By the time a couple of policemen had arrived at the scene the witnesses to the death of Jay Murakami had nearly all made themselves scarce, and the two or three who still hung about were, with one exception, singularly unhelpful. They had seen nothing, heard nothing, knew nothing, were strangers in the neighbourhood anyway.

"I never saw anything like it," the odd man out insisted. "I'd feel sorry for the poor sod driving the truck, except he seemed to have been in a hurry and I doubt if he even realized he'd hit anybody. The crazy guy just, well, sort of launched himself out into the road in front of him. What? No, sorry, but I wasn't bothering about licence numbers. I was too busy seeing if there was anything I could do. But he was a gonner."

The policemen were not naïve. They made the chatty witness wait while they checked through the contents of the dead man's pockets. Then, discovering that he was wearing a wrist-watch worth a small fortune on the black market and that there was a substantial sum of money on him, they took the helpful "bystander" at his word, noted down the name and address he gave them, and sent him on his way.

Their search of the body had given them something more important to attend to, namely the SCAP identity card they'd found. They called the military police at once, and were relieved to be able to hand over responsibility to them.

The envelope containing Polly's copy of the Operation Hi-Flyer notes was handed over to the gangster Masao Suekawa within the hour, and its contents were being discussed by friends of the Sugamo detainees Yoshio Kodama and Nobusuke Kishi later the same evening.

One of them was Fujiko Ueda's uncle, the member of the National Diet, who decided that it would be prudent to pretend when next he spoke to her that he didn't know Jay Murakami was dead.

18

The bodies of Mike Brooks and Jay Murakami were repatriated for burial in Ohio and Hawaii respectively. People remarked on the grim coincidence that two senior SCAP officers should have died on the same day, and there was some talk about organizing a joint memorial service for them. It came to nothing, mainly because Major-Generals Willoughby and Marquat, the heads of the two sections concerned, were barely on speaking terms, and official liaison between their staffs was minimal. In any case, Mike Brooks was reported to have been an agnostic who had rebuffed the chaplains when they tried to talk to him in hospital.

It turned out that Jay Murakami had on the other hand been an occasional worshipper at the Anglican church in Yokohama, and John Prothero circulated an announcement inviting those who had known him to honour his memory at a special service to be held there. It took place four days after his death, on a beautiful sunny afternoon, exceptionally mild for late January even up there on Yokohama Bluff overlooking the American warships moored in the bay. Some of the mourners commented on the weather as they made their way to the church from the special SCAP bus which had brought them from Tokyo. Others noticed the two-star pennant on the glossy black car that drew up where John Prothero and the Episcopalian chaplain were waiting by the roadside, and agreed that it was good of General Marquat to have decided to show up.

The general and Prothero were ushered to seats in the front row after the rest of the congregation had taken their places. Polly sat with Eleanor Curtis and Angie Brewster; Tom Berman with Arthur Reynolds a couple of rows in front. There were altogether about two dozen in the Tokyo contingent, plus a few other Americans based in Yokohama. Half a dozen Japanese sat towards the back of the church, keeping themselves very much to themselves, for the most part shabbily dressed, but silent and dignified in their impassivity.

Polly felt reasonably composed during the prayers and listened dispassionately to Prothero's short, beautifully delivered eulogy. He spoke of Jay Murakami's personal kindliness and love of justice, his devotion to duty and the special contribution his own Japanese ancestry had enabled him to make to the work of constructing the new, democratic Japan and of promoting understanding and friendship between it and the United States. It was all very seemly and appropriate, and Polly had no reason to doubt the sincerity of the speaker, but his remarks scarcely touched her feelings.

It was the words of the two hymns that brought hot tears to her eyes and made her voice quaver and falter until she had to fall silent, choked with emotion. "Dear Lord and Father of mankind, forgive our foolish ways" was familiar to her, the poignant melody always moving. The other hymn was new to her but obviously not to Arthur Reynolds, who sang out lustily.

These things shall be: a loftier race
Than ere the world has known shall rise;
With flame of freedom in their souls,
And light of knowledge in their eyes. . . .

Polly found the words almost unbearably beautiful. Someone – presumably Prothero – had chosen them with Jay in mind, but they evoked the memory of Mike Brooks so vividly that during the final verse she clutched at Angie's hand, and came nearer to breaking down in public than she had done since childhood.

As soon as the service was over, Fujiko Ueda slipped out of the church as unobtrusively as she had entered just after the beginning. She doubted whether any of Jay-san's friends had noticed or recognized her. To those who had been his guests at the house she had probably been more or less invisible, part of the furniture. Even the dark-haired woman who had disturbed her in the bedroom that evening and obviously taken in the situation at a glance had most likely forgotten all about her. Not that it would have mattered much if they had realized who she was, except that she couldn't have borne it if anyone had spoken to her in that awful, crude Japanese that a few of the Americans managed to acquire.

A slender, dignified figure in her black kimono, from a safe distance Fujiko watched the general being ushered to his car and seen off. She watched the other Americans standing about chatting animatedly for several minutes, before most of them piled into their bus. She saw Jay-san's boss Professor Prothero approach one of the Japanese who had attended the service and exchange a few words with him before going off in his own car.

The Americans had, in their strange alien way, been honouring a man they liked and respected. How different the ceremonies for her own former husband had been. No question in 1945 of sending even his ashes to Manchuria – if indeed in the bloody chaos of Okinawa his body had been cremated at all. There had been only the lock of hair and the fingernail clippings he had left with her for the purpose to be interred with solemnity, and the ritual prayers had been said. The date of his death had been uncertain: the forty-nine days of mourning calculated from that of the first ceremony.

At no stage had anyone spoken of her husband as a person, in the way Professor Prothero had spoken of Jay-san; and Fujiko herself could not remember much about his character or recall the endearing qualities he must have had. Yet she must not fail to observe specific anniversaries: still to come, the third, the seventh, the thirteenth and thirty-third by Japanese reckoning, a year earlier to a westerner. So that, as his widow, Fujiko should ritually honour her husband in the early summer of that year, 1947.

Perhaps his old Japanese parents in Hawaii would do the same in due course for the man she had worked for, seduced and betrayed: it would be good and right for them to do so. So far as his American colleagues were concerned, it was all over: the decencies observed, the man himself written off. But she would go on remembering, in pain and bitter remorse. She would remember Jay-san's concern when she cut her hand and he fixed it up, his generosity in getting her cosmetics from the PX, his unconcern with money. Above all she would remember his almost childlike delight when she made it plain that she enjoyed making love to him. At least she had not deceived him in that.

Her uncle had been quite sympathetic in his businesslike way. A street accident, did you say? Terrible, terrible, but that sort of thing can happen to anybody. What? Of course not, don't be so ridiculous, my dear, who could possibly have wished the man harm? Unless it was one of those leftists he cultivated. Perhaps it was just conceivable that one of them had taken it into his head that he was spying, only pretending to be a sympathizer. But no, that was too absurd for words.

Lost in thought, Fujiko failed to notice the man who approached her from behind, and she whirled round with a gasp of nervous surprise when he spoke.

"Excuse me, Ueda-san. Your uncle thought I'd probably find you here. I'm a friend of his."

He was youngish, better dressed than the Japanese men who had been at the memorial service, and looked her up and down with open and insulting appreciation. He spoke in a cultivated way, but not to have given his own name was ill-mannered in the extreme.

"Who are you?" Fujiko saw no reason not to be equally curt.

"A friend of your uncle, as I said. We need to know what's going to happen now. First, have you any idea who'll be moving into Murakami's house? Have you been given notice to quit, or is there a good chance you might be kept on as housekeeper?"

Fujiko stared at him with disgust but he went on, seemingly oblivious of her reaction. "We're all hoping we can continue to count on your splendid co-operation. An attractive woman like you ought to have no trouble getting on the same sort of terms with the new man – "

"Shut up." Fujiko kept her voice low, but virtually spat out the plain, unfeminine words. "Shut your filthy mouth and get out. And you can tell my uncle that if he wants to pimp for me he must do his own dirty work."

The man gaped at her for a moment in apparently genuine astonishment, hesitated, and then shrugged and made off without another word. Breathing deeply, Fujiko turned away and looked out to sea. The ships in the bay grew blurred as her eyes began to smart and at last, at last the tears came. Tears not of sorrow but of hate; hate for her uncle, for herself, and for the whole putrid business. Two hours later, in the kitchen at the house in Washington Heights, Fujiko Ueda hanged herself.

19

"I talked to Noonan," Masao Suekawa said quietly. The telephone was in a tiny room, hardly more than a cubicle, squeezed into a corner behind the bar of the "club" he owned not far from Ikebukuro Station, and he had learned to hear and make himself heard in spite of the background noise. The old autochange record-player at one end of the bar was on its last legs but he had decided against replacing it, at least for a few months.

Military police patrols did occasionally look in for a couple of free drinks, and one never knew when one of the top yakuza barons might take it into his head to pay a visit. Such "guests" would not approve of the ostentatious display of a black-market rarity. When he did judge the moment appropriate it would be easy enough to get one of the newest-style American record-players: they were beginning to become available in some of the biggest PX outlets, and there were few items on their stock lists that were beyond the reach of Masao Suekawa. The exceptions were such wonders as new automobiles, for even Occupation people with legitimate PX privileges wanting one of those had to put their names into the hat and hope they might get lucky in one of the periodic draws.

"Of course he's an idiot. And he's full of bullshit, but he has this new job that could turn out to be worth a lot to us. So much so that I want to suggest that we put our plans for him on ice for a while. . . . No, I know that, but I think you'll change your mind when you hear what I found out. Yes, boss, that's what I'm trying to do."

Suekawa fingered the disfiguring scar on his face, and scratched it gently with one of his self-mutilated fingers, a legacy of the days when he was beginning to work his way up the gangster hierarchy and had occasioned the displeasure of his superiors. He held the receiver at a little distance from his ear until he was given another chance to speak. It was stuffy and warm in the confined space, and sweating always made his scar itch. Sometimes he really hated the scar and thought about paying a plastic surgeon to pretty it up, but mostly he exploited it. People who needed to be leant on thought twice about being difficult when a man with a face like Masao Suekawa's was doing the leaning.

"Yes, I know those were your instructions, boss, and I know what you say goes. . . . But Noonan is actually investigating the lawyer, Berman. Yes, right now. A covert security check. And he won't be able to go on doing that if we sink him in Tokyo Bay the night we get the second Kobe shipment away." Suekawa caressed the scar again as he listened, his lips twisting slowly into a half-smile.

"Sure. He was very cagey to start with, but he's a natural bigmouth. It beats me that they ever put him into counter-intelligence. With a few drinks inside him he started to brag about the dirt he was picking up on a number of senior people, including Berman. . . No, he mentioned Berman spontaneously. . . . Who else? Just a second, I wrote down a couple of other names after he left. I was listening out for Berman's name, naturally. The others were unfamiliar."

He took a scrap of paper from his trouser pocket and smoothed it awkwardly with one hand. "I have them here. Not sure about the spelling. Something like Prodrow? What's that? P-R-O-T-H – Prothero, yes that was it. And a woman, Curtis, I'm pretty sure about that one, I used to know a Curtis in the States. Elaine or something like that. An economist. . . . OK, OK, I already said Noonan's full of bullshit. I know it could be just big talk. And he wasn't specific about what he claimed to have on any of them, except that he called Berman a 'faggot'. American slang for *doseijin*. If that's a fact then it opens up all sorts of possibilities, I should think. . . . Yes. Fine, I'll do that."

Suekawa's smile was broader after he put the phone down. That had made the man who fancied himself as such a big shot take a different line. Maybe in future he'd be more inclined to *listen* to what people in the know had to say before running off at the mouth.

Looking back on it, Polly thought she must have been in a kind of trance during the few days between being told that Jay Murakami had been killed and attending his memorial service – in fact, until she had choked over the words of the hymns, wept at the thought of Mike Brooks and clutched at Angie's strong warm hand. Then it was as if a door in her consciousness had burst open to admit a flood of rage, a passionate rage that on leaving the church made her want to stand outside and howl with fury instead of meekly allowing herself to be shepherded back to the bus. Though she had gone along meekly enough, for this huge emotion was so savage, so primitive, that it frightened her into continued silence. Nevertheless, it had been a silence utterly different in kind from that which had marked her earlier apathy.

Now, as she walked along beside Arthur Reynolds, both of them in civilian clothes, Polly felt alert in the way she imagined wild animals had to be every minute of every waking hour. The anger seemed to have quickened all her senses, making her awareness of potential danger on every side not so much terrifying as a normal aspect of the natural world, something one simply lived with. The little she could remember of what had happened in between had the quality of a rapidly fading dream, or a mediocre, instantly forgettable movie.

She must have eaten from time to time, she supposed. Dressed, undressed, bathed, used the toilet; even talked to people, without the smallest recollection of what she might have said. She had an idea that Angie had been with her for much of the time; and Eleanor, Eleanor came into it somewhere too. Big women, both of them, with Polly feeling like a child again between them in church. Yes, she could remember that now. God knows what they must have thought of her behaviour, anybody might have supposed she'd been in love with Jay to have reacted that way to his death.

". . . but actually I'm quite OK now, Arthur. Just mad as hell is all."

"With me?"

"Yes, among other people. I think you already realized that. I certainly hope you don't imagine I asked to meet you here because I thought you might like old books too."

"There are worse things to have a common interest in, Polly. But no, I assumed that you asked me to meet you in Jimbo-cho because it's not too far from Hilltop House but far enough to be unlikely that anybody we know will see us. It's also the sort of place where people can potter for an hour or so without drawing attention to themselves. Ah. Here's our old friend Thomas Hardy." He picked a tattered edition of *Tess of the D'Urbervilles* from a shallow box in front of the shop where they had paused. He glanced at the flyleaf. "I had no idea *Tess* had a sub-title. *A Pure Woman*. Maybe I should buy it for you. It seems very appropriate, somehow."

The book still open in his hand, Reynolds wheeled round and looked directly into Polly's eyes. "Mind you, I very much hope it's appropriate only in the sense that I'm sure you're a pure woman – as well as being as mad as hell. Because as you may or may not recall, poor Tess has a very rough time of it in the book."

"Is that right?"

"Yes. She ends up being hanged for murder."

"I didn't know that. I've never read the book."

"It caused a great furore when it came out. Shocking, wicked, immoral, everybody said. Then within, what, thirty years or so they were making me study it as a set text in school. The story of a woman sorely wronged by a man. Is that why you're angry with me, Polly? Because you think I may have wronged you?"

"I think you probably have, or maybe you're just planning to. I'm not quite sure."

"How can I persuade you you're making a mistake?"

Polly stared back at him. Hyper-sensitive though she now felt, she still found it hard to sense anything threatening about his mild, schoolmasterly manner even after he had chosen to talk about the apparently chilling book he held in his hand. He could hardly have arranged to find it so conveniently in the tray. But then again, well read as she knew he was, he could probably have found something relevant to her present situation in any book he picked up.

"By answering some straight questions," she finally said.

"Fine. Straight answers to straight questions. You won't of course know I'm answering them truthfully, but I hope you'll believe me. Shall we move on to the next shop before you begin?"

The whole street was lined with second-hand bookshops. Some were quite large, with room for a few browsers, others barely big enough to accommodate the proprietor and one customer. The great majority of the books on display inside and out were Japanese, piled high on every flat surface including as much as could be spared of the floor, but most of the dealers also offered a selection of books in English, German and French: for the most part tattered pre-war textbooks. Reynolds walked on slowly and Polly followed, studying him from behind. When he stopped she spoke again.

"You can begin by telling me about your friend the mysterious Jerry Nakajima." Reynolds had found a book on botany and was leafing through it, pausing at each engraved illustration. After a while he looked up, his expression as serious as her own.

"Eijiro Nakajima. Born in or near Osaka in 1908, second son of a senior naval surgeon. Didn't want to follow in his father's medical footsteps, but did enter the Japanese naval academy and performed very well there. So well that before long he was assigned to naval intelligence, and between 1937 and 1939 served as assistant to the naval attaché at the Japanese Embassy in Washington. We're not entirely sure what he got up to after that, though there's reason to believe he remained in intelligence work and was in China for at least part of the war. Shanghai. By the time of the surrender he was back in the Navy Ministry in Tokyo and a full commander, one up on me. Like a number of other quite senior Japanese officers, soon after he was cleared by the war crimes investigators he was hired as a SCAP researcher attached to G2. In his case towards the end of forty-five or early last year. Next question?"

"He has been cleared, then."

"Of course. Some of the interrogations were probably pretty perfunctory given the shortage of skilled investigators, but they gave him the nod. And G2 would have been glad to get hold of the services of a fluent English-speaking ex-officer with diplomatic experience."

"What's your own connection with him?"

"He's one of my most useful informants about the current Japanese political scene."

"In what way is he qualified?"

"Polly, I honestly do want to be frank with you, but you're straying into classified territory. I'm still trying to fix the assignment we discussed for you, to work with me. And I think I'm getting somewhere. So within a week or so you might well have access to information that will answer that question. Till then, I'm afraid you'll have to try me with something else."

"All right. How much does he make?"

"Salary, you mean? I really couldn't say. American civilians employed by the military government at about his level are on, what, around four, five thousand dollars a year. A Japanese wouldn't get anything like that much, nor in dollars either. Effectively about half, two-thirds perhaps? I could check for you if you really want to know."

"No need, that's about what I'd figured. OK, just two more questions, but the second one's a lulu, I warn you. If you can come up with plausible answers to both, well, I might just begin to believe you."

Polly had not so much overcome as forgotten about the constraints of military protocol. She was no longer a WAC sergeant addressing a senior Allied officer in a grossly insubordinate manner; she was a furious but newly clear-headed woman demanding honest replies from a man she had allowed to kiss her, put his tongue in her mouth and fondle her breasts, a man she had seriously contemplated going to bed with, and by whom she had been at the very least misled. Reynolds put the book back in the tray, took her arm lightly and led her a little further along the street.

"Go ahead. Shoot."

"First. How could he afford to take me – in a proper taxi – to an exclusive geisha house, pay for the services of two leading geisha, entertain me to what must be about the most expensive meal a Japanese can buy anywhere these days, and arrange to have the taxi waiting to take me home after? How can he afford to dress the way he does? To drink at the Press Club?"

"Two questions? That's about six already."

"Try answering them. The other one comes next."

"Well, he can drink at the Press Club because he goes there as my guest even when he's alone, signs for what he orders and I pay the bills. He probably dresses well because it's not too difficult for Japanese employed by SCAP to come by the odd bottle of whisky or carton of cigarettes, and you ought to know that items like that can be parleyed into all sorts of other things. Not a geisha party, though, I have to admit." He took a deep breath and looked around before going on.

"I can suggest an explanation even for that, though, and I will, at the risk of giving you some of that classified information I mentioned just now. My theory would be that his evening out with you probably didn't cost Jerry a penny except maybe the taxi fares, and possibly not even those. Jerry Nakajima is a very well-connected man, with friends in high Japanese political circles. The sort of people who can afford geisha parties with all the trimmings and would be more than willing to pick up the tab for him. In the way I'm content to pick up his very modest ones at the Press Club, and for very similar reasons, I dare say. Namely that they value him highly as a confidential channel of communication between themselves and people in SCAP. That is more than I should have said, and certainly all you're going to get on the subject until and unless you work with me officially."

"Thank you for that much. There's still the last question. The last for the moment, anyway. And the hardest."

"You can but try me. I'm not mad at you, Polly. Though I ought to point out you're trying your luck rather."

"It might be the only chance I have. So here goes. You obviously weren't surprised when I said Jerry Nakajima had taken me out. That makes it a lot easier for me to ask you this: why did you arrange for me to meet him, Arthur? After – well, after making me think you were interested in me yourself? Was it because you *wanted* him to get to know me? Because you guessed I'd be attracted to him? That given time he might be able to get me to talk?"

For the first time since they had met that afternoon she read an icy contempt for her in the Australian's face, and when he spoke after what seemed to be a long time it was very quietly. "Nobody has ever before either directly or by implication accused me of being a pander. If I didn't know you've been under great strain recently I should be sorely tempted to hit you. As it is, I'll say this, not to frighten you, but by way of answering your question: do not ever *dare* to suggest anything of the kind again."

"I'm sorry. I wanted so much not to believe it. And now you've convinced me it wasn't so. I'm sorry, I'm sorry I had to ask, but you must see that I was bound to think it possible. You do see, don't you? And you do see that I still have to know why you introduced us? I do believe you now, Arthur, but I'm sorry – you invited Nakajima to the Press Club that evening. You didn't even pretend he dropped in by coincidence."

"No. I wanted you two to meet, and made no secret of it. I'll try to explain, but before I can even begin to, you must answer at least one question yourself. And I'm afraid that to use your own word, it's a lulu. Polly, had you discussed this conspiracy Mike Brooks claimed to have uncovered with Jay Murakami before he was run over and killed by that truck? Maybe shown him the notes you mentioned to me? A straight answer to a straight question, please. You owe me that much, I think. After all, I came pretty clean with you." He stared into her eyes. "You hesitate, and I don't really blame you. I can only say that whatever you tell me, I would never knowingly do anything to harm your interests, and I may perhaps be able to help. I was – still am – a lawyer, after all."

"I do believe you. I have to, don't I? Yes. Yes, I had talked to Jay about it. Just the previous day. And I . . . no, that's all. I had talked to him in confidence."

"I see. And Polly, do you think the fact that he was killed in a traffic accident the very next day was in any way related to your conversation with Jay?"

"Yes. I'm appalled to have to say that I do. That . . . that's why I asked you all that about Nakajima. I was afraid – oh, Jesus, I don't know, but these politician friends of his – "

"You're quite sure you're not imagining things?" Reynolds reached out and caught Polly's arm to support her as her eyes closed and she swayed as though about to faint, the recollection of Jay Murakami's own words loud in her mind: "*. . . if something were to happen to you too. Don't look so horrified, I'm not suggesting anybody may be thinking of arranging an accident for you. . . .*"

"Thank you. I'm all right now. I just felt a little faint."

"This has been a difficult conversation for both of us. I'll walk you back to Hilltop House. I'm sorry, Polly, but if you're *not* imagining things, then you must tell me everything that's been going on. It may help you to know that Eleanor Curtis is very troubled, too. She and Jay were friends, I believe, and it seems he'd left a message with her secretary to ask Eleanor to get in touch with him first thing the following morning. Maybe you can work out why he might have done that. The secretary told Eleanor that Jay hadn't seemed his usual self. Preoccupied, you know, something on his mind. Does that help you at all?"

"That he wanted to talk to Eleanor? Yes, in a strange way it does. All right, Arthur. I'll tell you all I know."

20

"Let me just go over that bit again, may I?" Reynolds said. He, Eleanor Curtis and Polly were sitting in Eleanor's room at the Shiba Park Hotel on the evening of the same day. "Polly went to see Jay the day before he was killed, having been advised to do so by Mike Brooks shortly before *he* died. She confirms that, after being initially sceptical about what she had to tell him, Jay appeared to take her seriously. Now during the afternoon of the following day Jay tried to see you, Eleanor, but you were out, right?"

"Yes. He spoke to my secretary. Margaret told him he could probably reach me by phone here at the hotel towards the end of the afternoon. I was here for an hour or so until just after five-thirty, but he didn't call me."

"But he did leave a message at your office for you to contact him first thing next morning, which suggests that he wanted to see you urgently, but not all that urgently. And you have no idea what he wanted?"

"None whatever. I'd been in my office much of the morning. He could have talked to me then easily enough."

"Yes. So it could have been something quite unimportant; except that your secretary said that wasn't the impression he gave her. Do you attach any importance to that, Eleanor?"

"You know I do. Margaret is a very perceptive person."

Polly had been sitting quietly looking from one to the other and now cut in. "Major Brooks died that morning."

"He did, yes. But I don't see what that has to do with it, Polly. I think we have to accept that there are no suspicious circumstances whatever attached to Mike's death."

"Perhaps not. The point I'm making is that Jay might have wanted to talk to Major Brooks himself, and then discovered he was too late."

"Oh, I see what you're getting at. I don't think the news started going the rounds – in the Dai-Ichi Building at least – until towards

149

the end of the day. I remember somebody told me as I was leaving."

"And that could be why Jay didn't try to get in touch with Eleanor till later. And the reason he didn't call her here was perhaps because he wanted to talk to her in person, not over the phone."

"Well, maybe, maybe not. All we know for sure is that he left the office on foot more or less at the regular time. Then within an hour or so he was run down and killed by a truck not far from Shinbashi. The regular police must have found his ID on him because they called an army patrol. Now, according to what I've been able to find out through my own discreet enquiries, the Japanese police are content to write it off as a straightforward accident. The provost marshal's office is less convinced, but so far as I've been able to judge that's mainly because Jay came to SCAP from the FBI and did a certain amount of work under light cover. That, and the fact that there seems to have been a suspicious dearth of witnesses. However, it's a long way from that to establishing that it was a case of hit and run, even a simple one. I mean simple in the sense that the driver genuinely didn't see Jay but ran him down by accident and then made off simply to avoid trouble for himself. My guess is that the military police will go on asking around for a while and then close the file. But Polly thinks poor Jay was killed deliberately, don't you?"

"Do you honestly, Polly? It's a horrifying thought."

"Yes, Eleanor, I do. Because of what I'd told him."

"And what he might have been planning to tell me." Eleanor shivered and pulled her expensive dusky pink cashmere cardigan more closely round her shoulders.

"Yes. I've thought very hard about this," Polly said. "Jay told me he'd hunt around for some sort of verification of what I'd said. That's why I think it's reasonable to assume that the first thing he would have thought of doing would be to go to the hospital and check it out with Major Brooks. It seems to me that having found out the major had died, Jay decided to consult Eleanor. And I'm ready to do that myself now if you are, Arthur."

"Forgive us for talking about you as though you weren't here, Eleanor. Polly has understandably been very cautious indeed about all this. Two people in the know have died within hours of each other. That may be pure coincidence; nobody was expecting Mike Brooks to live long anyway, and in Jay's case it obviously *could* have been the tragic accident people are saying it was."

"All the same I can see why you're suspicious as well as upset, Polly," Eleanor said. "I've been very concerned myself, knowing Jay wanted to see me a couple of hours before it happened. It did cross my mind that his death might have been intended, but that was because I knew he was in touch with various trade union organizers. Not all of them were supposed to know exactly who he was. In fact I hinted as much to John Prothero."

"What was his reaction?"

"Total disbelief. He seemed almost angry with me for even suggesting such a thing, but that was probably because he must have been more stunned by the news than any of us except Polly. And he's obviously under great pressure. Jay was his deputy after all, and we all know that Labor Division is going frantic in these final days before the general strike. This has completely thrown them all. Well, are you going to tell or not? If not, at least give me some idea why Jay might have intended to confide in me."

Eleanor looked first at Arthur Reynolds, who had been playing with his empty briar pipe after manfully declining Eleanor's casual invitation to go ahead and smoke it if he wanted to. He cocked his head to one side, eyebrows raised, and turned expectantly to Polly.

"Yes, I guess it is up to me," she said. "In a way it was me that started all this after all. Eleanor, does the name Operation Hi-Flyer mean anything to you?"

"Not a thing. Should it?"

Polly forced a grin. "No. In fact if you'd said yes I think I should have gone clean out of my mind. It didn't mean anything to Arthur either, and he's in a position to know about most of the schemes GHQ likes to call by that kind of code name."

"I can confirm that," Reynolds said. "I've checked, and there is no official file under that name or anything remotely resembling it listed as being anywhere in the archives. Nor anything which would suggest to me that the material Polly's referring to is held under a different name in the high-security files."

"Arthur and I have discussed this, and I agree with his conclusion that Major Brooks must have invented the name himself. We think he amassed a lot of miscellaneous data over a period and at some point thought he discerned a logical pattern emerging from it. That he built up a hypothesis and tested it in various ways, refining it all the time. It might have been a kind of intellectual exercise at first – he was brilliant at crosswords, anagrams, any kind of puzzle like that.

And eventually he became horrified by the implications of what he had discovered, so horrified that he decided they ought to be made known. He was just about ready to take action when he collapsed and was taken to hospital."

Polly paused as if to gather strength, took a deep breath and went on. "Basically, Major Brooks – I'm sorry, you both called him Mike I know, but I can only ever think of him as Major Brooks – he believed that a number of highly placed people, both Japanese and American, are conspiring to make sure that there will never be anything but a right-wing government in Japan. That they intend to crush any opposition especially from the trade unions, to keep the industrial cartels intact and to build up a powerful army again as soon as possible, no matter what it says in the new Constitution. No, wait, let me go on before you say anything, I might be able to save you some breath. When I first told this to Jay he acted bored and told me this was nothing new, that plenty of people were well known to favour those objectives."

Reynolds cut in. "And he was right, of course. My initial reaction was the same, and I'd be willing to bet yours is too, Eleanor."

"Well, yes, I suppose it would have to be. . . ."

"Precisely. Mine was perhaps even more cynical. I work for Willoughby, remember. The great anti-communist crusader. I've heard him holding forth – *ad nauseam* and not in the least confidentially – on the subject of the Russian menace and his vision of Japan as America's strongest ally in countering it. It's not just bluster, either. The Prussian is a determined man with a formidable intellect. It's well known that he and General Whitney over there in Political Section hate each other's guts. Mind you, only a mother could love Whitney."

"One of his people told me they call him the stuffed pig with a moustache," Eleanor put in unexpectedly, and giggled. Then she seemed to feel ashamed of her levity, and looked serious again.

"Most apt. Even Willoughby doesn't go so far as to accuse Whitney himself of being a Red, though. On the other hand he is genuinely convinced that SCAP as such – Whitney's side and yours, Eleanor, or rather Marquat's – is crawling with communists, fellow-travellers, pinkoes generally. And he wants them rooted out, their liberal policies frustrated, and so on and so forth. Even before all this I doubt if any of us imagined that he'd be any too scrupulous about methods, either."

"I couldn't agree more," Eleanor said. "I was interrogated by some unspeakable Counter-Intelligence Corps man myself just last week. He was seeing Reds everywhere and trying to get me to inform on my colleagues."

"Right. So I wasn't particularly impressed either when Polly told me Brooks claimed to have evidence that his so-called Hi-Flyer conspirators included some unsavoury characters from the far right of Japanese politics who in turn had connections with organized crime. I was well aware of the existence of links between GHQ and such people. Better than most, probably, because that's the territory I prowl myself in my official capacity. But you don't have to have access to classified information to know that the hoodlums on the streets who beat up leftists while the police look the other way take their orders from gangsters."

"Well, Polly, how *did* you persuade this cynic to change his mind?"

"I told him that Major Brooks had noted specific details of a plan to get a group of top Japanese war criminals – Class A suspects – released from jail and then almost immediately back into positions of influence. At least one of them – Nobusuke Kishi – into mainstream politics and then into office as prime minister of Japan within a matter of a few years. Hence the name 'Hi-Flyer', I suppose."

"Yes. At that point I was persuaded that if it was true, Mike had uncovered the chapter and verse of something worth getting excited about. The rest, with all respect to Polly, might constitute a certain amount of useful ammunition for a liberal journalist like Mark Gayn or Dwight Rogers. Possibly even win one of them a Pulitzer Prize. All the same I can't think that even the most carefully researched exposé would significantly influence the way things are headed in Japan. The liberals in SCAP are undoubtedly in retreat, the Emperor seems safe in his palace, and in the fullness of time the Japanese will very likely decide to revise their fine new made-in-America Constitution and flex their military muscles again."

Eleanor sounded shocked. "I simply can't agree with you there. It's inconceivable to me that the bombs on Hiroshima and Nagasaki haven't ruled out any question of rearmament for all Japanese. There's overwhelming public support for the Peace Constitution. The people are sick to death of militarism."

"It will be nice if you turn out to be right, Eleanor, but I don't think you are. Anyway we can only guess about that and time will tell. What you say does encourage me to think you agree with Polly and me about this other business. It's quite different, in my opinion, because we're talking about the here and now. For all its obvious faults the International Tribunal is still sitting, and a second round of trials is a distinct possibility. If hard evidence of a genuine conspiracy to put Mike's so-called high flyers back into circulation can be put into the right hands, then there is a real chance it could be frustrated."

Eleanor blinked and rubbed her eyes. "Well, obviously I'd want to see that happen if possible, and I'm sure poor Jay would have agreed. I presume you think he was planning to ask me to pass the information to my father?"

Polly looked at Reynolds, the ghost of a smile on her face. They had talked about Eleanor on the way to see her, and Polly had predicted that she wouldn't need to have things spelt out in detail.

"Yes. Some time ago now, the major told me he'd thought about various ways of handling the material, and one of them was to try to persuade you to have your father ask some awkward questions in Washington."

"I could certainly ask him, but not without producing the hard evidence you talked about. What *is* the evidence, and how hard is it?"

"The evidence is a document Major Brooks wrote out by hand. Three pages of notes. Giving names, dates of clandestine meetings, other circumstantial details. I have those notes in a safe place."

"I don't want to be impolite, Polly, but I have to say I don't think my father would consider that to be conclusive."

"He might if he knew that I'd made a copy of those notes and given it to Jay. You see, for a number of very good reasons I think somebody found out shortly before Major Brooks got sick that he had drawn up an incriminating report of some kind. Then after he was hospitalized, he or they thought I might have it. The reason I think so is that right after that, odd things began to happen to me."

"Such as?"

"Such as being pulled out of my job in a hurry, and having my room searched. Then I believe the same person unknown somehow or other figured out I'd given Jay a copy, and had him silenced. You'll probably think I'm paranoid when I say this, but I also believe it possible that Major Brooks's death was somehow hastened. Even if you discount that, all the other circumstances would at the very least suggest that the people involved think a document of some kind exists and that it could be used to damage them."

Eleanor's hand went up to her mouth and there was fear in her eyes as she slowly lowered it again. "Dear God, Polly, how can you be so matter of fact? You must be terrified!"

"I have been. Maybe I should still be, but I'm not."

"She's mad, Eleanor. Hopping mad, she told me. American usage. I was taught to use the word in the British way, to mean crazy. I may say I think she's that too. I also think she's rather brave, don't you?"

"I'm not brave, I'm indignant at being pushed around myself, and outraged at what happened to Jay. And whether or not you two are willing to help I'm determined to do something about it."

Reynolds reached for her hand and squeezed it gently. "I've already told you I want to help, and I get the impression Eleanor does too."

"Yes, that goes without saying. I think I can persuade my father to take this seriously. There may be a better way though, not instead of bringing him in but in addition. Tom Berman."

"Why him in particular?"

"Because I had a long talk with Tom not too long ago. Arising from my – brush with the counter-intelligence man I told you about, Polly. I wanted to find out what he'd been asking Tom about me, but we ended up talking about all manner of things." In spite of her anxieties and preoccupations, Polly noticed with some surprise that Eleanor wasn't blushing. "Anyway, I gathered in the course of conversation that now the prosecution have finished making their cases against the first batch of defendants and the defence are having their turn, the pressure's off Tom's team. So they're working on a submission to the Commander-in-Chief about further prosecutions, of other Class A detainees in Sugamo. In view of that, I think Tom could put this information to good use right away, don't you?"

Polly looked dubious. "I suppose so, yes . . . but do you have any idea how he'd be likely to react? I mean, I've only met him a few times, but he strikes me as being, oh, I don't know – "

Reynolds interrupted. "Ambitious, Polly? A bit of a politician? Unlikely to risk sticking his neck out? Sorry to cut in on you, but I think I know what you're getting at there. As one who was once a lawyer and hopes one day to return to the profession I keep an interested eye on those prosecutor chaps. I'd say Master Berman has a good opinion of his own abilities, and on the whole that it's justified. On the other hand he's not exactly likeable. You know him better than I do, what do you think, Eleanor?"

"Tom has an incisive mind and a lot of valuable experience. I'm sure he must be a very able lawyer, and he has the looks and the confident manner to make a very effective one. Arthur implies that he's motivated mainly by considerations of career advantage, and might be wanting in integrity. I'm not so sure about that, but even looking at it quite cynically I should have thought it would be very much to his professional advantage if he could achieve a successful prosecution. A prosecution which would be bound to be accompanied by a lot of spectacular publicity. As a matter of fact, my feeling is that behind the stylish public image there's probably a sad and lonely man, and a very likeable one. So I disagree with you completely on that point, Arthur."

"I like your logic. It would certainly do no harm to Tom's future for him to play the saviour of democracy. I wish I could share your view that he's fundamentally a nice fellow. Maybe he is, but I must admit that I instinctively keep my back to the wall when I'm talking to him."

Eleanor didn't react immediately, but after a moment she gaped at Reynolds, and her neck and face did then become suffused with blood.

"I . . . I'm very uneducated about these things. Are you saying that . . . that you think he might be – "

"A pansy? Sorry, forgive my bluntness. A homosexual. Yes, I must admit I do have a sneaking suspicion along those lines. It could be that I'm completely wrong, and in any case whether or not a man is that way inclined should have nothing to do with one's assessment of his worth. In other words I'm not proud of saying what I did, but the fact is he does rather give me the creeps."

"Arthur could be right about him," Polly said. "I certainly don't sense he has much interest in women as women. Isn't all this rather beside the point, though?"

Eleanor still looked profoundly ill at ease, but closed her eyes momentarily and then spoke more freely. "No, it could be very important: something that hadn't occurred to me before. Listen, this counter-intelligence investigator. Noonan. He seems to have a general interest in those of us who inevitably meet Japanese left-wingers in the course of our work. Myself, John Prothero, Jay before he died. And I'd assumed that he only went to see Tom to pick up any gossip he could about us. But suppose Tom himself is being investigated? His work doesn't involve any outside contacts at all. And

I simply cannot believe that he's a covert left-winger. On the other hand, if counter-intelligence suspect that he may be ... well, what you think, then he'd be considered a security risk, wouldn't he?"

"He certainly would. Well, we can hardly confide in him if the snoopers are about to recommend cancelling his clearance, can we? Unless you're about to produce another brilliant argument, Eleanor."

It was Polly who broke the lengthy silence which followed. "It's not an argument, but I do have an idea. It's something I'd like to try out on Eleanor first, though. Arthur, would you very much mind going down to the lobby for a few minutes? It won't take us long, I promise, but it'll be easier for us if you aren't here."

21

At the end of the concert at the Hibiya Public Hall, Polly Horvath stood up reluctantly, feeling slightly dazed. As she made her way slowly out of the building she thought she might be coming down with some sort of flu, but by the time she reached the outside her head had cleared. Then it occurred to her that the strange feeling must have been due to the fact that she hadn't thought about Operation Hi-Flyer for nearly two whole hours, and that during the Grieg piano concerto at least she'd even forgotten that she was in Japan.

It was a fine, clear evening and she was well wrapped up, so she decided to walk over to Tokyo Station and see if she could find a taxi there. If not, she could take the local train: it was just a few stops to Ochanomizu Station, close to Hilltop House. Perhaps she had been able to forget things during the concert because she had gone alone, following another lengthy session with Eleanor who was revealing a hitherto well-concealed talent for intrigue.

Arthur Reynolds knew she planned to go to the concert and had offered to take her; so, independently, had Angie, but Polly had made excuses and they both seemed to understand why. She probably wasn't in personal danger any longer, and if she was, then to hell with it. Arthur and Eleanor both knew that if anything happened to her, Angie had instructions to produce the Brooks dossier and hand it over to one of them; and either would know how to make effective use of it.

Polly's heart did miss a beat a few minutes later as she was approaching the poorly lit station forecourt and felt a light tug at her sleeve, but she breathed again when she saw that the person who had accosted her was a young girl, ten or eleven years old at most. She had a grave, solemn little face that made her look as if she had forgotten how to smile if she ever knew, and she avoided Polly's eyes while whispering something incomprehensible.

"I'm sorry, I don't understand. *Wakarimasen.*" Polly smiled help-lessly as she spoke, and then noticed that the child was wearing clean but threadbare clothes and was shivering with cold. The Japanese girl spoke again, a little more clearly so that Polly could just make out the English words.

"You buy, lady? Japanese kimono. Very cheap." She produced a cloth-wrapped bundle from under her other arm and began to open it as she offered it to Polly. "Only ten dollar."

Polly looked at the pathetic bundle and wanted to weep. Hardly aware of what she was doing she took off her warm woollen scarf and wrapped it round the girl's neck, then searched in her purse. She had between twenty and thirty dollars in military scrip, and seventeen yen in Japanese currency. She kept the odd seventeen yen and gave all the rest to the girl, wrapping the cold little hand round it and pushing the bundle back at the same time.

"No, no, you keep, I don't want," she said, and impulsively hugged the child before virtually taking to her heels and running towards the station.

The image of the sad little face in the cold night refused to fade, and Polly's thoughts were still dominated by the girl when she got off the train at Ochanomizu and turned out of the station. This was perhaps why she was taken completely by surprise when she was seized from behind. She didn't even have time to scream before a large hand covered her mouth. She could produce only a muffled moan. She kicked and struggled furiously and tried to bite the hand that was stifling her, but within seconds she was dragged bodily into an unlit alley and held there without effort.

"Keep still and be quiet, Polly. I promise I'm not going to hurt you, but we must talk. Now when I take my hand away *don't scream*. This is important, believe me." The pressure on her mouth was cautiously reduced and then, when she remained silent, the hand was taken away. Polly whirled round within the confines of the other encircling arm and confronted her captor, still struggling to free herself.

"You *bastard*! What the *hell* do you think you're doing?"

"I'm afraid you're becoming a nuisance, Polly," Nakajima said, his arm still firmly round her body. "You've shown yourself to be more resourceful than anybody expected, and a certain person wants to form a personal impression of you. I'm taking you to see him now. After that it will be decided what to do about you, so a lot depends on this meeting."

"I'm going nowhere with you. Let me *go*, damn you." Nakajima's arm tightened round her as Polly began to struggle again.

"You will go with me, believe me. But I'd hate to have to hurt you in the process. You'll find this hard to believe, but in the past few days I've been doing my best to look after your interests because I like and admire you. Come with me quietly, Polly. It's better for your self-respect that way. I followed you from the concert hall, you know, and watched you giving the money to that little girl at Tokyo Station. That was a nice thing to do."

When Joe Noonan arrived at the club in Ikebukuro, to his surprise Masao Suekawa personally welcomed him, took him straight to the bar, and when they both had drinks raised his glass to him in a sketchy salute. "Remember that attorney you mentioned? Berman? Well, you guessed right, Noonan. He is a fag."

Noonan preened himself. "Never been wrong yet. Spot one a mile away. What makes *you* think so though? You got something on him could be useful to me?"

"You made me curious so I had a guy talk to the janitor where Berman lives. Berman thinks he's so smart, keeping it on the premises."

"He's doing it with the janitor for chrissake?"

Suekawa was undoubtedly in an affable mood. "The janitor's an old guy with about three teeth left, but don't knock it till you've tried it, Noonan," he said. "No, Berman's boyfriend's a kid works at the lobby desk. That janitor doesn't miss a trick, though. Seems the kid works evenings three nights a week, goes up to Berman's room after he gets through around ten, ten-thirty. So you want something to put in your notebook, drop in on them, right? Make a third, you know?"

"Wowie! Just what I needed, a fruit right there in Prosecution Section! I'll nail that bastard and run him out of town before he has time to get his pants back on. Hey, friend, I really appreciate this."

Suekawa shrugged. "We owe you, I guess. You keep us happy, we do you a favour now and then."

"Well, thanks anyway." Noonan visibly pondered. "This janitor, he speak English?"

"Are you kidding? You characters really are something. You come here, try to run a country like Japan, want to know what's going on, doesn't occur to you it might be smart to learn the language? No, he speaks English the way you speak Japanese, Noonan. Not even *sukoshi* bit, as you Yanks like to say. *Zenzen wakaranai*, in other words."

"Uh huh. Listen, Suekawa-san, could you – your guy, I mean – find out what nights this boy works? It would help me a lot."

"God help the New York police department. No wonder they let you go. You think we didn't ask? Tuesday, Thursday, Saturday. Think you can remember that without writing it down? You better get moving before Saturday though, because you'll be busy at Hama Rikyu that night. Getting the second shipment off to Kobe."

The shabby little inn called the Kikuya was a far cry from the elegant teahouse to which Nakajima had taken Polly to lavish food and entertainment on her. The tatami mats in the entrance were old and stained, and there were holes in the *shoji* screens inside, the torn paper hanging down in tatters. A faint but perceptible smell of urine pervaded the chilly gloom, and Polly had to make a great effort to suppress a wave of nausea when she entered.

The man she assumed she had been brought to meet was sitting quietly sipping green tea in a small, poorly lit room. Here, to her relief, the predominant smell was of burning charcoal. He was wearing a dark blue woollen kimono with a padded half-length outer garment over it, looked about fifty and had a round, plumpish face. He remained seated when Nakajima urged Polly into the room but inclined his head briefly in acknowledgment of her presence, pointing to one of the two threadbare cushions which had been placed on the tatami for them. He remained silent while the elderly woman who had led the way poured tea for them from a tin kettle on a tray beside him. Then she retreated, closing the door behind her. When she had gone, the man in the kimono spoke to Nakajima in Japanese.

Nakajima listened attentively until the man paused, and then turned to Polly to interpret. "You have possibly guessed who this gentleman is. His name is Kishi, and he is . . . one of those you have been concerning yourself with recently. He says he's sorry this meeting has to take place so late in the evening, and is grateful to you for coming. He hopes you're not finding the cold weather too troublesome, and that you're enjoying your stay in Japan."

Polly gaped in disbelief, momentarily incapable of speech. Then, as so often in the past few days, furious indignation swept over her. "Good God! You jumped me like a common hoodlum, hustled me into a car, brought me here by brute force and now this . . . this jailbird thanks me for coming and asks after my *health*? How the hell did he get out of Sugamo anyway?"

"We're only about a block away from the prison, and he'll go back in an hour or so. It isn't the first time an arrangement of this kind has been made."

"You realize this confirms the whole thing? He must have some buddies damn high up in SCAP to be able to slip out of jail for a cup of coffee."

Nakajima began to interpret but there was the hint of a smile at the corner of the mouth of the man in the kimono and he interrupted with a gesture. "I understand," he said. "My English is very poor but I understand you if you speak slow. You are a strong lady. Not afraid."

"You're damn right I'm not afraid, mister. Not any more. You wouldn't dare have me murdered too, you must know by now that if anything happens to me you're finished." She turned to Nakajima. "And so are you I very much hope, you worm."

"Nothing's going to happen to you, at least not in the sense you mean, Polly. We take your point. One or two impulsive people have recommended crude measures but it's too late now. I'd never have permitted it, anyway."

"*You* wouldn't have? Gee, that's really big of you."

"Would you mind just listening for a moment instead of sounding off, Polly? Whether you like it or not, what I believe you think of as Operation Hi-Flyer is on schedule. Nobody's infallible and accidents can happen, but believe me when I say there's nothing you and your friends can do to stop it, even with the aid of the document you have."

"You want to bet? Anyway, if that's so, how come you're so keen to get hold of it?"

Nobusuke Kishi intervened. "I have read a copy of the paper, Madam. It is interesting."

Polly turned on Nakajima. "*You murdering bastard*! You had Jay Murakami killed to get your dirty hands on that paper."

He shook his head wearily. "No, not I, Polly. I hate what happened; it was unnecessary anyway. As a matter of fact it was an American who initiated that business."

"An *American*? You're a goddamned liar!"

"It's the truth. A highly placed civilian playing a very subtle double game. That doesn't make it any better, but I want you to know. Jay Murakami ran a lot of risks, he was a professional and did so knowingly. Not quite professional enough in the end, I'm afraid. I respected him and I'm sincerely sorry he's dead."

"I too did not wish this," Kishi said.

"Maybe you didn't. Who cares, with any luck you're going to be hanged anyway," Polly said, but it was getting harder and harder to cling to the buoy of fury which was all that prevented her from sinking into confusion and despair. The idea that Jay had been murdered at the behest of an American, a SCAP colleague, was shattering.

Kishi merely shrugged at Polly's words, and Nakajima spoke again. "As Mr Kishi says, we have seen the copy you made of the document Major Brooks drew up. Even though his job gave him privileged access to a lot of confidential information, it was the product of a remarkable intellect."

"A good blueprint," Kishi said, nodding in what looked uncommonly like approval, and Polly looked from one to the other before shaking her head in renewed disbelief.

"What in the world am I doing here? You know you can't get your hands on the original. And you admit it's no good trying to shut my mouth too."

Nakajima answered. "You're here, as I told you earlier, because you're a nuisance. No more than that. And because Japan's going to need friends like you in the years to come, Polly. It's true we were very anxious to find out what was in that document, but now that we know, I can assure you there's very little Reynolds or anybody else can make out of it. Who's going to believe the fantasizing of a man in the last stages of alcoholism? Where's the proof that these secret meetings Brooks claimed to know about actually took place?"

"Who will believe you, Madam, if you say or write down you have spoken to Class A detainee Kishi in small Japanese *ryokan*?"

The words spoken by the quiet, avuncular man to whom Nakajima so obviously deferred did more to deflate Polly than anything either of them had said previously, and her shoulders slumped. Nakajima quickly took advantage of her vulnerability.

"I said just now that Japan needs friends like you, Polly, and I meant it. There are in fact two reasons why you're here. The first is that this gentleman has been impressed by what he has heard of your determination and your integrity, and was curious to meet you. So curious that he and others went to a good deal of trouble to make it possible. The second is so that we can if possible persuade you to abandon any attempt to embarrass us by trying to make use of what you think you know. I put it like that because Brooks didn't get it all right by any means. Nevertheless his notes *could* be embarrassing if they got into the wrong hands. No more than that, but we are anxious to avoid publicity of that kind."

Polly spoke sullenly. "You can't scare me off. You could probably have me shipped back to the States tomorrow, but that would just make me all the more hard to handle, wouldn't it? So what's next, you going to try to *buy* me off?"

"That's ridiculous. I don't know you as well as I'd like to, but you're obviously not open to bribery. No, it's very simple. We just want to try to convince you – as some of our American friends are already convinced – that Japan's future is best left in the hands of the Japanese, and that even with the best of intentions you can only do harm if you try to interfere."

"For heaven's sake don't give me that. Left in the hands of the Japanese? Which Japanese? Decent democrats who want to live in peace like the people Jay Murakami tried to help, or the war criminals and crooks who hire thugs to beat them up on the streets? People like you two, in fact? What a choice!"

"Arthur Reynolds said something very similar not long ago, Polly, and I told him you don't have to be nice to be right. There are ugly scenes on the streets, certainly, and terrible crimes have been committed, by our people as well as the other side. As recently as last July three dozen Formosans rioted: they were shot down by the police. Seven killed, twice that many injured. Yes, I've seen Japanese hoodlums attacking Koreans and Chinese in Tokyo, and I've seen it happen the other way around. What perhaps you don't know is that there are communist thugs on the streets too." The older man nodded in agreement, the bland face otherwise expressionless.

"Yet in the past six months there hasn't been a *single* attack on Allied personnel or act of sabotage anywhere in Japan. Shall I tell you why not? It's because *we* are keeping the peace as far as you people are concerned, that's why. You can walk out of the PX on the Ginza carrying packages that cost you a few dollars but would be worth a fortune to a Japanese, but nobody will lay a finger on you. Hasn't it ever occurred to you to wonder why? When you know that half-starved people on trains from the country to the cities risk getting their throats cut for the sake of the pathetic little bag of rice and scrawny chicken they're bringing back for their kids?" Nakajima's voice had been getting louder and louder as he spoke, and he was leaning forward, quivering as the words poured from him. Suddenly he seemed to regret the outburst, and paused.

"Big agonies, small agonies," he went on after a moment, much more quietly. "Like that little girl tonight sent out in the dark to humiliate herself by trying to sell something for a tenth of its value to get food. You were good to her, but she'll be hungry again next week." Then he fell silent, rubbing a hand over his eyes.

"Mr Nakajima speaks well, Madam. Japan has proud spirit, not only body. So, very hungry people give precious food to well-fed guest. Many, many problems Americans cannot solve, so my friends solve some for them, quietly, you see. Please come back in five, ten years. You will find Japan peaceful, enough to eat too, but not if the communists win. You are a strong lady and can help us, please. Now excuse me. Mr Nakajima will take you safe home." Kishi hoisted himself up into a kneeling position, from which he bowed low to Polly. Unseen by her, Nakajima made his own farewell in the same manner.

Then he was on his feet and at her side, helping her to her feet. This time when they reached the entrance of the inn Polly was not surprised to see a taxi waiting for them outside. Nakajima tried to make conversation during the drive back to Hilltop House, but she remained obdurately silent.

A much larger car arrived at the inn called the Kikuya ten minutes after she and Nakajima had left, and its driver waited patiently with the window open slightly. In the stillness of the Tokyo night he heard the sound of voices just inside the inn before the rattle of its sliding outer door, and was standing to attention beside the car when two middle-aged men emerged. The one in Japanese dress was short and stocky; the other, a tall westerner, was in civilian clothes but looked every inch the military man he was. From the next room he had been able to hear every word of the conversation between Kishi, Nakajima and Sergeant Polly Horvath. General Charles Willoughby had even more than usual to think about in the car on the way, first, to Sugamo prison to return his companion to the custody of the specially selected duty officer, and then back to his own house.

22

Master Sergeant Joe Noonan straightened the tunic he so seldom wore, set his forage cap at a jaunty angle on his narrow head and opened the door immediately after rapping on it. "Ready when you are, Lieutenant! Jeep's outside, camera's loaded, flash-gun tested. Let's go!"

The young lieutenant behind the desk looked up at him with distaste, but stood up and reached for his cap. Without a word he followed Noonan out of the Teikoku Sogo Building where the Counter-Intelligence Corps headquarters was housed. When they reached the jeep Noonan tenderly laid the camera and flash-gun he had been carrying on the back seat, and took the wheel as the officer clambered in beside him. Only after he was settled did the officer finally say anything.

"Your information better be good. It's after ten-thirty and I'm bushed."

Noonan drove away with great panache, the tyres squealing in protest as he rounded the first corner. "No sweat, sir, sorry this is the way it has to be, but an hour from now you'll thank me. This is one big fish we're about to hook."

"I'll believe it when I see it," the lieutenant grumbled.

Noonan was in an ebullient mood and would have been happy to chat on the way to the Shufunotomo civilian staff billet, but if this kid officer wanted to act high and mighty, let him, the stupid jerk. He had his own thoughts to while away the time. Oh boy, he sure had made a hit with that Curtis broad! She'd sure taken her time thinking it over, but had she come through with the goods in the end, calling *him* and asking if he could spare her half an hour! And then coming to the Teikoku Building in person, kind of shy but hell, that was understandable in the circumstances, seeing as how she had a very different song to sing. Want to apologize for reacting hastily, Mr Noonan. Realize you have a difficult and highly sensitive job to do, wouldn't want you to have gained any impression that I'm not a wholeheartedly patriotic American, only too glad to co-operate with the security authorities.

Then some more names of Jap professors to add to the file, didn't mean a thing to him but great for filling out a report. Oh Mr Noonan, I really don't care to speculate about my American colleagues, but I guess, yes, I have to say that I believe the late Mr Murakami was in touch with a number of communists . . . I mean, you know, privately.

After that, how cleverly he'd brought the subject around to Berman to get the kind of corroboration he needed to make the case stand up! Kind of sexy situation, too, watching her blush as he got her to admit after a hell of a lot of beating around the bush that, well, yes, she *had* heard some rumours that Mr Berman wasn't, well, quite normal, but please, *please* Mr Noonan don't quote me because, well, you're a man of the world of course, but to be quite honest I don't know anything about that sort of thing and could be entirely wrong.

Yes sir, she might have started out with the idea of covering her sweet ass because she really was a pinko and was scared in case big bad Joe Noonan might put a query mark on her personnel file. Could be, but she was also one frustrated lady, that's for sure. Embarrassed by the subject but you could see she was real interested at the same time, squirming in the chair and breathing kind of heavy with her mouth half open, like she couldn't wait for it.

Specially when he told her not to worry, he had plenty other evidence to confirm what Mr Tom Berman was up to, and planned to clinch the matter that very evening. Personally. That put a sparkle in her eye, realizing that Joseph Xavier Noonan didn't need to send for the Marines when he wanted action. Well, she'd have to wait a little while for the action *she* obviously wanted, but that was all to the good, make her appreciate it all the more. Maybe when the time came it'd be fun to slap her around a little first, that kind of aristocratic dame went for that. Yeah, make her ask nicely. Beg for it. On her knees, even –

"*Watch it*, Noonan! Goddam it, you want to kill us both?"

"Sorry, Lieutenant, wheel kicked there, must have been a hole in the road."

When they reached the Shufunotomo billet a few minutes later Noonan went ahead, holding the camera and flash-gun behind him. Opening the door no more than a few inches, he glanced inside. No problem. The Japanese porter on duty was a middle-aged man, and the only other person in the lobby was talking to him in halting Japanese, probably leaving a message for somebody. He was a man probably in his late thirties but younger-looking, with crinkly fair hair. Noonan recognized him, it was the limey, no, Australian naval officer attached to G2. Been around for ever, people said, like the old man's Bataan Boys. Noonan beckoned to his lieutenant to follow and marched boldly towards the stairs, the camera now on the blind side of the porter and the Australian, whom he treated to his foxy grin. "It's OK, Commander, we're expected," he said breezily, and led the way up.

When they reached Berman's corridor the officer looked up and down its length. There was nobody else about, but he whispered anyway. "Has it occurred to you that if he's doing what you think he's doing he's had the sense to lock the door?"

Noonan shrugged. "Maybe, maybe not. These doors aren't much better than cardboard, and the locks are Mickey Mouse. A breeze compared with some I've bust in." In his present state of euphoria he felt omnipotent, and when they had tiptoed to the end of the corridor and paused outside the door which had Berman's name typed on a card thumbtacked to it he smiled patronizingly at the much younger man before bending down and squinting through the keyhole.

"There's a light on but no key in the lock," he mouthed, and double-checked the settings on the camera before producing a flash-bulb from his pocket, moistening the terminal with his tongue to improve the electrical contact, and screwing it into place.

When everything was ready he very slowly turned the door knob and edged the door forward a fraction of an inch, another smile slowly spreading over his face with the realization that the door was unlocked. Then he flung the door fully open.

"OK, Lieutenant, take a look at this!" he yelled in triumph as a bare-chested Tom Berman sat up straight in bed with a look of stark horror on his face and his partner burrowed under the covers. Noonan raised the camera. "Drag that sheet clear, Lieutenant, we've got 'em cold!" Looking distinctly uncomfortable, the officer crossed to the bed and took hold of the covers. "Right, *now*!"

The timing was perfect. The flash exploded just as the sheet came away to reveal the naked Berman and the equally, magnificently naked Eleanor Curtis.

23

"Sit down over there, Sergeant Horvath. The general's with the Chief right now, but he shouldn't be long." Polly did as she was bidden and looked around General Willoughby's ante-room with as much interest as the smart young captain at the desk in the corner gave her. Polly presumed she was supposed to be impressed by the casual reference to General MacArthur, and had to admit to herself that as a matter of fact she was. Nevertheless, she settled herself comfortably in one of the armchairs, determined, in spite of the fact that her heart was pounding and her throat felt dry, to appear completely at ease, as though she were accustomed to calling on general officers.

"You've met the general before, have you?"

"Not exactly met, sir. I've seen him often enough, of course, when I was working for Major Brooks."

"Uh huh, of course, I guess you would have done. That was a sad business. The major was a very nice guy, but. . . ."

Polly had no intention of gossiping about Mike Brooks with this officer who was probably about her own age. "Yes, Captain, he was."

He tried again, this time with an encouraging smile. "The general has an exceptionally busy schedule today."

"He does?"

"Yes. I had a tough time juggling things to fit you in when he said he wanted to see you."

"No doubt. I guess he doesn't have sergeants report to him personally all that often any way."

"It wasn't that easy to find you, either. I hadn't realized you weren't still in the same job. I tell you frankly, Sergeant, I was damn glad I raised you at Hilltop House. My head would have rolled if I'd had to tell him I couldn't locate you."

"Wouldn't have been your fault, sir. I'm on furlough. Was thinking about a trip to Nikko as a matter of fact, but I could hardly play hard to get with General Willoughby." As the minutes ticked by it was becoming less difficult for Polly to behave with apparent nonchalance. Stonewalling this young man was quite satisfying. He probably thought he knew his master's business as well as Willoughby himself and was obviously not enjoying being kept in the dark about the reason for the presence in his office of a non-commissioned officer as an invited visitor.

All the same, as the minutes ticked by Polly began to wonder how long she could keep her end up. Then, just as the silence was becoming awkward, the door was opened and both she and the captain shot to their feet and stood to attention as General Willoughby swept in, followed by Captain Henderson, the officer who had taken over Major Brooks's job in such a hurry. Polly felt rather than saw Willoughby assess her at a glance.

"Sergeant Horvath, yes?"

"Sir!"

"At ease, Sergeant. Come through to my office. John, coffee for three."

Polly followed the two officers. If she had been apprehensive earlier when the summons had come, and thoroughly intimidated by the time she had been escorted to the G2 holy of holies, she was now in a state of near panic. Only by hanging on to the recollection of the look on the captain's face when he had been commanded to bring coffee for her could she pretend to anything like composure.

Both men were bare-headed but otherwise in full uniform. Willoughby was so much taller than she that when he turned to face her she found herself gazing almost directly at the colourful rows of medal ribbons above his left breast pocket. "I said at ease, Sergeant. Sit down, I want to talk to you. You've met Captain Henderson."

He circled his desk and sat down behind it, indicating a straight chair placed so that he could face a visitor across an expanse of highly polished wood with nothing on its surface except a pen tray and a leather-bound blotter on which he placed the folder he had been carrying tucked under one arm. Meantime Henderson moved quietly to the far corner of the room where there was another chair and sat down, out of Polly's range of vision.

It was the first time Polly had been literally face to face with the man people referred to as the Junker General or the Prussian, and the proximity did nothing for her composure. The scrupulous military courtesy with which he had greeted her and even the touch of warmth suggested by the demand for coffee were belied by the coldness of his stare now. The trace of German accent which lingered in his speech underlined the absurdity of a situation in which a general and a WAC sergeant were sitting staring at each other in silence with a watchful captain as witness, waiting for another captain to bring them some coffee.

As the seconds dragged past it suddenly struck Polly that it was like being in some corny war movie, and she dug her nails into the balls of her thumbs to suppress a powerful urge to giggle. Mercifully, the tension was soon broken by the appearance of the general's aide carrying a tray.

"Set it down there, John. Close the door behind you." The general watched him depart and then whirled back to glare at Polly again. "Something amusing you, Sergeant?"

"No, sir. Sorry, sir."

"Cream and sugar?" Stupefied, Polly watched one of the most powerful men in Japan pour a cup of coffee for her from a silver pot.

"N-no, sir," she stammered as he picked up the cream jug and looked at her enquiringly. "Thank you, sir. Black, please."

Willoughby pushed the cup and saucer across the desk towards her and glanced at the silent man in the corner. "Help yourself, Henderson." Then he stared at Polly again. "I saw your face. The captain out there doesn't know what the hell is going on, it bothers him and you were enjoying the fact."

"Yes, sir, I guess I was."

"Right. So you've had your fun. Fun's over now." The haughty expression disappeared as Willoughby's face reddened and the quiet conversational tone was abruptly replaced by something between a scream and a snarl. "*Just who do you think you are, Horvath!*" It was neither a question nor a statement; it was an assault, and Polly instinctively cringed. The storm passed as quickly as it had arisen, however, and the general spoke normally again. "Well, Sergeant?"

"Sir?"

Willoughby leant back in his chair and held up one finger. "Item. You have been fraternizing with a senior officer on my staff." Another finger flicked up. "Item. You have been fraternizing with a senior Japanese member of the staff of the War Data Department, informally attached to G2." Third finger. "Item. You purloined a confidential document from the safe of the late Major Michael Brooks –"

"Major Brooks approved my action, sir."

The voice became quieter, taking on an almost caressing quality. "Do not ever again presume to interrupt me when I am speaking. Knowing that Major Brooks was critically ill and unlikely to survive, and with this document in your possession, you recklessly embarked on a totally unauthorized course of action. This involved lying to your military superiors and conspiring with certain members of the civilian staff of SCAP and other military personnel. I cannot at this stage even guess at the final number of offences with which you could be charged; but several of them would unquestionably involve court martial proceedings."

Willoughby picked up his cup with unexpected daintiness and sipped. Polly seized her opportunity. "Permission to speak, sir?"

"Granted."

"Sir, I should like to say only that I should welcome the opportunity to give evidence on my own behalf before a court martial." Waiting for lightning to strike, she first hesitated and then drank some coffee too. Nothing happened, except that her hand was shaking, which made the cup rattle in the saucer. Willoughby opened the folder in front of him on the desk and turned over a few of the sheets of paper inside. When he did speak it was almost as though to himself.

"Preferably with Lieutenant-Commander Reynolds of the Royal Australian Navy as defending officer, no doubt." Closing the file again he looked up. "But that couldn't be, of course, as you well know. Commander Reynolds would not be permitted to serve in such a capacity in US Army proceedings. Nor is there the remotest prospect of your being assigned to work with him, for him or indeed in any capacity in G2." He looked at his watch.

"Right now, Commander Reynolds is, I believe, on his way to Atsugi. There he will board an aircraft bound for Manila and thence to Australia. I understand that the commander will be resigning his commission as soon as he is back in his own country. Does that surprise you?"

Polly looked down and bit her lower lip hard to force back the tears that pricked at her eyes, and then flung her head up again in defiance. "Not really. He knows too much, doesn't he?"

The aristocratic face briefly reddened again and there was a protracted pause, but this time no outburst. "Presumably you are impertinent because you think you have nothing to lose. In the circumstances I will overlook that remark, though you are mistaken. I have yet to decide what to do about you."

"I thought you planned to court-martial me, General."

"I might. I see from your record that you have some working acquaintance with the law, Sergeant. So it shouldn't be necessary for me to point out to you that military law can be a very flexible instrument in the hands of those who administer it. Here in Japan, ten years or so ago, hotheads in the army and navy who played politics used to exploit court martials as a means of gaining publicity for their opinions. But they could do that only because it suited the generals and admirals to let them. You obviously have the notion that you could do something like that, emerge from the proceedings as some kind of national heroine. You couldn't be more wrong. If I have the book thrown at you, you'll be crucified."

"I can only justify what I've done to the best of my ability, sir. I might make a better case than you imagine."

"You are so very sure you're right, aren't you? Cards on the table, Sergeant. I . . . I am aware of the kind of arguments Eijiro Nakajima has put to you about the situation in Japan and the vision he and his friends have for the future of this country. Tell me, did nothing he said make the slightest dent in your confidence?"

"You surprise me by even asking that, General. I wouldn't have expected you to bother yourself with rights and wrongs."

"I am a realist and far from tender-minded, but it's not only the so-called progressives who have principles. Answer me."

"Sir, I have little reason to be impressed by the arguments of a man like Nakajima. Personally, I despise him for fooling me into thinking he was attracted to me when really he was just trying to find out how much I knew. Furthermore, I detest the company he keeps, the ruthlessness and greed of the politicians he wants to see running this country, and the crooks they employ to see they get their way."

"Do you indeed?"

"Yes, sir, I do. I think that in the last analysis Nakajima is very probably a crook himself. There are some things about him I can respect and even admire, like his sensitivity to beauty and his deep understanding of Japanese culture. However, on balance I'm not convinced he really does believe what he claims to. So he hasn't changed my mind about politics, though I'll admit he has made me see that things aren't quite so simple as I used to think."

"No, they aren't. And none of us has clean hands, and dealing with you isn't going to be as straightforward as I had assumed. I'll tell you something, Sergeant. Keep it to yourself for the rest of today, but it'll be announced tomorrow anyway. I just came from the C-in-C. He has today signed a directive banning the general strike which was to have begun the day after tomorrow." Willoughby raised his eyebrows. "Now, as an expert on the Japanese political scene, what do you think will happen?"

Polly ignored the sarcasm. "It's an insane idea. It will inflame the ordinary Japanese even more, and the strike will go ahead."

"You're wrong again. I will tell you what will happen. The overwhelming majority of the people concerned will show up for work. The left will scream and shout, and then turn on each other. The trade union movement will fall apart: as of today it has no real future in Japan. It is very gratifying that the Supreme Commander has seen fit to act upon my advice." The general looked at his watch again and stood up. Polly's reaction was a simple reflex: she jumped up and stood to attention, as did Captain Henderson.

"There will be no charges against you. Personnel admin will be instructed to offer you a choice of assignments, none of them punitive in character. Alternatively, if you prefer to apply to be released from the service an honourable discharge will be arranged. You're a political innocent and an intolerable nuisance, Sergeant, but you're a brave, honest woman and I have no wish to persecute you. This conversation did not take place. Dismissed."

"Well, that's it," Suekawa said as the black shape of the fishing boat merged into the darkness of the night. He didn't speak again until its red, green and white navigation lights had dwindled in apparent size to become first Christmas-tree decorations suspended incongruously over Tokyo Bay, and then pin-points, before finally disappearing.

"You did OK on the deliveries. Two good shipments assembled, loaded and on their way. I hear you got your ass scorched when you tried to set Berman up, though. That why you're so quiet tonight?"

Noonan had hoped that word of the fiasco hadn't reached the gangster. The thought of the money he stood to make out of the evening's work helped a little, but it would take something very different to counteract the bitterness of his mortification. "Me set Berman up? That fat bitch set me up. She's not through with me yet though. I got plans for her. Long-term plans."

"Face it, Noonan, you blew it. You led with your chin, heard what you wanted to hear and she was too smart for you."

"She's a commie-loving whore and I'm going to get her and the fag she's covering for."

"Not according to what I hear. What I hear is, Berman had a little talk with your lieutenant the morning after, and your lieutenant knows what's good for him. What's good for him is to make very sure everybody who matters in CIC knows not to mess with that fine American patriot and horny old stud Tom Berman. Nor the real bright lady with the great tits who warms his bed. Matter of a lady's honour, right? What would not be good for the lieutenant is for Berman to file a complaint about the pair of you or have a quiet word with his old boss General Whitney. Know something, Noonan? Wouldn't surprise me Berman keeps a copy of that picture you took in his billfold."

As it sank into Noonan's awareness that Suekawa seemed to know everything that had happened during the course of that disastrous evening and since, he also realized that the two men who had helped the crew of the boat with the loading of the supplies now on the way to Kobe were still very much in attendance: were indeed standing one on either side of him.

"What the hell, Suekawa-san," he said with an attempt at an easy-come-easy-go sort of laugh which was a complete failure. "So it didn't work out. That green kid of a lieutenant isn't about to try to hurt me and have me rub his baby face in it too. Hey, it's late, I better get back to Ebisu Camp now."

"You're right about the officer. He doesn't need to do a thing about you. You're all washed up anyway." The gangster gave a little laugh that chilled Noonan's blood. "All washed up, that's good. Except the idea is you won't be. You're right about something else too, it is getting late."

He said something in Japanese to the two men. They closed in immediately and seized Noonan's arms while Suekawa went behind him, gagged him with a piece of cloth, and tied his wrists behind him. Then the struggling American was half carried, half frogmarched to the little quayside and bundled into a flat-bottomed boat. All three of the Japanese clambered in too, and Suekawa untied the mooring rope while one of his men positioned himself by the single sweep at the stern. It was a quiet, effective means of propulsion and they were soon well out in the bay.

"The guy at the back knows the tides and currents around here a lot better than you know how to keep your big mouth shut," the gangster said in a conversational tone. "So we won't be seeing you again. You're – how do you say – expendable. Because you're dumb. Stupid. You could have been useful, really useful. We could have done good business, but you had to sound off, didn't you? You talked big to a dame way out of your league because you wanted to get into her pants. And what happens? Instead of being pleased with *you* my boss is mad at *me*, and I don't like that at all. So you don't have to wait for your payoff, you get it right now."

CHRISTMAS EVE, 1948

24

Two or three hours had passed since the seven plain rectangular wooden boxes containing the bodies of the convicted war criminals hanged shortly before midnight were unceremoniously loaded on to two US army trucks and despatched to Yokohama for cremation. The Buddhist priest who had consoled General Tojo and the others during their last hours had left. Not surprisingly, though, the Sugamo prison's administration block was still a blaze of light; and things were going on outside the compound, too. For some time a variety of vehicles had been arriving, their drivers parking in the shadows a discreet distance away from the main gates and cutting their engines and lights immediately.

Some of the vehicles were taxis, some private cars. There were one or two passengers in most of them in addition to the drivers, and a few people got out and walked up and down to warm themselves. For the most part they behaved as though the others were invisible, but here and there two or three huddled briefly in conversation.

After a while, bright light spilled out as the prison gates began to swing open, and almost at once many more people got out of the cars and gazed towards them. By the time the first man came into view and paused outside the prison entrance, looking around with a bewildered expression on his face, some twenty or thirty people were there to stare at him. Then, as others came out of the compound and joined him, the scene lost its first tableau-like quality. The onlookers surged forward to greet the men and seize the battered suitcases and cloth-wrapped bundles they were carrying.

In all, sixteen of them emerged, and within a minute or two they had been singled out and greeted by those who had come to meet them in the chill small hours. Almost everybody bowed repeatedly, some very low and some more hesitantly, but there were no tearful embraces, no handshakes. Soon it was nearly all over, and with a great slamming of car and taxi doors, revving of engines and switching on of headlights, the majority of the released detainees were driven away.

A few people remained, including three of the men from the prison. After barely exchanging greetings, they had drawn a little apart from their friends and relatives and were talking quietly together. One other person joined them in their brief conversation. Then Nobusuke Kishi and Ryoichi Sasakawa turned away to rejoin their friends and were each led to one of the remaining cars: large, well-cared-for limousines, like the one to which Eijiro Nakajima ushered Yoshio Kodama.

"I am very much happy for you, and to hear it on Christmas Eve too! It's a wonderful nice Christmas present, nicer even than this great parcel of fine coffee!"

"I'm so glad to be able to tell you in person, Father. I was going to write to you, but then I had the chance to come to Tokyo for the holiday so I waited a while. Thank you for hearing my confession today. Working down there in Kyoto, I've missed being able to come to you."

Father Leydekkers raised a finger as if to chide her. "A priest is a priest. Every one of us is just as bad as all the others, Miss Brewster. Or should I call you Sister already?"

Angie smiled at him. He seemed to have shrunk physically in the past two years and looked far from well, but his eyes were as bright as ever. Just as the dingy little sitting room still reeked of kerosene, and the coffee was barely drinkable. "Of course not. You know better than that. In a few months, I hope."

"So, so. Very good. Much different from the army, eh?"

"Is it? I remember you told me once, right here in this room, that you Benedictines know all about house arrest . . . I guess it'll be a little like that for me in the convent."

"Not so much, I think. You have the girls to teach in the Sacred Heart School, isn't it so?"

"I'm no teacher, Father. A year and a half as a military government social worker after I quit the army doesn't count for college credit, you know, and I'm too old to start hitting the books now. No, I reckon Reverend Mother will decide that my place is in the kitchen. Maybe let me do a little counselling now and then if I don't break too many dishes."

The old man shook his head. "Still wanting to do penance, are you? After so long? And even though anyway you committed no sin?"

Angie looked away, but the pain in her expression was still obvious to the priest. "I loved her, Father. And I wanted her. Sinfully."

"You think you should be excused temptation? That people can switch off desires? That was a crazy, impossible thing Saint Paul said – forget it. I know you loved her, sure. But you never even told her, isn't it?"

"No, but she probably guessed."

"If she did, then she should be proud. I remember my advice to you when you first told me, the time you came back for the envelope. Sadness, distress, of course, because your friend was going away, OK. But guiltiness, no. And I say it to you again six or seven thousand times since then."

"Father, I don't think you've even *seen* me more than three times since then."

"Poof! You know my meaning. Anyway, enough, I close my ears to your nonsense! You have news from her? She is well?"

"Yes, I got a letter from her enclosed in a Christmas card just a few days ago. She and her husband are in London, would you believe it? Arthur seems to have done the right thing when he decided to join the Australian diplomatic service. Polly says he's just lucky to have moved up so fast, that he happened to be the right age for quick promotion, but I don't believe a word of that. No children yet, but she's young still. She has plenty of time. . . ."

"Now then, now then. Don't cry, my dear. Here, you can use my handkerchief if you want." Father Leydekkers delved into the pocket of his habit and produced it, then paused and peered doubtfully at it. "Oh dear, it's a little bit dirty I'm afraid."

APRIL 1976

25

Polly checked the time by the clock set into the bedside unit in her room high in the new tower block of the Imperial Hotel. Almost seven o'clock, nearly time for the news on the English-language cable television channel for foreigners. After a brief hesitation she opened the little refrigerator beside the dressing table. She tried not to make a habit of drinking alone, but the circumstances were exceptional. She took out a miniature bottle of Gordon's gin, tipped the contents into a tumbler and topped it up with tonic water, swallowing a generous mouthful before crossing the room to turn on the television. Then she emptied the rest of the tonic into the glass, placed it conveniently beside the armchair and sat down to watch.

The report of the arrival at Haneda International Airport of one of the most outspoken members of the US Senate Sub-committee on International Industries was brief and placed towards the end of the bulletin, but it was worth waiting for. Senator Berman looked confident and composed. Obviously an old hand at facing flash-bulbs and questions shouted from all sides, the Senator dealt with the reporters affably and adroitly. Yes, it was always a pleasure to be back in Japan, especially at cherry-blossom time. No, the members of the sub-committee had at no time sought to embarrass the Japanese government or former prime minister, Tanaka. Their investigation was into the way the Lockheed Aircraft Corporation carried on its business in a number of countries; Japan yes, but also Italy, the Netherlands and elsewhere. It was not for a member of the sub-committee to comment on the reaction in Japan to the conclusions they had arrived at. Yes, of course. The United States government would surely co-operate, if requested to, in any investigation launched by the Japanese authorities: the relationship between Japan and the United States was like that between two mature and sensible people, close friends and partners in a great enterprise. Such people did not allow themselves to get over-excited when faced with a problem; they got their heads together and sorted it out.

Judging from the look of relief the television cameraman captured on the American Ambassador's face as he and his VIP guest were eventually escorted to the ambassadorial car for the twenty-minute drive to his residence at Toranomon, Polly thought he was probably well pleased with Senator Berman's performance. She stood up, switched off the TV and went over to the window. It overlooked the Takarazuka Theatre, and Polly had a clear view of the huge posters advertising the current attraction. This seemed to be a period drama, featuring one of the all-female company's most glittering stars as a samurai and another as the heroine, a poor peasant girl in attractive rags.

As Polly gazed down at the familiar building in the street that now looked so different in its affluent brightness, she remembered that in the old days it had been called the Ernie Pyle Theater, and what Angie had said one time as they emerged from a symphony concert there. *"Ernie Pyle! What kind of a cruddy name is that for a concert hall? This guy Pyle's just a war correspondent, for heaven's sake. How come he gets a concert hall called after him?"*

Dear Angie. So good to have been able to be at the requiem mass for her in Kyoto the previous day. Sister Celine, she had for some inexplicable reason chosen as her religious name. Or more likely it had been bestowed on her by the order: surely Angie herself would have secretly thought it was a pretty weird name for a larger-than-life American nun. Still, Polly had noticed that the Japanese Reverend Mother's pronunciation made it come out as Sister Serene, which was by all accounts what Angie had become long before she died in her seventy-eighth year.

The telephone rang and Polly hurried to answer it. "Hello? Yes, of course it's me. No need to apologize, the earlier the better. I'm all ready, but would you like to come up and have a drink here first? Fine. See you in a couple of minutes." There was time to dispose of the evidence of her drink and check her make-up before the melodious chiming of the doorbell had her hastening to peep through the fish-eye lens set into the door. Then she flung it open and took a step back.

"Hello, Jerry."

"I'm so glad to see you again, Polly." Nakajima closed the door behind him before gently putting his hands on her shoulders. "You look wonderful."

She looked up at him. His hair was completely white but there was still plenty of it; and if he had put on a little weight in the past two years, an expensive tailor had made it look as if it belonged.

"Don't be silly. I'm getting to be an old woman. Fifty-five last birthday."

"Don't *you* be silly. You always seem to forget that I'm twelve years older than you. In my second childhood."

"Let's not argue about it. Do I get a kiss or don't I?"

"You most certainly do."

"I was sorry to hear about Arthur, Polly."

"Don't be. If you could have seen the pain he was in towards the end you'd understand why it was then that I wept for him, not afterwards. It's been more than a year now and I'm used to being alone."

"I'm surprised you didn't decide to go back to the States after he died."

"What, after over twenty-five years as an Australian citizen? Whatever would I do in Minneapolis? No, I have plenty to occupy me in Sydney, and the Australian foreign service is reasonably generous to the widows of its retired ambassadors."

"It's good of your Ambassador here to invite me to dinner this evening too."

Polly looked at the badge in Nakajima's lapel, the golden chrysanthemum mounted on a pad of rich indigo velvet that identified him as a member of the Upper House of the National Diet. "I was doing him a favour when I told him he had to. A former Cabinet Secretary's a much bigger fish than me. He'll enjoy the chance to pump you about the Lockheed scandal over the port."

"Well, I suppose he can try. Incidentally, did you know Eleanor Berman's in Tokyo?"

"Yes, I've just been watching her on the news. Senator Berman. I still can't get used to it even after, what is it, five or six years?"

"I wasn't surprised. She was already so popular in her own right that the state governor more or less had to nominate her to serve out Tom's term after he was killed. And by the time she ran for re-election she'd made such an impact nationally that the result was a foregone conclusion. Do you plan to meet her while she's here?"

"I'd like to of course, but I can't see her being able to fit me into her kind of programme. I left a message for her earlier today with the Ambassador's secretary to say I was staying at the Imperial for two more days, but . . . would you like another drink, or shall we go?"

"We should be going, I think. My car's waiting."

"Is that Lady Reynolds?"

"Yes, speaking."

"One moment, ma'am. I have Senator Berman for you. . . . Go ahead, please, Senator."

"Polly? Polly, is it really you? I could hardly believe it when I got your message."

"*Eleanor*! Yes, it really is! I'm so glad you called now, another ten minutes and I'd have been out. I'm sure you're furiously busy, but I just had to try to get in touch when I saw in the paper you were coming. I saw you on TV yesterday evening, you look wonderful."

"Come *on*, Polly, we've known each other too long for you to try to kid me. I'm just delighted you're here in Tokyo. Listen, we simply have to meet. This Lady Reynolds stuff really impressed me, so I had the Embassy fill me in about you . . . anyway, whatever else, you must know from your own experience as an Ambassadress the kind of schedule I have. But could you possibly bear to come over here to the Residence late this evening? You know the way formal hospitality is in Japan, everything early but finishing around nine-thirty? The Ambassador couldn't be more understanding, he's promised we can go hide in a room on our own *and* he'll send a car for you. You will come? Please?"

It took time for the first fragile filaments of conversation to touch, grow stronger and show that an interval of nearly thirty years was capable of being bridged; but privacy and alcohol both helped to relax and open up the initially guarded messages they exchanged. After an hour two well-dressed women in late middle age were wiping tears of laughter from the eyes through which the young Polly Horvath and Eleanor Curtis looked affectionately at each other's unlikely successors, the one so opulent and queenly, the other so neat and trim.

They were over the solemnities: the horror of that day when they were leaving their hotel and Eleanor saw her smiling husband shot down by a crazed gunman, and the more protracted agony Arthur Reynolds had endured as the cancer fed on his body and poisoned his once generous spirit. They had talked of the manifold mystery of love, too, of Eleanor's unexpectedly happy fellowship with Tom Berman; of her acceptance of his bisexuality and the way his initially selfish gratitude to her had developed after their marriage into an honest respect and admiration which, in turn, released her from the prison of her shyness and "warned me that I had it in me to be the public nuisance I've become since dear Tom was killed".

Polly shook her head slowly with a rueful smile. "Life really is something, isn't it? That day in your room at the Shiba Park Hotel when I asked Arthur to leave us alone together I was all set to volunteer myself as the one to be discovered in bed with Tom. It hadn't even occurred to me to think of you . . . I thought I was pretty experienced, and you seemed so innocent, in spite of being such an intellectual."

"I was innocent, sexually. But I realized I'd make a far more credible partner for Tom than you. And as a civilian I wouldn't be breaking any rules, whereas you would have."

"Just think, if it *had* been me we might have ended up marrying each other's husband!"

The way Eleanor looked at her made Polly regret having said that, but the awkward moment soon passed. Then had come the silly trivia, the do-you-remember-the-time-when nonsenses that brought back the sound of boogie-woogie, the weirdness of zoot suits, the stridency of Technicolor, the slippery texture of artificial silk and the bliss of wriggling out of those awful girdles at night, the taste of Japanese fish sausage and – oh God, yes, the way the honey-wagons stank in the warm weather as they trundled right through downtown Tokyo with their loads of night-soil.

Laughter dying then, a pause, fresh drinks and a more reflective Eleanor on the subject of Jerry Nakajima.

"But when did it *start*, Polly? That's what I'd like to know."

"Around twenty years ago. In fifty-seven, right after the impossible happened and Kishi really did become prime minister within ten years, just like they'd planned it. We were here, Arthur was a counsellor by then and rushing about showing the Aussie flag all over Japan. And as I told you, things were no more than OK between us."

"Any particular reason?"

"It was as much my fault as his. He'd begun to take himself over-seriously, get a little pompous, and I loathed being an embassy wife. Because we had no children they tried to land me with all manner of ridiculous committees, coffee mornings . . . and when I was on parade at official functions I'd have to trail along behind Arthur wearing one of those stupid rosettes like a prize cow at a state fair."

"Wasn't it even worse after he became Ambassador – in Thailand, didn't you say, or was it Malaysia?"

"The formal occasions, yes, but at least as Ambassadress I could pass the other stuff down the line. Arthur's deputy's wife was *insane*, Eleanor, she actually enjoyed all that garbage. Anyway, before that here I was eating my heart out – you know there was a woman psychiatrist in Tokyo at the time, a German I think or maybe a Swiss, and she was treating literally dozens of diplomatic wives who were going frantic? Well, Arthur was in Nagoya or some such place when I got this phone call. He didn't say who he was, just 'Well, Polly, I suppose you can finally destroy that Operation Hi-Flyer file now, can't you?'"

"That must have shaken you."

"You can say that again. Of course I knew at once who it was. It was awful, I wanted to curse and swear at him but at the same time my stomach was *churning* at the sound of his voice. I stammered something, can't remember what, and then he said 'We have a long-standing date, you know. In January 1947 you promised to let me take you to see a Noh play. Now, what about Thursday afternoon? The Kanze company are doing one of my favourites.' I know I must have been out of my mind, but I said yes."

"And don't tell me you ended up in a short-time hotel?"

"*Eleanor!* Whatever do you take me for?" Polly busied herself with her glass for a few seconds, and when she spoke again it was in a very small voice. "That didn't happen until two days later."

"Wow, and you've kept it up twenty years? It was that good?"

"Yes. It was good. You see, with him I wasn't Mrs Reynolds the counsellor's wife, I was myself, Polly. He used to tease me about having this dream about discovering the real Japan. He claimed it no longer existed, but busy as he was he showed it to me all the same. Kabuki, Noh, *bunraku*, festivals in little out-of-the-way temples, other simple, fascinating things about Japan that had been staring me in the face and I'd never noticed ... and yes, I have to admit it, he was fantastic in bed. Of course, it ought to have ended when Arthur and I were transferred in fifty-nine, but one way and another I managed to get back here for a few days on the way to somewhere else at least every couple of years. That way we never had long enough together to get tired of each other."

"And Arthur didn't mind?"

"I still can't be absolutely sure whether he ever knew. I never told him but he was a very perceptive man. I don't see how he could have failed to guess when the discontented shrew he was married to suddenly turned into a happy woman. But Arthur was also a very nice man who knew that I loved him, and an experienced professional spook from way back who knew how and when to keep things to himself."

"Polly, did you know Nakajima had been working for Yoshio Kodama all that time? I mean, for years? In Shanghai during the war, and then while Kodama and Kishi were both in Sugamo and Tom was desperately trying and failing to persuade Joe Keenan to recommend that they should be prosecuted?"

"I found out eventually from Jerry himself, yes. It's an odd thing to say, but I think part of him had wanted Tom to succeed and was rather sorry when he failed. Anyhow, all our running around in the old days had come to seem rather pointless in the Japan of fifty-seven, with MacArthur long since fired and the Occupation over and done with. It was hard for me to remember what it was we'd all got so excited about. I realize now that the truest thing I ever said about Japan was the time I told General Willoughby that Jerry had made me see that things weren't as simple as I thought."

"Never mind that, Polly, I could argue with you but I won't. The important thing is this. Do you know that Nakajima has never stopped working for Kodama? That he's still one of his most influential placemen?"

"That's ridiculous. Jerry doesn't have to work *for* anybody. He's one of the most important politicians in Japan in his own right."

Eleanor studied her with a strange little smile. "Tom and I haven't wholly failed, you know. Not yet. Even Mr Hi-Flyer Kishi himself burned his wings in the end, didn't he? When he treated the Opposition in the Diet like a bunch of nobodies and bulldozed the security treaty through? He got his come-uppance. Had to put off the Eisenhower visit because he couldn't guarantee Ike's safety, and lost so much face he had to resign. Sure he's still around, but he's a spent force, and the Japanese still have the Constitution we gave them. And if Yoshio Kodama were Houdini himself he could never get himself out of this Lockheed mess, because I've handed over some exceedingly interesting material to the Japanese authorities and I'm not through talking to them yet. I figure Tom would have wanted me to do what I can to get that bastard at last. I have to tell you something else, Polly. I'm going to nail Eijiro Nakajima to the wall along with him."

Postscript

Later in 1976, the multimillionaire and power broker Yoshio Kodama was prosecuted on serious corruption charges. In spite of ingenious and protracted legal manoeuvring, he was utterly discredited long before he was eventually convicted. The careers of Kakuei Tanaka (prime minister from 1972 to 1974) and a number of other senior Japanese politicians were also destroyed as a result of the Lockheed bribery scandal.

Kodama is dead, as is his fellow Sugamo prisoner Nobusuke Kishi (prime minister from 1957 to 1960). The last surviving former Class A detainee is their friend Ryoichi Sasakawa. This colourful entrepreneur, financier and international philanthropist is one of the richest men in Japan, and still active as he enters his nineties.